Game Changer

THE HIDDEN ATTRACTIONS NOVELS

Playmaker

Game Changer

Game Changer

A HIDDEN ATTRACTIONS NOVEL

DEANNA FAISON

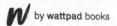 by wattpad books

W by wattpad books

An imprint of Wattpad WEBTOON Book Group

Published in Canada by Wattpad WEBTOON Book Group, a division of Wattpad WEBTOON Studios, Inc.

36 Wellington Street E., Suite 200, Toronto, ON M5E 1C7 Canada

www.wattpad.com

First W by Wattpad Books edition: August 2025

ISBN 978-1-99834-130-6 (Trade Paper original)
ISBN 978-1-99834-131-3 (eBook edition)

Library and Archives Canada Cataloguing in Publication information is available upon request.

Printed and bound in Canada

1 3 5 7 9 10 8 6 4 2

Cover design by Dylan Bonner
Typesetting by Delaney Anderson
Author Photo © Deanna Faison

To those who always feel a step behind.

It's okay to take the scenic route.

Playlist

The Pretender
Lewis Capaldi

Heather
Conan Gray

Please Notice
Christian Leave

making the bed
Olivia Rodrigo

Drunk in My Mind
Benson Boone

imperfect for you
Ariana Grande

But Daddy I Love Him
Taylor Swift

Before You
Benson Boone

One

ETHAN

It used to be that when I looked in the mirror, all I saw was a failure.

Someone insecure.

Someone afraid of the unknown.

Someone with no goals. No aspirations. No *motivation* because anxiety suffocated them like a thick piece of barbed wire wrapped around their throat.

It started in high school when I joined varsity football with my best friend, Cameron. I was talented but Cameron was better, and before each game, I'd think of all the plays I'd inevitably fuck up, disappointing the hundreds of people on the bleachers. That would lead to me sneaking off to the locker room to hang my head between my knees with my throat feeling like it was closing and my heart racing a million beats per minute.

Now, seven years later, anxiety has become an old friend—one that only comes around once in a while to remind me that even if I think we're growing apart, it'll never truly leave. But it's the start of my junior year in college, and I'm determined to make *something* of myself no matter how daunting the task may seem.

After community college, I decided to take a gap year, start over somewhere new, and create a fresh beginning for myself here at State. What else was I supposed to do after my extracurriculars were out of the way and I still had no clue what I wanted to do with my life? Cameron is starting his senior year now, basically a shoo-in for the NFL when he graduates, and my little sister, Maddie, is a sophomore studying to become a fucking *doctor*. And I'm . . . well, I'm unpacking boxes in my new dorm room with a knot in my stomach and clammy hands because I can't help wondering what the hell I'm doing here.

Attending Arizona State University seemed like the right thing at first. Continuing my education was a logical move, but now that I'm here, the mind that's supposed to propel me forward is doing the opposite.

Do you actually think you can graduate?

Why would you succeed at this when you've royally sucked at everything else?

You lost your virginity to the girl of your dreams, and she still didn't want to date you.

You're a loser.

A weak, spineless—

No. I refuse to fall back into that mindset when I've worked so hard over the past year to change my perspective. I'm taking medication now. I've gone through countless counseling sessions to create a better mental space, and this is the year I'll find my life's purpose. I'm making it my mission to accomplish that, and thinking negatively won't help.

"Are you Ethan?"

Lifting my eyes from the box I've been staring into for the past ten minutes, I see a tall, lanky guy about my age poking his head around the plastic bin he's holding. He's got a goofy smile on his face and he's wearing braces, which makes me smile back because it reminds me of Cameron when he was younger.

"Yeah, man. And I'm assuming you're Leonardo?"

He cringes. "Leo. Just Leo. Leonardo makes me seem like even more of a nerd than I already am." Setting the bin on the twin bed across from mine, he adds, "Hope you're okay with *Star Wars* posters, because those babies are packed in here." He pats the bin for emphasis.

I shrug and reach into my box to pull out a stack of video games. "So long as you're okay with me having these."

"*Dude.* Is that the new *Cowboy Slayer* that came out last month?" His bin is forgotten as he closes the distance between us to look at the other titles in my hands. "Oh, we're going to be *great* roommates."

The knot in my stomach loosens slightly.

At least one thing worked out in my favor today.

Leo is talkative as hell while we unpack the rest of our things. He reveals that he's part of the AV club here, which fits the bill given his button-up polo with outlines of various radios and laptops on it. Black-rimmed glasses stand out starkly against his pale, freckled skin. He's quirky, but at least we're into the same things.

Leo rambles on about his love for anime while I send a quick text to my parents to let them know I'm settled in. They wanted to help, but I preferred they didn't. I love my parents, but they can be overdramatic about these kinds of things. My mom is the type who'd bake a batch of cookies and deliver them to everyone on the floor, and my dad would tell embarrassing childhood stories about me to my new roommate.

It's not until I'm putting the sheets on my mattress that I hear a familiar throaty laugh. It's a sound I've memorized by heart. A laugh that no matter how hard I've tried to forget over the past five months, I just can't. The way it sounded pressed against my ear, and the little gasps that followed. Those sounds have haunted me every night since the best one of my life, and I'm still wondering why everything fell apart so damn quickly afterward.

I know, without a shadow of a doubt, who is about to pass by my wide-open door.

Maya Garcia, the woman of my dreams, saunters down the hallway with three other girls glued to her side. Those honey-brown eyes lock on mine, and she freezes on the spot, one of the girls running into her back at the abruptness. Her full, pink lips pop open in surprise before she swallows thickly and says to the girls, "I'll catch up with you guys in a few, okay?"

They scurry off giggling when I join her in the hallway, shutting the door and leaving a confused Leo behind.

Coming to State wasn't only a way for me to do something with my life, but it was also a way to escape my small town of Wickenburg, which is home to every memory I have of her. It's a small enough place that everyone knows everyone, and my anxiety was only heightened whenever I went to the store, the coffee shop, the movies. I didn't want to run into her, and although State is only an hour away, I thought it'd be enough distance to escape her.

But now she's *here*.

Right in front of me.

"How have you been?" she asks, shifting awkwardly. I lift a

brow, but before I reply, she says, "That was a stupid thing to ask. Sorry."

My eyes flick to the way she chews on her bottom lip, wishing I was the one doing it instead. In fact, I *remember* doing that five months ago.

A thousand questions are on the tip of my tongue, but I ignore them and go for something safer. "I thought you were in the cosmetology program?" We went to the same community college before this, and I assumed she'd be off gathering clientele after graduating from the program, not transferring to the same four-year university as me. She already accomplished what she set out to do, right?

"I was. I mean, I finished the program, but my parents wanted me to get a"—she finger quotes—"*legitimate* degree, so I'm majoring in business. I didn't know you were transferring here too. Have you chosen a major yet?" Something akin to hope lines her features, but although I'm working on it, I'm still the same guy she took a chance on only to wind up disappointed.

"Nope. Still trying to figure it out."

Her smile falters before she drops her eyes to her white-painted toes, clad in a pair of sparkly sandals. It's late August, and the heat is slowly but surely becoming more bearable, but it's still well into the nineties. I can't blame her for wearing the shortest ripped jeans shorts she can find with a pink crop top that showcases her silky tan skin, but all it does is make me want to ask her what I did wrong to make her disappear without an explanation. We slept together after years of pent-up tension and then, just when I thought we were getting somewhere, she bailed on us before we even had a chance to start.

Was the sex bad?

Of course it was, idiot.

You lost your virginity to her.

Positive thinking! I mentally snap at myself.

"Well, I'm sure it'll come to you," she says. She hikes up the duffel bag slung over her shoulder, wincing from the weight of it. I reach out to take it from her, but she shakes her head and lets out another giggle that calls to the depths of my soul. "No need. I'm actually . . ." She scans the hallway before landing on the door next to mine.

Oh no.

Fuck no.

There is no way the universe would be this cruel to me.

"I guess we'll be seeing a lot of each other," she says. It's meant to be a joke to lighten the mood, but I don't have the energy in me to laugh. Despite my broken heart, I want the very best for her, but I came to State to try and *forget* her. To grow up and figure out what to do with my life. I didn't intend on living next to the one person who, for the first time in my life, had me telling my anxiety to go fuck itself so I could take my chance with her.

And now anxiety is coming back to seek its revenge. One look at her angelic face is threatening to undo months of healing when I promised myself I'd never go back to such a low point.

Maddie warned me about this happening, but I ignored all the red flags. I knew when my sister brought Maya home from school in the eighth grade that she would be dangerous, and I'm not talking about her looks. Sure, she's stunning and could be a supermodel if she pursued it, but her looks aren't what drew my attention when we first met. I was a sophomore in high school at the time, and she was way too young to catch my interest in that way.

It was her fiery personality that had me intrigued when she

followed Maddie into our living room like a tornado and proceeded to chat away like she wasn't nervous at all.

Maya is the life of the party. Outgoing and fearless, she lights
up any room she walks into. She's the center of attention whether
she wants to be or not, and as we got older, she embedded herself
in my mind until no other woman would suffice.

It was a stupid dream that she'd ever give me a chance. I'm
five eleven with a dad bod, which is nowhere near her type. I
saw her exes on social media, and all of them were tatted, buff,
and towered over her. She never dated them long; a few weeks at
most. And that should have been my first sign that her sleeping
with me didn't mean it would become serious. Maya likes to have
fun. She likes to flirt. She likes the chase.

I got so caught up in her game that I forgot the rules entirely.

"Hey, Garcia." A guy interrupts us, tugging at her silky black
ponytail before he winks and continues on his way. Her cheeks
redden in response, and all it does is make me more infuriated.
Garcia. She's already made connections and it's only our first day
on campus. Then again, looking the way she does while simultaneously being a social butterfly would have anyone kill to be her
friend. Maya is a lot of things, but she's loyal to the very core, and
my sister is lucky to have her as her best friend.

I just wish that loyalty extended to me.

"Well, I should get going." She flicks her eyes over me briefly,
a sad smile tugging at her lips. "It's good to see you, Ethan."

"I wish I could say the same." It's out before I can stop it, and
I don't miss the hurt that flashes across her face. Maya being here
is just another reminder of why I *shouldn't* be here. I've fucked up
everything good in my life, and a bachelor's degree will just be
another item on my never-ending list.

A tanked football career.

Grades that will never compare to Maddie's.

Sleeping with Maya and letting her slip through my fingers before I could call her mine.

Before the anxiety threatens to consume me whole, I open the door to my room and shut it with my back, leaving her out in the hallway alone. I would feel like an ass, but I'm not the one who said it couldn't work between us two weeks after we slept together and then proceeded to never even text me again. Now she wants to act like we're old friends? Like nothing happened?

Like she didn't moan my name and shatter against me three times in one night?

Leo glances up from the book he's reading. "*And* you pull hot women? Yeah, this is going to be the best year *ever*."

And just like that, Leo gets added to the list of people I'm inevitably going to disappoint.

Two

"Mamí, Papí, I have to tell you something."

Palms slicked with sweat, I sit opposite them in our living room, which can hardly be classified as such. We've lived in the same trailer since we came to America, so our "living room" consists of a tiny two-seater couch and a television that might as well belong in the 1990s.

My dad's forehead wrinkles in confusion. "¿Qué pasa?"

I've been sitting on this news for a week, and as nervous as I am, I have to tell them at some point. Ethan isn't just another guy to me. He's someone I want to get serious with, and in order for that to happen, I need to tell my parents.

"I'm seeing someone," I admit. "And it's going really well."

Two dates in, and I'm the happiest I've been in years. Ethan treats me like I'm a freaking princess, so all I can hope is that once my parents hear this, they'll want to meet him too.

Mamí's face brightens. Even after working herself to the bone *with three jobs, she remains youthful. Everyone says I resemble her, and I've always considered that a compliment. If I can age like her and still not look a day over thirty? I'll take it.*

"What's his name?" she asks in her thick accent.

"Well, actually . . ." I wring my hands together. Here goes nothing. "It's Ethan. You know, Maddie's brother?"

My heart falters at the disappointment that falls over her face, replacing her smile. My parents have made it clear they'd prefer me to end up with a man with a stable career. One who would be able to support our future family without having to go through the hardships they went through to make it all these years in America. A doctor, lawyer, veterinarian. Anything that pays six figures a year.

And it's not that they're gold diggers or anything, but they've made me understand how much sacrifice it took to provide me with the life I have. The last thing they want is for me to have the same experience. It's why they came here in the first place, so I don't take any of it for granted.

"No," my father says. "The boy who is friends with Cameron Holden?"

Okay, granted, Ethan doesn't have the greatest track record regarding his friend circle, but in his defense, he's been friends with Cameron since they were kids. Ethan didn't know he'd turn into a girl-obsessed player when they got to high school.

"There's more to him than that," I plead. "He treats me well, and—"

My father, the complete opposite of my mother, displays the hard work he's done for years on his face. It's wrinkled and worn from days spent laboring in the sun, and he looks tired, with heavy bags lining his eyes and gray strands peppering his cropped black hair. It makes me feel guilty for preventing him from going to bed by having this conversation, but this is important to me, and if I don't do it now, I'm afraid I'll never get the courage to bring this up again.

"If he wanted to treat you well, he'd do steps to take care of you. Not mess with girls all day. He was smoking that night we picked you up, right?" *It's* take steps, *but my parents' English is subpar at best. They can have a basic conversation, but I grew up having to translate for them for any major document signings or visits to the bank. Now that I'm transferring to a four-year college, they're taking classes to become more fluent since I won't be around as much to help them.*

Everything isn't about money to me. I've seen people live happily without a six-figure paycheck, but saying this to my parents never does any good. How could it when they've struggled for so many years? I can understand why it'd be a factor. My wants and needs have never seemed important when I've watched them run themselves into the ground to ensure we can pay our electricity bill and have food in the house. Even now, asking their permission to date a man I know they won't approve of makes me feel selfish.

And Ethan was smoking a blunt that night when my parents picked me up my freshman year after a sleepover with Maddie. He was around the side of the house attempting to hide it from his parents, and it didn't help that he put it out as soon as he noticed my parents' car. The image was embedded in their heads, and they automatically labeled him another party boy, like Cameron.

What could I say in his defense? At the time, he was with a different girl every week, and he was smoking. But they don't know him like I do. If they just met him and gave him a chance, they'd realize he's not the same as Cameron. He's far from it.

But it doesn't matter if Ethan isn't the guy he seemed. Explaining this to my parents would be fruitless when, at the end of the day, he still doesn't know what he wants to do with his life. If he can't prove to my parents that he'll be able to take care of me emotionally and physically, my parents will never approve.

"Bambina." My mother's use of my childhood nickname brings tears to my eyes. Her eyes soften in a way that lets me know that no matter how hard I try, they aren't going to budge on this. "We want the best for you. Do you understand?"

But what if he is the best for me?

It's on the tip of my tongue, but I swallow the words and give a curt nod instead. I was raised to respect my parents. Whatever they say goes, so it's useless to try and fight them regarding something they'll never change their minds about. I'll always be the obedient daughter. It's why I'm going to college for a degree I don't even want. It's why I'm allowing them to dictate my future now, despite every ounce of my being wanting to scream at them and fight for this.

They took themselves away from their families, away from a community they loved profoundly, and everything they've ever known to give me a better life than theirs. And while being with Ethan would make me happy, I can't sit here and promise that he'd never betray me and fall back into his partying habits. People make mistakes. It's bound to happen in any relationship. But my parents want someone perfect, with no flaws, and I don't know if they understand that perfection is impossible to come across.

"So, you're saying no?" I whisper through my tears. "You don't approve of him?"

My mother leans over to pat my hand, but a hint of regret shines in her eyes. "You will see when you have kids one day."

Papí nods in agreement. "Te amo, princesa, but no. We want the world for you, and Ethan isn't grown up enough to give you it."

~

"So, let me get this straight. You guys *weren't* dating?"

Propping my phone against the tiny desk beside my bed, I spread my makeup across it and sigh excessively at Maddie's endless questions. I love my best friend, I do, but the last thing I want to discuss is my hookup with her *brother*, and the way her eyes are sending me pity looks through the screen makes me want to end this topic of conversation as quickly as humanly possible.

"We hooked up, went on a few dates, and then I called it quits. You know how I am, Maddie. Long-term relationships aren't my thing." The lie rolls smoothly off my tongue, but my stomach sours all the same.

Ethan was more than just a hookup.

"Oh, come on," she deadpans. "You expect me to believe that? We've known each other since the eighth grade. You tried to hit on him by asking him about *sailing* this past spring break! I've never seen you try so hard with anyone."

She's right. I've never had to put in an effort for any man, and I'm not trying to be a cocky bitch by saying that. It's just the truth. Men have always done the work for me, but Ethan needed convincing. Maybe that's why I felt such a connection to him in the first place. He's the first guy I had to work for. The first guy not to comment on how hot I was within the first ten minutes of meeting me. It was refreshing.

Then, this past spring break, I made a move on *him* and sealed the deal, but sleeping with Ethan wasn't what I was expecting. His touch felt like heaven. His lips on my skin felt like he was kissing me not for my body, but for my soul, and when we locked eyes . . .

It was too much.

Too real.

Too terrifying.

"It doesn't matter why I ended things." I clear my throat and twist the cap off my mascara, but her unnerving gaze practically burns a hole in the side of my head as I face the compact mirror to apply it. *"What?"*

"Nothing." She moves her phone back and lies down on the comforter of her tiny twin bed. She's doing big things in Connecticut, studying at Briarwood to become a doctor, and although we still have weekly FaceTime sessions, they're not the same as seeing her in person. After running into Ethan for the first time since everything happened, I holed up in my dorm room for two days out of fear of bumping into him again. It would be nice to have her here to binge Ben & Jerry's and watch Lifetime movies with to fill the gaping hole in my heart.

"So, how's university life?" she asks, thankfully changing the subject. "Are you handling being away from your parents okay?"

That could be another reason I'm in a slump. In all my twenty years, I've never spent this much time away from my parents. The plan was to graduate from cosmetology school and work at a salon close to home, but my parents refused. They said having a proper education was important. After all, what would be the point in them going through so much just for me to become a cosmetologist? It hurt when they were disappointed about my passion, but I understood it. They worked three jobs and we could barely scrape by, so if I have to get a bachelor's degree to make them proud, then so be it.

"It's weird," I admit. "Mixed emotions, I guess, you know? I'm used to helping them with the chores around the house and making them dinner and stuff, but being away at university allows me to just live for myself. I'm not sure what that looks like yet." After a beat, I add, "I did get that waitressing job at the bar I was telling you about, though. It's only about a ten-minute walk from campus, and it'll help with their bills while I'm away. Make things easier on them."

Maddie's baby-blue eyes soften and her lips tilt into a sad smile. "You're a selfless person, you know that?"

"I'm really not, but for my parents I am. I owe them everything." *And that's why I ended things with your brother* is what I want to add but don't. I knew before I messed around with Ethan that he hadn't yet figured out his life and who he wanted to be, but in all fairness, I didn't expect our hookup to be loaded with so much emotion either. I thought we'd have a fun summer of fooling around, but I should have known there would be feelings involved, since we'd known each other for so long.

Telling Ethan the real reason I called it quits would embarrass him, and the last thing I wanted to do was hurt him even more. Unfortunately, Ethan, with his flighty path through life and facade of being a player—regardless of whether it was in the past or not—isn't going to meet my parents' expectations. It was better to sever the cord early, before things became serious between us.

And yet, seeing him two days ago felt as painful as the last time we spoke five months ago. Time doesn't seem to be healing *anything* when it comes to Ethan Davis.

"What are you getting all dolled up for?" Maddie twirls a blond curl that fell out of her messy bun, and tilts her head to the side to study me. "You look hot."

My ruby-painted lips lift into a grin. "Well, I was going to wait for my roommate to arrive so I could meet her, but she still isn't here. Some girls I met the first day invited me to a party off campus. They met some guys who are part of a fraternity, and it's supposed to be a rager since it's the last one before classes start. You know I'll never pass up a good party."

She laughs. "Trust me, I know."

"What are *your* plans for the night?" I tease. "Reality television? A good book?"

Her eyes dart away from the camera when a door closes in the background, and then her phone falls to the side as her boyfriend, Cameron, tackles her on the mattress. She squeals with laughter as he trails kisses down her neck, his large hands on either side of her stomach. "I fucking missed you," he groans. "Sorry I'm late. Practice ran over, and the drive took longer than expected."

My heart falters at the sight, and my chest swells with happiness for two people who almost didn't take a chance on each other because of Ethan. Cameron is Ethan's best friend, and with Maddie being Ethan's little sister, Cameron didn't want to risk losing him. I'm glad they finally said fuck it and started dating anyway, because now they're happier than ever, and so in love it's almost sickening.

"Hope you know I wasn't all talk in my texts." His voice drops lower. Huskier. "And now that I'm here . . ."

"Should I go?" I ask, applying a last bit of blush.

Cameron's head snaps up. He clearly hadn't realized his girlfriend was on a FaceTime call, but with Cameron being Cameron, he doesn't let it faze him. "Sorry not sorry, Maya. I fully respect your girl time, but I've only got your best friend for the next forty-eight hours, and I don't plan on wasting another second."

I roll my eyes. "I get it. We were just wrapping up anyway. Just like *you're* about to do in the next few minutes. At least, I hope so. Better safe than sorry."

He rolls his eyes, accustomed to my teasing by now. "Oh, before I forget." He grabs the phone to bring it closer to his face, wearing an arrogant smile. "I don't know what the hell is going on between you and Ethan but fix it. He's fucking depressed."

"What makes you think he's depressed?" I try to hide my concern but fail epically. It's evident in the way my voice goes high pitched. "And what makes you think his mood has something to do with *me*?"

"Oh, I'm sorry. I guess his other ex moved next door to him for the school year."

"I'm *not* his ex."

Cameron's eyebrows lift, and he's still wearing that fucking smirk. "My mistake. Fuck buddy, then?" He laughs when my eyes narrow into slits. "Is that too meaningless? Should I go back to *ex*?"

"Hey, Maddie, have I ever mentioned that your boyfriend is annoying?" My voice is playful. They know I don't mean it, which is why the lovebirds laugh in response. "*Anyway*, I'll let you guys go. Burn some calories for me."

"Have fun at the party!" she shouts in response. Cameron hangs up her phone, leaving me alone in an empty dorm room, and the silence eats at me. I meant it when I said this is the first time I've been on my own without my parents overseeing my every move, but it's so much freedom that I almost don't know what to do with myself.

Temptation. Drugs. Alcohol. These things surrounded me before when I snuck out to parties as a teenager, but now? I don't have to worry about my parents finding out. I'm free to choose whatever path I want.

But the biggest temptation of all?

Knowing Ethan Davis is on the other side of this wall.

Three

ETHAN
Five years earlier

Preseason training is the worst. Coach had us do suicides for the last fifteen minutes of practice, and every muscle is aching when I get home. After working out in ninety-degree weather the only thing I want is an ice-cold bottle of water, and possibly an ice bath.

Summer in Arizona is hotter than hell, but thankfully September is right around the corner, and the cooler months won't suck as much when Coach punishes us for not hitting the weight room like we were supposed to.

But it's my senior year, and even though there's talk of me getting a scholarship to play at State, I'm not set on it. Football is my passion, but having all the focus on me at every game is getting to be too much pressure. Granted, the focus is mainly on Cameron, who's gearing up to take us to the championship this year, but I still feel it as a linebacker. Because whereas Cameron controls offense, I'm the center of attention when it comes to defense, and I feel the expectation to be the greatest every single day.

"Oh. Hey, Ethan. Long time no see."

I drag my eyes from my phone, and my mouth drops open. Maya Garcia is standing in my kitchen, seemingly taking up every bit of space in the room without trying. I haven't seen her since before the summer started. My parents sent me to a football training camp with Cameron, and I just got back four days ago, before preseason begins.

How is it possible for a person to change so much in the span of twelve weeks?

It's all I can think about as I try to take in the new version of Maya, my sister's best friend. My *little* sister's best friend. I've always thought Maya was cool to be around, but I've never . . . well, I've never had my dick react to her like this, and it shouldn't. She's two years younger than me. She's about to be a fucking sophomore, for crying out loud.

But she's wearing a pair of tight yoga pants and a crop top that does little to cover up her body. When did she get so curvy? When did her hips start to look like they were made for my hands to grab onto?

"Um . . ." I'm staring at her like an idiot, and Maya's glossy lips tilt into the cutest smile I've ever seen.

"How was camp?" she asks. The microwave is humming in the background, the steady sound of popcorn popping. She and Maddie frequently have movie nights, so I'm assuming they're preparing for one.

Where is my sister, and why am I begging for her to come downstairs? It's almost like I need a shield to protect me from Maya, and nothing will douse my raging hormones better than having my little sister join us.

"It was good," I reply. "What did you do all summer?" Because

20

she had to have done something to go from girl next door to a curvy fucking bombshell. My eyes can't leave her full, pink lips, and I fight with every ounce of my being not to imagine those lips wrapped around my—

"Nothing, really. Hung out with Maddie mostly. Oh, and I've discovered a love for yoga. It keeps me calm, you know?"

Yoga can't possibly be the reason her ass seems to have grown three times in size.

"And flexible," she adds, and when she finishes that statement with a wink, I shift behind the island to discreetly fix my jeans. Jesus. Maya has always been loud and vibrant, and has never been ashamed of it, but this is the first time she's dropped sexual innuendos around me, and I'm not used to it.

"Oh?" It's the only thing I can think to say. It's the only safe question that keeps me from teetering into territory we shouldn't. This is my little sister's best friend. I'd never make a move on her. Maya Garcia is the one girl—woman, now, judging by how much she's grown up—who's off-limits to me.

"Mm-hm." She flicks her eyes over me, which feels scrutinizing. I'm not fit like Cameron, who has a glistening eight-pack. My stomach has a layer of fat covering whatever pack is beneath it, and while I'm not technically overweight, I'm not in shape either. It joins one of my many insecurities along with the height ordeal. Being five eleven sucks ass. So close and yet so far from what girls prefer. "You've gained muscle. How much can you bench now?"

"Almost three hundred." It's something I'm proud of. I hit a new goal at training camp, surpassing even Cameron, who lives and breathes the gym.

"Wow. That's impressive. You'd be able to bench me."

Christ.

The images flash before I'm able to stop them. I've never had sex before for a multitude of reasons. Partly my body insecurities, but also because no one has made me feel quite as crazed as the girl before me. Before seeing this mature version of her, she had me hooked on her fiery, blunt personality, but now . . .

Now I'm thinking of all the sex positions I want to learn with her and only her.

Judging by the look on her face, I'd almost assume that's what she wanted me to think after saying something like that, but I know better. A girl who looks like that would want nothing to do with me. She could have any guy she wanted.

Maya takes a step closer, and the heat in the room rises to a fucking inferno. It's hotter than it was doing suicides in the desert, and while I survived out there, I'm not so sure I can do the same here.

"Popcorn ready?" *Maddie pokes her head into the kitchen, and eyes us curiously.* "Everything okay?"

"Yeah." *Maya nods and spins around to open the microwave like that built-up tension was just a figment of my imagination, and maybe it was. Maybe I'm losing it.* "Just catching up about our summers."

I clear my throat and grab what I came in here for, needing the water now more than ever. "I'm gonna head back upstairs. Cameron's coming over in a few."

Maddie's nose wrinkles in disgust. "Great. Can't wait to hear about his conquests of the week." *The two had a falling out after Cameron's mom passed three years ago, but neither of them talk about it. We all used to be tight, but since Cameron got to high school, he's became a different version of himself. The kid who collected Pokémon cards turned to sex and partying the second we entered freshman year, which ultimately led to my sister despising him. Not that I can blame her. I'm still getting used to the new version of him too.*

"We'll be in your room the whole time," Maya reassures her. She dumps the popcorn into a bowl and flashes me a devastating smile. "See you around?"

I nod as they disappear upstairs, hating the way my eyes stay glued to her ass in those yoga pants. Maya is so much more than a nice body, but damn, if I don't appreciate every one of her new-found curves.

~

I wake up to the shrill sound of my ringtone. My eyes shoot open in the pitch blackness of the dorm room, just the faint light of my phone illuminating the space. After a quick glance at Leo, I feel thankful he fell asleep with his headphones on. The last thing I want to do is become a noisy roommate.

"Hello?" My voice is scratchy from sleep, and I answer without looking at who it is. The sound of pulsating music blaring in the background makes me pay more attention, and when I pull the phone away from my ear, my heart drops. "Maya? Are you okay?"

It's three in the morning. What the hell is she doing out this late, and why is she calling me? Alarms flash through my head when a drunken sob echoes through the speaker.

"I got a little too drunk," she admits. "My friends drove here, but they left, and I have no one else to call." I'm already out of bed and pulling on a pair of sweatpants when she adds, "You don't have to come. The last thing I want is to hurt you even more, and I swear I wouldn't call if I—" She hiccups, and if I wasn't so concerned about her safety, I might have smiled at the cuteness of it. "I promise if I had someone else, I would call them instead, but my friends went home hours ago, and I *can't* call my parents because—"

"I already said I'd bring you home, sweetheart." A guy's voice makes all the hairs on my body stand on end. I'll be damned if some random guy with questionable intentions takes her home.

"Where are you?" I blurt, grabbing my keys off the dresser. "I'm on the way."

She repeats the address slowly, like she's really trying to focus, and when she mentions a *fraternity*, I want to break every fucking speed limit to get there as soon as possible. What the hell is she thinking being drunk like that at a *frat house*? Who knows how many guys are surrounding her? I don't trust other men. I've heard firsthand in the locker room just what goes on at these types of parties, and I don't want Maya getting caught up in one of their twisted games.

"Stay where you are, and don't let anyone convince you to go home with them. Okay?"

"I won't," she slurs. "Promise."

Nothing is more terrifying to me than when the line goes dead.

Four

MAYA

I took my newfound freedom a tad too far tonight.

Okay, maybe a shit ton.

I've been sitting on the grass for what feels like an eternity because standing became too much. Everything is spinning, and closing my eyes only makes it worse. So now I've focused my gaze on the mailbox to try and gain a semblance of control again. Drunk people litter the yard, attempting to find their way home.

This guy Daniel hasn't left my side, and I don't get the vibes that he's trying to look out for me. He's repeatedly attempted to persuade me to let him drop me off, which I wasn't keen on. I'm drunk as a skunk, but not drunk enough to overlook the dangerous situation I've put myself in. And now Ethan Davis is coming to get me, like a knight in shining armor.

God, I've really fucked up tonight, haven't I?

I should have gone home with Destiny and Callie, but I foolishly thought I'd enjoy a couple more hours of partying. I've only known the girls for a few days, since we all just moved into the dorms, so I can't blame them for leaving me. I hide my liquor well until I reach a certain point.

Needless to say, I passed that point a long time ago.

"It's almost four," Daniel says. "Come on, let me drive you. I'm sober."

I clench the grass with my fingertips, needing something to tether me to this world before I pass the hell out. My brain is foggy and isn't working correctly, and Daniel smells like stale beer and cheap cigarettes.

Why did I call Ethan? I broke his heart, but, if I'm being honest with myself, I haven't been able to stop thinking about him. Severing the connection between us was better than continuing things only to break his heart again when my parents found out, but with him living in the room next door? Keeping my distance is way easier said than done.

"Come on," Daniel urges. He grabs my elbow and attempts to tug me up from the grass, making everything spin more. I place my hands on my knees and hang my head to try and get a grip when I hear another set of footsteps approach.

"I suggest you take your hands off her." I don't recognize the cold voice, but my world rights itself with one perfect glimpse of Ethan Davis. The man always wears a hoodie and a pair of sweatpants, which I know is because he feels self-conscious, although he has no reason to be. Sure, he's a little huskier than men I've dated, but it's something I've always liked about him. His hugs are warmer. His arms are stronger. And right now? Ethan looks like he's about to tackle Daniel, like he's playing a football game.

Daniel's wary eyes meet mine. "Is this who you called?"

"Take. Your hands. Off her," Ethan reiterates. I've never seen him like this. Who knew the soft-hearted boy could have a terri-torial side? And it doesn't make sense when I'm not his to claim, but him standing there with his arms crossed over his chest, all broody and caveman? It has my hormones in a full-blown *fit*.

I decide for Daniel by shrugging my elbow out of his hand and taking a tentative step toward Ethan. The world tilts, but Ethan's hands hold me steady. He runs his thumbs over my arms, and dips his head down to look at me. "Hey, you okay?"

"Yes. Everything is just"—I wave my hand in a circle as if that'll explain it—"spinning."

Daniel, who realizes he's not getting lucky tonight, *huffs* a sigh of frustration and stalks back inside the frat house. Solo cups and random bits of trash litter the ground around us, and it only takes Ethan five seconds of contemplation before he hoists me into his arms.

My thighs wrap around his waist, and for a heartbeat, I allow myself to enjoy it and not ask questions. I hook my arms around his neck and gaze into his eyes. They remind me of the icy blue hue you'd find in a bonfire, filled with rage and simmering with something I can't quite put my finger on.

"Christ, Maya. Do you know what could have happened to you?" He carries me to the sidewalk, avoiding the trash along the way, and my guilt replaces the moment between us.

"I wasn't thinking," I admit. My eyes feel heavy, fluttering shut as I fight to stay awake. "You don't have to carry me. I can walk."

"In those heels? Not a chance. I had to park a block away." He tugs on one of the neon-pink stilettos for emphasis, and I suck in a breath at the feel of his calloused hands caressing my ankle. *This was a bad idea.*

A *very* bad idea.

"Thank you for coming to get me," I whisper. "I'm sorry if I woke you up."

"Don't ever apologize for that. You know I'll always be here if you need me. I'd rather you call me in the middle of the night than attempt to drive home drunk or find a way home with someone like that idiot back there." His grasp grows tighter on my thighs, keeping a respectful distance from my ass. I almost wish he'd slide his hands up just an inch higher so he can feel the satin thong that matches my heels.

You are drunk! my subconscious snaps. *A stupid, flirtatious drunk. You always have been.*

Ethan's scent surrounds me like a sensual caress. Cedarwood mixed with a hint of spice. I want to nuzzle my face into his sweatshirt and bask in this moment, and I'm so drunk that I let my forehead fall into the crook of his neck despite every warning I give myself. "You smell *so* good," I groan.

His chest rumbles with a laugh. "And *you* are very drunk."

"How do you know?"

"Because I know *you*, and you're a ridiculous flirt when you've had too much to drink. It's the sign to look out for with you."

I want to tell him that he's wrong. Maybe I was a flirt in the past, but at every party I go to now, the only person I want to see is him. I miss him. I miss our late-night conversations at their house when Maddie went to sleep and I had nothing better to do than stay up. I'd join Ethan in the kitchen, and we'd have a bowl of ice cream and talk until the wee hours of the morning. Then we fucked and everything changed. I had to choose between my parents and him, and it'll always be them.

Instead, I say nothing, because staying silent is better than telling him I was too chickenshit to tell my parents they were wrong about him.

When we make it to his car, he tucks me into the passenger seat and reaches over to buckle me in. I want to sink my fingers into his disheveled blond hair, but I refrain and close my eyes instead.

"You okay?" he whispers.

My eyes flicker open, and time comes to a halt when Ethan's gaze dips to my lips before slowly working back up to meet my stare. I'm suddenly aware of how quiet it is a block away from the party. How there isn't a single soul on these streets to interrupt us if I was to do something incredibly stupid like make a move on him again.

Ethan doesn't bother to wait for my answer. He breaks the tension by shutting the door and clambering into the driver's side. My heart flutters when he passes me a bottle of water sitting in the cupholder. "You should drink this," he says. "It'll help."

And for the next five minutes, I sip my water while he drums his fingertips on the steering wheel. I shouldn't be bothered by the silence, but our friendship was never like this. It was teasing, flirtatious, and *fun*. I want to get back on common ground; I just don't know how. Flirting with him would send the wrong impression when we can't ever get back to the place we were in five months ago.

The world isn't spinning nearly as much when we make it back to my dorm room. I'm expecting Ethan to tell me goodbye, but instead, he follows me into my room and eyes the empty bed adjacent to mine. "You don't have a roommate?"

"Not yet. Maybe she'll get here on Monday when classes start." I collapse onto my bed, hair fanning out around me, and the breath stalls in my lungs when Ethan approaches and stands over me in a way that shouldn't be as domineering as it is. His eyes remain locked on mine as he grabs my foot and fumbles to get the strap of my heel off, then doing the same with the other. Then he examines my dresser, his eyebrows scrunched up in an agonizingly cute way. "Where are the makeup things?"

I tilt my head to the side. *Makeup things?*

"Yeah. Those things you use to wipe off your makeup."

"Ethan." Is my vision blurry from the alcohol or my tears? "You don't have to do this."

"Please." He scoffs, continuing to scan and remaining oblivious to the emotional reaction I'm having. "You're a licensed cosmetologist, Maya, and you fail to realize we grew up around each other. Your skincare routine is right up there with your fascination with *The Bachelor*."

That gets a laugh out of me. "What can I say? I'm a sucker for romance and glowy skin." I point to the spot beside my lipstick case. "It's that orange pack."

I sit up, and after he grabs a wipe, Ethan steps between my legs and tilts my chin up. I'm utter putty when he gently wipes my makeup off, taking his time and ensuring there's none left behind. He runs one last swipe over my lips, his thumb tracing the motion afterward. My pulse skyrockets from the contact, and I'm afraid if he doesn't step away from me right now I'm going to drag him onto this mattress with me.

"You should be good now," he says raspingly, his voice rougher than normal. He steps away and turns for the door.

"Wait," I blurt. "I really don't want to ask you to do this, but I can't reach the zipper of my dress." I'm not lying. Destiny had to get me into the skintight number before we left together, and without her here, it'll be hopeless trying to get out of it.

Ethan clears his throat and instructs me to turn around, and all I can think about is that night in the hot tub when I taught him how to fuck. When he surprised me by bending me over and nipping at my ass, almost like he's wanted to do it for years.

I'm a sweltering, wet mess when he steps behind me and tugs the zipper down. The dress falls to my feet before either of us can catch it, and although I shouldn't, I relish the strangled noise that leaves his throat. I'm not wearing a bra, which means the only thing he sees is my ass in a neon-pink thong.

The last thing I want is to lead him on, so I spin around and scramble to pick up the dress. Ethan juts a hand out to stop me. He does a slow, heated perusal of my exposed skin—like he didn't get a good look before and is trying to etch it into his memory now.

Alcohol still runs through my veins, and my hormones are overpowering the logical part of my brain. Ethan *stopped* me from putting on the dress, though, and that awakens the flirtatious, horny part of my brain that should be shut off.

"Do you like it?" I ask.

He *huffs* a laugh, no sign of anger or irritation. But that's how Ethan is. He's too good of a guy, always thinking of others.

Too good for me.

"The thong is cute, Maya. Very you."

There. A glimmer into the past of a friendship I longed for. Or not a friendship, since this is definitely not what friends do, but it's us, and I've missed it. The humor. The banter. The flirting. I don't wish we'd never slept together, because that night is something I'll cherish forever, but do I wish things could be different? Of course I do. If he could battle his anxiety and take a chance on himself to find what he's passionate about, maybe then my parents would see what I see in him.

But he's still living life by the seat of his pants, so despite my body urging me to tell him to come show me just how cute he thinks this thong is, I have to sober up, listen to my head, and be rational about this. Starting things back up with Ethan will only result in heartbreak.

"Do you need anything else before I go?" he asks.

"No," I whisper, ignoring the way my heart clenches. "Thanks, Ethan."

And when the door clicks shut behind him, I'm left with a nauseated feeling that has nothing to do with the alcohol and everything to do with how wrong it feels to be without him.

Five

ETHAN

Four years earlier

It's getting pathetic how obsessed I am with Maya. You'd think after knowing her for two years, I'd find a way to shake my interest in her, yet I'm downstairs watching television at midnight, wondering if she'll wait until Maddie goes to sleep and come join me for a bowl of ice cream.

I have no clue when this tradition started. She was up late during one of their movie nights and I guess she got hungry. Maddie was asleep already, and we ended up in the kitchen at the same time. I got out the cookies and cream from the freezer, and Maya said it was her favorite flavor. Before I knew it, I'd grabbed two spoons from the silverware drawer, passed one to her, and we'd shared a bowl of ice cream.

Now it's become a recurring thing. I stay up watching whatever is on television, and eventually Maya makes her way downstairs. I haven't told her this is something I look forward to on the nights she sleeps over, and she hasn't said anything, either, but I also feel like

I can't say something. It doesn't feel right. She's a sophomore, and I'm a senior. This attraction I've developed for her and whatever these ice-cream nights mean is scary as hell. Granted, we're only two years apart, but that feels like a lifetime when I'll be going to college next year and will be on a different journey than her.

I keep telling myself she's like this with every guy, but lately I've been wondering if maybe she thinks of me as something more than her best friend's older brother. I wonder if she wants me to become something more than that.

But it isn't the right time. Maybe in a few years I can make a move. When we're both older, Maddie might be more understanding. Until then, I plan on suffering through this fucking infatuation with her and everything she does.

As expected, the bottom step creaks before Maya tiptoes into the kitchen, smiling softly when she sees me watching a random sitcom. All the lights are off, so it's just the faint glow of the freezer when she pulls out the ice cream and waves it at me. "Hungry?"

I shrug as if I haven't been waiting for the past hour and a half. "I could go for some ice cream."

Joining her in the kitchen, I inwardly groan at the skimpy silk set she calls pajamas. I've noticed she's a fan of neon colors because they emphasize her tan, so I'm unsurprised at the vibrant green material. "You seemed off tonight," I say. "Earlier at dinner."

She pauses with the ice-cream scoop in her hand. "Why do you think that?"

"You weren't as talkative." I'm more of an observer and a listener, which is why I could tell by Maya's demeanor at dinner with my family that something was wrong. I watch everything she does, though, so my observations could be because I'm a stalker who can't seem to take his eyes off her.

"Maybe I don't always want to talk," she replies.

"That's not true, and you know it. If anyone loves talking, it's you. What gives?"

With a defeated sigh, she passes me a spoon and sets the bowl between us on the island. "It's stupid, but you know how Maddie was talking about going on the class trip to Disneyland? I lied and said I hated amusement parks when, truthfully, it's the one place I've always wanted to go. I didn't bother asking my parents because I know they can't afford it."

I nod thoughtfully while attempting not to be distracted when she swipes a cookie chunk from her bottom lip with her tongue. From what Maddie's told me, Maya's parents aren't wealthy. She lives in a trailer park that she's embarrassed about, so Maddie doesn't go over to her house much. It's easier if Maya comes here.

"I don't know," she continues while I process her confession. "It makes me feel guilty for being jealous, you know? My parents bust their asses to make ends meet, and I want to complain about going to Disneyland?" She shakes her head in frustration. "God, even saying it out loud sounds—"

I cut her off before she can finish. "You shouldn't feel guilty for wanting to go somewhere fun. It's okay to be upset, and I'm sure your parents would understand if you told them, and who knows? Maybe they'd find a way—"

"You don't get it." Tears form in her eyes, and the sight nearly brings me to my knees. "The trip is five hundred dollars, Ethan. That kind of money could pay for our groceries for an entire month. Even if my parents did find a way to pay for it, I wouldn't want them to. That's why this year I'm going to get a job and help them out. I'm sixteen now, and although it won't bring in a lot of money, it'll be something to help, you know?"

Right now, staring at Maya stealing another bite of ice cream from the bowl, I'm seeing her in an entirely new light. Yeah, she's outgoing and the life of the party, but she's got the biggest heart, one I already admire, and she deserves to go to Disneyland, dammit. No one deserves it more.

"What?" she asks, breaking me out of my trance. "Why are you looking at me like that?"

"I'm not looking at you like anything," I lie, as I go in for another scoop. "I just hope you make it to Disneyland one day."

~

Two weeks later, Maddie is chattering away at dinner about how thrilled she is that Maya can go on the class trip to Disneyland with her. Apparently, the teachers picked one exemplary student in the class to go on the trip for free, and they nominated Maya.

I eat my spaghetti in silence while Maddie explains that Maya was so happy she cried. It's an effort to hide my smile, but when I get back to my room, it takes up my entire face.

Working at Perry's ice-cream shop during the summer came in handy, and when I found out Coach was one of the chaperones on the trip, it didn't take much convincing to get him to help, since I had the cash. I don't know how he came up with the whole nomination thing, or how he convinced the staff to vote for Maya.

All I care about is she's going on a trip she wholeheartedly deserves.

~

Happy Endings is the closest bar to campus, and it lives up to its name. Rumor has it that any person who walks into Happy

Endings looking to get lucky will, indeed, find their match—whether for a lifetime or just a night. You wouldn't think that after setting foot in the place. The music is really loud, and the entire place looks like it's in serious need of a deep cleaning, but I guess superstitions exist for a reason.

My sneakers stick to the beer-clad wooden floors as I search for Mark, a former teammate of mine from high school. We were close back then, and stayed in touch even after he got a full ride to play for State, and when he discovered I was transferring he almost threw a damn party. *Literally.* The star offensive tackle is known for more than his skills on the field. The dude can throw a mean rager when he wants to.

Neon signs practically blind me as I squint at the booths in the back, but it doesn't take me long to find him. Mark is one of the biggest guys I know. Six foot three, fucking jacked, and makes the booth he's sitting in look like a high chair.

"Dude, I can't believe you're officially here!" He rises from the booth—which shakes due to his weight—and claps me on the back. His shoulder-length blond hair is pulled into a man bun on his head, making him the spitting image of Thor with his scruffed beard cropped close to his chin and around his mouth. "It's so good to see you, man. How have you been?"

"I've been all right. Excited for classes to start tomorrow. You?"

"I'm more excited for football season. Preseason is cool and all, but I'm ready to kick some serious ass." I slide into the booth across from him, and drum my knuckles on the sticky table because I can feel in my fucking bones what he's about to suggest. "You should come to a game this season. Check out the team."

I despise the look of pity on his face. It says *Why did you give*

DEANNA FAISON

all of this up? And it'd be easy to confide in Mark. He didn't have the greatest childhood, so he'd probably be able to relate to my constant state of anxiety, but it's not something I'm comfortable sharing. Hell, even Cameron didn't find out about all of this until a few months ago, and he's my best friend.

I presented myself as someone I wasn't when we were in high school because I was afraid Cameron wouldn't like the real me. He wanted to fuck and party, and I felt most comfortable at home playing video games. The two of us wouldn't have been able to mix. But after telling Cameron the truth, I felt like an idiot for wearing a mask all those years when he was the one person who would never judge me or leave my side. He would have been my best friend no matter what, but he was going through the loss of his mom at the time, and it seemed more important to make sure he was okay rather than dump my emotional baggage onto him.

"I think I'm going to steer clear of games this season," I admit.

"Oh, come on." He gives me his best impression of puppy-dog eyes. "It's my senior year."

"I think your ego will be just fine if I'm not in the stands. I'm sure you have countless cheerleaders filling those spots."

He chuckles, and I swear it rattles the booth. "You know I don't play dirty like that. I'm a one-woman type of man." I do know this, which is why we were close in high school. He gave me a reprieve that Cameron couldn't. It wasn't Cameron's fault he loved everything to do with girls, but Mark was someone I could just chill at my house with and binge *Fast & Furious* while we smoked a joint rather than attend whatever party was happening that night.

"Look." He leans forward in the booth, resting his elbows on the table. "If you won't make it to one of my games, why don't you come out to one of the youth football practices? I'm an assistant coach, and the kids would love someone else to watch them and give them advice."

"You want *me* to advise kids?" *I have nothing to offer them* is what I want to add. I bailed on playing college ball out of fear of leaving my comfort zone. Fear of being a disappointment to everyone. Kids have nothing to learn from me. If anything, they should do the *opposite* of what I've done.

"They're a wild bunch, but they're also a hell of a lot of fun. They make you realize why you fell in love with the game to begin with."

I can't remember why I fell in love with football. I know it *was* my passion, but at some point between getting on varsity and graduation, everything felt so serious. It felt like my future was riding on every game I played, and that was a lot of pressure I didn't know how to handle. I lost sight of the reason I started.

"Is this some ploy to get me to try out for the team? Because it's not going to work."

He uses his fingers to make a cross on his heart. "No games. Just watching kids have a blast. And *if* you feel there's any advice you can give, then by all means, speak up. It'll be nice having an extra set of eyes out there."

I groan. "Fine. I'll agree to one practice *if* you stop with the fucking puppy-dog eyes. They're creeping me out."

"So they worked? Cool. I'll text you the address and—"

Two menus are abruptly slapped down in front of us.

The waitress's arms are crossed over her chest, and her foot is tapping impatiently. "What the hell do you want?" The question is directed at Mark, who doesn't seem fazed by the woman's attitude one bit. It only seems to fuel his good mood.

"Tabi has claws today, I see," he muses.

"You do realize my name isn't spelled like the *cat*, right? Or did all those football collisions knock loose a screw or two?" She swipes at a bead of sweat trickling down her forehead. Not that I can blame her, it's stifling hot in here. Maybe that's Happy Endings' key to living up to its superstition—making people so dehydrated that they're thirsty for just about anything.

"I assure you my head is exactly where it needs to be. Ethan, do you know what you're going to drink?"

Tabi looks at me as if she's just suddenly realizing there's another person at the table, and a silent apology passes between us. There's a tiny apron around her waist that she pulls a notepad out of, gazing at me expectantly as if that weird-ass interaction didn't just happen.

"Um, I'll take a Michelob Ultra so long as it won't get spit in or anything."

Her lips tilt into a grin. "No worries. The only drink that will be spat in is Mark's."

"Which is why I only order bottled beverages." Mark winks and passes her back the menu.

"You come here often?" The place is practically deserted for an early afternoon. I know that the ratings for this place are poor, and their food ratings are even worse. I highly doubt this is an establishment that has a dish Mark craves, but when his eyes slide from Tabi's wide-set hips and linger on her full chest a beat too long, I suspect it's a *person* he craves and not the food.

"He's here every Saturday, Monday, and Friday afternoon." She narrows her hazel eyes at him. "The *only* shifts I work."

Mark places a palm over his heart as if he's flattered. "That's a little conceited of you, Tabi. I can't help it if your shifts are on the days I don't have practice. I get hungry."

"And you're just *desperate* for frozen fries and day-old burger patties?" she asks.

"What can I say? I'm a sucker for freezer-burnt takeout."

Tabi *huff*s in defeat and stalks off to the other side of the restaurant, and while Mark's gaze lingers on her retreating back, I respectfully look the other way. The waitresses at Happy Endings might have the skimpiest uniforms known to mankind. A pair of black booty shorts and a neon-pink crop top with a palm tree logo make no sense when their only location is in Arizona, but who am I to judge? They're the most popular bar on campus for a reason.

"You never ordered your drink," I say.

"Don't need to. Tabi already knows my order."

"And are you and Tabi . . . ?"

He snorts. "Fuck, no. She'd gut me before I could make a move. So would her father." When he realizes I'm still confused, he adds, "She's the coach's daughter. Aside from that, she's my least favorite fan."

"Why?" Mark is a lot of things. Funny, easygoing, smart. But he isn't mean, and he isn't a fan of fucking around with women to make them respond like Tabi just was.

"It's complicated between us. You know Ronnie took me in when I was in high school, so he's the only reason I'm playing for State now. If he wasn't the coach, I'm not even sure I'd have gotten a full ride." He shakes his head as if attempting to get back on track. "Anyway, Tabi's his only daughter, and he didn't exactly ask her permission for me to move in with them. She's got a lot of resentment toward me. I get it. However, I've always loved getting beneath her skin."

"Hate to break it to you, but it doesn't seem like the feeling's mutual."

His eyes glisten with mischief. "That's what's so fun about it, but anyway, enough about me. I'm surprised you came today. You aren't the type of guy who drinks beers on a Monday afternoon."

I'm not, but today is an exception when I'm dying for something to make me forget Maya and that neon-pink thong. The image has been burned into my memory for two days now, and it took all my willpower not to give in to the temptation of another memorable night with her. I'm not that kind of guy, though, and I couldn't even pleasure *myself* when it felt wrong. She was drunk and flirty like she always gets when she's under the influence, and my only job was to ensure she made it home safely. Maya isn't mine—she made that clear five months ago—so even thinking about her ass is off-limits.

"Drinking isn't my thing anymore," I admit. "But certain circumstances call for—"

"Hey! Who ordered the—oh! Oh my god. What are you guys doing here?" Maya fucking Garcia is holding a tray with a beer and a bottle of water on it, looking godsent in her skimpy uniform. Her long black hair is in two French braids that cascade down her back, and her face is glowing and perfect when her brown eyes latch onto Mark. She's purposely avoiding eye contact with me, but I can't say I blame her. Especially if she remembers our last interaction.

"Damn, when did you start working here?" Mark asks. "I didn't even know you'd transferred to State."

She grins proudly. "It's my first semester. I did the community college thing for two years, graduated from the cosmetology program, and now I'm pursuing a bachelor's in business. How about you? From what I hear, the team has a good shot at the championship this year."

"Possibly. You know I never like to get my hopes up. Being too conceited is a recipe for failure."

Finally, her eyes slide to mine before she averts them to the tray. "Who, uh, ordered the Michelob?"

"Me." I clear my throat when she sets it down in front of me, and I swear I drink half the damn bottle before she places the water in Mark's hand. I hate how awkward things are between us when it never used to be this way. We had good banter and even better chemistry, but it seemed like when we finally gave in, it only made things worse. For whatever reason, having sex complicated things, and although I don't regret that night, a part of me wonders if we'd still be close if we'd never slept together.

"Do you guys want anything to eat?" she asks.

"No, I'm all right. Thanks." I'll pass on freezer-burnt food.

Mark grins before he says, "You can ask Tabi for my order, and you can also tell her putting another waitress at our table isn't slick. She's not getting away that easily."

Maya arches a brow. "Well, you'll be pleased to know I'll be working night shifts on the weekends, so she'll be all yours again next week. She's training me before classes start."

Don't get me wrong, I'm an advocate for women wearing whatever the fuck they please, but it doesn't sit right with me that she's going to be wearing that Happy Endings uniform at night. Will she bring a change of clothes? I know she doesn't have a car, so how the hell does she plan on getting home? She's not going to *walk*, right?

God, I have no reason to be protective. She isn't mine to

worry about, but I can't help it. A piece of my heart will always belong to her, and there's nothing I can do about it. Believe me, I've tried.

Mark stutters. "I don't want her to be all *mine*, I just meant—"

In typical Maya fashion, she rolls her eyes and gives him a little wave. "Save the lies for someone naive. See you guys around. Oh, and Ethan?" My eyes snap to hers, noting the way her cheeks are redder than they were a few seconds ago. "This shade of pink is a close second to my thong, don't you think?"

Fucking hell.

Her flirtatious remark is my own fault. I don't know what I was thinking when I held her back from putting her dress on. I just, god, I missed her. I love staring at her. And it'd been months since I'd seen her.

I deserve that. I'll admit it.

I had no business stopping her.

With her hips swaying, she disappears into the kitchen, leaving me utterly dumbfounded. Her teasing and sexual innuendos have always been part of our banter and humor, but that was before we had sex. Now her flirtatious remarks only bring a twinge of longing.

Is she flirting with me as a friend or as something more? Or is it payback for the way I behaved? She certainly wasn't opposed to leaving her dress off, but that doesn't mean she wants me. Does it?

Fuck. My head is already throbbing.

I won't be able to survive mixed signals from her. Not when I've been certain that she was the only girl for me since the second I lost my virginity to her. It sealed the deal in my eyes, but then she ghosted me. Now I feel like an idiot for mentally signing a dotted line on us while her signature remained vacant.

I shift uncomfortably in the booth as I try to adjust the semi in my jeans, and Mark says, "Well, *now* I know why you wanted to drink on a Monday afternoon. Should I get another round for you?"

"*Please*," I grumble. "And while you're at it? Make it a double."

Six

MAYA
Five months earlier

"Is there a reason you're acting like an inmate who just escaped prison? Christ, Ethan, slow down! What the hell is wrong with you?" His gentle grip on my wrist guides us through the tables in the fanciest restaurant I've ever been to, the red exit sign coming into view seconds later. Ethan suggested this dinner in the first place, which is why I'm only more confused when he tugs me outside and continues striding toward the car, leaving Maddie and Cameron behind. "Ethan!" I whisper-shout. "What is going on?"

He whirls to face me, his eyes dipping to the low-cut neckline of my dress before he heaves a sigh of frustration. "Get in the car. We need to talk."

Ethan Davis, who normally has a better handle on his emotions than anyone, looks like he's about to lose his shit, and to be honest? It's kind of hot. He's raking a hand through his shaggy blond hair, his jaw is clenched, and his blue eyes are running wild.

Out of the two of us, I've always been the one to act irrationally.

Prime example: suggesting a game of chicken in the pool yesterday and telling him I planned on getting wet regardless of if we won or lost. I say and do things without thinking whereas Ethan meticulously plans everything he's going to say before the words leave his mouth.

He opens the door for me, placing his hand on my exposed lower back to help me inside. My skin ignites in flames at the bold contact because even though I flirt with him nonstop, he's never reciprocated. I know why: I'm Maddie's best friend. But Maddie knows I have a crush on her brother and, as of last week, is all for us hooking up. The one roadblock in our way has vanished, but I don't know if Ethan knows that.

What I do know is I'm loving this version of him. The one who can't seem to keep his hands off me. Shy, tentative Ethan is coming out of his shell, and I like it.

"What do you want to talk about?" I'm breathless when he shuts the driver's-side door and starts the engine. His fingertips drum on the steering wheel in time to a rock song playing quietly on the radio.

"Is this one-sided? Is—" He stops himself, his lips forming a thin line. "Are you into me, or am I delusional? Because sometimes . . . sometimes you'll flirt, and I can't tell if that's just your personality or if you're trying to make a move, and I haven't wanted to say anything because I didn't want to make things weird between us, but lately I . . . fuck, I can't get you out of my head, Maya, and I'm sorry if this is coming out of left field, but—"

"You think I'd hit on you for the hell of it?" I tilt my head to the side, watching his throat work on a swallow.

"Well, I'm me, and you're you, so . . ."

"What does that mean?"

"It means I've seen the losers you've brought around for years. They look nothing like me. They're tall—"

"So are you."

"Handsome—"

"So are you."

"But—"

"I'm sorry. Are we actually debating whether I should or shouldn't find you attractive? We've tiptoed around each other for years, Ethan. You can't sit in this car and seriously tell me you've doubted that I've been into you this whole time. How could I have made it more obvious?"

He squeezes the steering wheel before dropping his hands. "I'm not trying to debate it with you, I'm just in shock, I guess. I didn't expect you to say yes."

"You've brought other girls around, too, you know. I see the parade of cheerleaders you and Cameron work your way through every month."

Ethan's jaw ticks, but he doesn't tell me I'm wrong, either. He can't. When he's around Cameron, he's a different person. He's lively, energetic, and outgoing. He's different when it's just us in the kitchen at midnight sharing a bowl of ice cream. The real Ethan is hesitant, but he's got the biggest heart and would take the shirt off his back for anyone. It's like he wore a mask in high school and could finally take it off when he got home. It didn't make sense. It still doesn't.

"Okay, so, we're into each other," he says, ignoring my statement about the cheerleaders. "Where do we go from here?"

I furrow my brows. Why is Ethan acting like he's never done this before? He knows what comes next. We're in a car alone for fuck's sake. It doesn't take a rocket scientist to figure out the next step of the plan. "Where do you think we go from here?"

He shakes his head. "I don't know. We have to tell Maddie first."

Little does he realize Maddie isn't a factor anymore, but that's a conversation he needs to have with her himself. I know Ethan, and until he hears it from Maddie, he isn't going to believe it.

"Maddie aside, do you want to know what I think we should do next?" I move over the console to place a hand on his thigh. His eyes shoot down as if he's etching this in his memory for eternity, watching as I move my hand slowly to the crotch of his jeans, where his erection is already waiting for me. I'd be lying if I said I haven't longed for this for years. Ethan and I have always had sexual chemistry, but we've both been too afraid to make the leap.

"Maya." His voice is gravelly, filled with warning as I palm his erection. Little by little, the temperature rises in the car, and my thighs are clamped together in an attempt to gain some sort of friction while he raptly watches me palm his cock. He glances over at my thighs, which are exposed since my dress has ridden up.

Leaning in close with my lips pressed against his ear, I whisper, "This is the part where you kiss me."

Whatever tether is holding Ethan back snaps. One second I'm on my knees in the passenger seat, and the next he's pulled me onto his lap to straddle him.

His lips meet mine with a force that has me moaning instantly. I'm shocked at how much passion is behind it. I'm thrown by how I've gone without kissing him for this long. His hand drags up my back to wrap in my hair, holding me at the base of my skull while he completely devours me. My mouth opens for him, allowing his tongue to collide with mine, and damn, is it good. No wonder all the girls in school wanted to sleep with him.

I'm grinding against his growing erection when suddenly his

hands land on my hips and he rips his mouth from mine. "Fuck, fuck, fuck," he mutters, inhaling deeply through his nose. "We need to stop."

"Stop?" The word is foreign to me. I have never had a man tell me to stop what I'm doing. I've never had any complaints, but maybe my pasta had too much garlic at dinner. Shit. Does my breath smell? Am I bad a kisser? I've never been told that before, but . . .

"I just need a second," he pants. "To breathe."

"Um, okay?" I slide back over to the passenger seat and put my seat belt on in a total state of confusion. What happened? Did I say something wrong? Do something he wasn't comfortable with? I'm racking my brain while Ethan mutters under his breath and pulls out of the parking lot, and the entirety of the drive back to the Airbnb is spent in silence.

Twenty minutes later, Ethan opens the sliding door that leads out to the patio, where I'm currently sulking in the hot tub. His parents went to bed hours ago, and Maddie and Cameron aren't back yet. I didn't want to be in the bedroom across from Ethan's because even that felt too close. My blood is still humming from our kiss, but my heart is broken all the same.

I should have known it was a bad idea to come on this spring-break trip with their family. Yes, Maddie is my best friend, but the older I get, the harder being around Ethan becomes. And after he pulled away from our kiss, I'm pretty sure I've royally fucked this up between us.

Why do I feel like this? I've never been upset over a man's opinion. I can tell myself all I want that Ethan is just another guy, but deep down, I know he's more than that to me. Our midnight ice-cream time and brief moments around his sister have been enough to drive me crazy, and although I played it cool earlier in the car when he confessed his feelings, I was relieved this game between us was finally over.

And then he went and started the game clock over.

"Can I join you?" he asks.

I shrug, swirling the water around in front of me to play with the bubbles. "Your parents booked the place. I can't dictate where you can and can't sit."

With a frustrated sigh, he enters the hot tub with swim trunks and a T-shirt on. He wore a T-shirt in the pool yesterday, too, and it bothers the hell out of me that he thinks he needs one. "Look," he starts, "I didn't want you to stop kissing me earlier. What I said came out wrong, and I'm sorry you took it that way. I just—"

"You just what?"

Steam passes between us when he locks eyes with me and says, "I had to stop because I'm a virgin and I didn't want to embarrass myself by coming in less than ten seconds."

Silence.

Nothing but dreadful silence.

I pop my mouth open to say something but then snap it shut because what the fuck am I supposed to say to that?

"This is why I didn't want to tell you. Nobody knows. Not even Cameron, so if you could keep this secret between us then I'd appreciate it."

"How?" It's the only response I can think of. "I've seen you with countless girls, Ethan. You've escaped with them upstairs at parties only to come downstairs looking all disheveled. You expect me to believe you're a virgin? I wasn't born yesterday."

"Think what you want, but I'm telling you the truth. It was easy to make it seem like I hooked up with other girls. Escape to the bathroom, flick water on my face, mess my hair up. It takes a lot of effort to keep a facade up, but I did it."

"For what?"

"More like for who. Cameron lost his mom, and to cope with the loss, he turned to partying and sex. I didn't want to lose him, so I became the person he needed me to be." Ethan says that sentence like it isn't a big deal. Like changing his entire personality to please one person hasn't affected him. "He never asked me to do it, but I knew if I didn't do those things with him, he'd find himself in a deeper hole, and I wasn't going to let him lose himself entirely."

"That's . . ."

"Selfless?" he suggests.

"No." I shake my head, blinking away tears. "I was going to say that's lonely. You've been faking this personality, but who has been there for you? Who checks in on you?"

"Well, I can think of one person I sometimes share ice cream with at night. I'd like to think she knows the real me."

I smile softly. "Oh? She sounds incredible. Tell me more."

He closes the distance between us and drags my body against his. Water laps over the sides of the hot tub, falling through the cracks of the deck and onto the grass below. "She is incredible, and I'm not going to be an idiot any longer by hiding things from her if I actually have a shot here."

I do something I've always wanted to do: I rake my fingers through his hair, loving the way his eyes fall closed. "You do have a shot," I whisper. "I've never been with a virgin before, and while your lack of experience doesn't deter me, I just thought you should know. If you still want this, I'll teach you what to do. We can figure it out together."

Why is that turning me on? It's so rare to find a guy who's never had sex before, and knowing I'm about to teach him what to do and be the only girl he's ever been inside of? Yeah, it's definitely doing something for me.

"And you won't judge the hell out of me if I finish quickly?"

I giggle and roll my eyes. "Will you shut up and kiss me already?"

His lips taste even better than before, minty freshness melding with my tongue. I have no idea what I'm doing offering to take his virginity, but Ethan is kissing me and being downright distracting, so I'm going to roll the dice and see what happens.

Thinking things through isn't my strong suit.

"Take this off," I pant, grabbing at the soaking-wet fabric of his T-shirt.

"Okay, but I don't look like—"

"You look exactly as you're supposed to." My fingers wrap around the hem, and after a jerk of his chin for confirmation, I peel it over his head and toss that shit to the side. So long as we're doing this, he's never going to wear a T-shirt in the water again.

I allow my eyes to rake over his chest, trailing past his sternum and into the water where his abdomen meets the band of his shorts. Ethan is panting heavily, purposely avoiding eye contact, like he's terrified I'll run away in fear at what he looks like. Where do these insecurities of his come from? His body isn't bad at all. Sure, he doesn't have an obvious eight-pack, but his stomach is sexy as hell. More to grab onto. More of a stabilizer while I ride him into oblivion.

I push him onto the bench of the hot tub and straddle him, running my fingertips over his stomach in gentle, caressing strokes. "I love what you look like, Ethan. Don't hide from me."

His eyes open as if he's seeing me for the very first time, and *now that the insecurity of his body is handled, a new version of Ethan comes to the forefront. Blazing desire ripples through his gaze when he says, "Well, since I took my shirt off, maybe you should return the favor."*

There he is.

I've never had doubts about my body or dealt with insecurities, so the removal of my top is accomplished in less than five seconds flat. It floats in the water beside us as Ethan takes his fill. He's always avoided checking me out, almost like he was afraid I'd think he was a creep or something, but now that I'm allowing him to look? He's staring at me like he's a man who's been stuck in the desert for weeks, and I'm the first glass of water he's seen.

Goose bumps pebble my skin in response.

No one has looked at me this way—like I'm a work of art. The guys I've been with before only wanted to sleep with me to rave about it in the locker room the next day, but not Ethan. I can tell that the dirty details of what happens between us tonight will be secret forever.

"You're fucking beautiful, Maya," he says. "Goddamn. I mean it. You're perfect."

A knot forms in my chest, but I refuse to break down crying in a hot tub right now. "Wait until you see my pussy," I reply to lighten the mood. "That's pretty perfect too."

He rolls his eyes, accustomed to my dirty mouth. "I have no doubts."

Since this is his virginity, I have to take the wheel for the first time in . . . well, ever. I lift my hips and reach down to the band of his shorts, only to hear a sharp intake of breath. I wonder how long he's waited for this, and I wonder why he's agreeing to lose his virginity to me, of all people.

"Is this okay?" I pull the band back with two fingers, and when I get another nod of confirmation, I pull out his hard length and hold it in my hand. Ethan's cock is so thick I can hardly wrap my hand around it. The thing has a heartbeat of its own, and when Ethan glances into the water, he inhales deeply through his nose, then rests his head against the back of the hot tub.

"I'm not going to fucking last," he blurts. "Not at all."

"It's going to be fine," I whisper, giving his cock a long, hard tug. The steam is swirling around us, a perfect ambiance for the heated state I've worked myself into, and I'm so wet I'm probably dripping at this point. Teaching him is so much hotter than I thought it'd be.

I move off him briefly to remove my bikini bottoms and let them float next to my top. Then, when I'm straddling him again, I rub his cock along my slit, my core clenching when his moan sounds like he's being tortured. "Do you feel how wet you get me?" I whisper into his ear. "How could you be self-conscious when my clit is throbbing for you?"

"Fucking hell," he groans.

"How long have you wanted your cock inside of me, Ethan? How many times have you thought about it?" It's so tempting to slip him inside of me, but I keep reminding myself I need to take this slow. Or is that just a stigma? It's not like it'll hurt him.

"Too many times," he pants. "Way too many." His hands slide to my ass, and I gasp when he gives it a firm squeeze. He thrusts his hips to drag his cock along my slit, and the feeling is pure heaven. My head rolls to the side, and I feel my release counting down like a ticking time bomb until he suddenly stands up and hoists me up so my stomach is over the ledge of the tub, my ass hitting the cool night air.

"You want to know what I've thought about? This." He spreads *my legs wide before he falls to his knees on the bench, making him directly eye level with my ass.*

"So, you're an ass guy?" *I halfheartedly laugh before his teeth meet my skin, then cease any sort of laughter. He sucks my flesh like he's worshipping the ground I walk on, leaving hickeys all over the damn place, but all I want is for him to move to my pussy. I want his mouth between my legs.* Need *his mouth between my legs.*

Has he done that to anyone yet?

I'm tempted to ask, but then he pulls me back into the water until we're in the position we were before. My legs are shaking as I straddle him, and now I'm wondering how the hell he's flipped the tables on me. I was supposed to be teaching him how to fuck, but something tells me he's going to do just fine in that department.

A turned-on Ethan is a controlling Ethan.

And I love it.

"Did you get your fill?" *I tease.*

"Hardly, but if I continue looking at your pretty pussy any longer, I'll come, and I have a virginity to lose."

Have I met my match?

It takes me a second to recover, and Ethan seems amused at how surprised I am. "Where do you want to come, Ethan? I'm on birth control."

He flicks his gaze to my breasts before dipping between my legs in the water. "I'll come in you . . . on you . . . the choice is yours."

"Um, okay." *When the hell did I get nervous? Why is my pulse skyrocketing when I grip his cock again? Why does it feel like I'm overheating when I slip him inside of me?*

More importantly, why does it feel so right?

Ethan's jaw drops at the sensation, and when he looks at me, I . . . fuck, I told myself I wouldn't cry, and I'm not going to start now. *His face is a canvas of emotions, leaving me with no doubt about what he's thinking. I can see how much he cares for me. I can feel the connection between us like it's a physical, attainable entity.*

Words fail us both when I start to ride him. His hands scrape down my back until finally settling on my ass, squeezing and touching like it's the last time he'll ever be able to do so. This is his first time, but it's not mine, and I can't help it when my hips take on their own rhythm. I'm barreling close to release with him staring up at me like I'm a fucking goddess.

"Fuck, where do you want me to—"

"Come in me," I gasp. "Please come inside of me."

His grunt fills the silence, and it's enough to topple me over the edge. I pant his name over and over again while I ride out my high, feeling his cock jerk inside me as he has the longest ejaculation I've ever felt a man have. I collapse onto his chest, allowing him to hold me close and press a kiss to the top of my head.

For me, intimacy has never come in a form other than sex, but lying on Ethan's chest and listening to his heartbeat while his fingertips trace my spine? It's bringing feelings I never realized existed up to the surface.

It's his virginity that was lost.

So why does it feel like it was mine?

Seven

ETHAN

It's the first day of classes, and I'm not sure whether I'm relieved or disappointed Maya wasn't in any of mine. Not that I expected her to be. State has a huge campus, so the odds of her living next door to me *and* sharing a class were slim to none, but I still found myself scanning the students in the room for black glossy hair and skin that rivals the dunes in Egypt.

I don't know why I want to see her when she's giving me hot and cold signals. Well, in her defense, I haven't tried to reach out to her either after Happy Endings, but what would I say? I don't want to bring up what happened between us because it's fucking embarrassing. We went on two dates, and then she ghosted me out of nowhere. It doesn't make sense.

The Coffee Lounge is the one spot I know I'll be visiting frequently on campus. After a full day of classes, I'm exhausted, and if I have any hope of completing my assignments, I need all the caffeine I can get.

The sound of espresso machines and the smell of coffee beans instantly relax my mind. Potted plants line the walls and open windows, and multiple tables are scattered around the space. It's the afternoon, so it's not busy. Only a few students with their laptops in front of them occupy the place.

But the girl in front of me has me debating whether or not I need the caffeine. With her perfect ass hugged tightly by a pair of denim shorts, I'd recognize her body anywhere. After all, I've fantasized about her hips for years. I've always felt like their Coke-bottle outline was made for my hands.

"Caffeine boost?" I say when I step behind her in line.

Caffeine boost?

That *is what you come up with of all the things to say? God, you're an idiot.*

She tenses for a split second before she glances over her shoulder and shoots me a smile. "The first day was rough. I hate everything about school, but it's necessary, so . . ."

Why? Because of her parents? I've always known they've been strict with her. Maya's parents moved here from Mexico when she was five to give her a better future, and Maya does everything humanly possible to make them proud. I've only met her parents in passing, never officially, but I know enough to understand they put a lot of pressure on her without realizing it. Maya's determination to make them proud is admirable, but I wonder if she's ever thought about chasing her dreams instead. She's already a licensed cosmetologist. Why doesn't she see where that takes her?

But I'm not one to offer any life advice when I don't even know what the hell I'm doing with mine, so I keep my mouth shut.

"Do you want to sit together?" she asks.

"Yeah." My reply is instant, and it's an effort not to cringe. It's so fucking obvious that I'm down bad for her, but it doesn't seem to put her off. With her brown-sugar espresso and my Americano in hand, we find a secluded table in the back.

I watch her hands wrap around the cup before she brings it to her lips, fascinated with the sight. There isn't a thing Maya Garcia does that I'm *not* utterly obsessed with. The woman is perfect to me. She's my dream girl.

"I'm glad we ran into each other," she says. "I wanted to apologize for yesterday, but didn't know how."

My brows quirk up. "Apologize? What for?"

"I feel like ... I don't know. I feel awful about how things went down between us, Ethan. You deserved more of an explanation than me disappearing out of your life, but believe it or not, it was just as painful for me to walk away as it was for you. I miss our friendship. I miss our late-night talks over ice cream, but sleeping together made everything more complicated, and now that we aren't sleeping together anymore, I feel like I have to watch what I say around you. The thong comment? I said it without thinking, but as soon as it left my mouth, I realized how wrong it was. That's how our friendship was before, you know? But the last thing I want to do is lead you on. I don't know what to do or where to go from here."

"Then why did you ghost me?" It's out before I can stop it. I usually think things through before I react, but I've thought about this every day since she walked out of my life five months ago. "Was it something I did?" My voice drops lower into a whisper. "Was the sex bad?"

"What? God, no. Our sex was . . ." She sighs and shakes her head. "Would it make you feel better to know my walking away had nothing to do with you? It was my decision."

"But now you want to be friends again."

"Is that so wrong? We're living next door to each other. It'd be nice if we could at least see each other without all this awkwardness. And I'll totally understand if being friends again is too much for you. I don't blame you if you'd rather keep your distance, but I don't think I'll forgive myself if you don't at least know that I miss you in my life."

So, our falling out had nothing to do with me, but she doesn't feel comfortable enough to share the reason? It doesn't make me feel better in the slightest. It just waters the seed of doubt I've let fester inside me since she vanished, and now she wants to be friends. How can I possibly be around her without wanting to kiss her again? My heart isn't ready for that. But am I prepared to let her go completely? Am I ready to not have her in my life at all? Whether I want to admit it or not, living without her had me transforming into the cold, lifeless version of myself I was before I met her. Being friends wouldn't be everything I want, but it would be *something*, and isn't something better than nothing?

I've never been one to make irrational decisions. Well, except when Maya told me to kiss her five months ago. I didn't think twice before my lips met hers, but even then, I stopped it and went back to the house to have a moment of clarity to be sure it was something I wanted to take the risk on.

This isn't a minor decision, especially when my heart is on the line.

It's better to be safe than sorry.

"Can I think about it? I don't know if being friends is something I'll be able to handle, and I'll have to give it some thought before I give you a final answer."

Her full lips twist into a sad smile. "I wouldn't expect anything less. I'm just grateful you're considering it." A liquid sheen coats her eyes, and for the life of me, I can't understand why she looks so upset about this. If she said the word, we could be together. I would forgive her without any questions asked.

What the hell happened to make her run away?

The urge to lean over and wipe away her tears is insufferable. I'd do anything to take away her pain, and because of that, even though I'll go back to the dorm to think about her proposition, I already know what I'll decide.

Maya means the entire world to me, and if I have to choose between something or nothing?

It'll always be something.

Eight

MAYA

The first week of classes went by in a blur.

I was practically bored to tears listening to my professors drone on and on about product-line planning and implementation. My hands itch to dye someone's hair a bright purple. I crave the feeling of being the reason someone's self-esteem skyrockets. Makeup, hair, nails—I love them all. There's a sense of freedom that comes with beauty. People can be whoever they want to be.

Maybe that's why I was so inclined to break my parents' rules and sneak out to parties. It didn't happen often since they kept a close eye on me, but on those nights, I'd never felt more alive. I could be whoever I wanted to be—but the older I got, the more I realized I still had no idea who that person I wanted to become was.

This is probably why I'm getting ready for another party even though the one last weekend went so poorly. I'm using this freedom to go buck wild, and I know it won't end well for me. Still, Ethan not giving me an answer makes me want to take three shots to the face to try and forget I suggested anything in the first place.

I knew there was a high probability he'd turn me down. Why would he want to be friends when I'd ghosted him? I don't deserve his forgiveness or his friendship. And, sure, I could tell him that my parents disapprove of him, but Ethan is an emotional guy. It was easier to ghost him and tell him nothing at all than tell him the truth and risk hurting his feelings even more.

I at least expected an answer, but when I ran into him yesterday, four days after I proposed we be friends again, he just gave me a weak smile and brushed by me as if I had never said anything at all.

It's what I deserve, right?

A taste of my own medicine?

But he doesn't realize that I *had* to end things. He wouldn't understand. He doesn't know what the pressure is like to be the first generation of *everything*. The first person in the family to graduate high school. The first person to graduate college. I'm the daughter my parents rely on. Their translator. The one who helps them around the house because they work themselves to the bone holding down three jobs. Their daughter, who feels selfish for going out to a party tonight because it makes her feel like she has a semblance of control in her life when the truth is she's in a downward fucking spiral she can't get out of.

Blinking away tears, I coat my face in setting spray once my makeup is finished, and that's when I hear it. *Moans* coming from the other side of the wall.

I'm rooted to my chair as distant thumps soon coincide with porn-star sound effects, and it shouldn't make me want to flip this damn desk over, but I'm quick to anger. I'll own that. Maybe that's why I slam my makeup case down and screech my chair back, slide my slippers on, and stomp over to Ethan's fucking door and bang the hell out of it.

It's not like he isn't allowed to fuck, but it's just I *taught* him how. I don't know why I thought he wouldn't move on at some point. Maybe it's because I haven't. I haven't been able to kiss anyone else. Touch anyone else. Even *think* about anyone else without him and that night invading every section of my mind.

The door swings open to reveal a fully dressed Ethan. His neck is red and splotchy, and dammit, I can't help myself when I look behind him to see what girl he brought into his tiny twin bed.

But the bed is empty, and the moans are still—

"Close the door," his roommate groans. He pokes his head above the comforter before a cheesy smile crosses his face. "Oh, it's nice to officially meet you. I'm Leo, and this is—"

"Casey." A girl giggles from beneath the covers.

Oh my god.

"Um, you too? I'm Maya."

"I've heard," he replies. "Now, if you'll excuse us . . ."

"Right. Sorry." I whirl around to head back into my room but Ethan grasps my wrist and closes the door behind him, leaving Leo and Casey to have their fun. I feel like an idiot when he lets go and leans against the wall with his arms crossed over his chest. He wants an explanation, but it's too embarrassing to admit I was jealous for no reason.

Leave it to me to act irrationally.

Again.

It seems to be a trend for me.

"I was just on my way out." He reaches into his pocket and

pulls out a perfectly wrapped blunt. "This is probably the only thing that'll help me forget what it sounds like to wake up to Leo fucking some random girl." After a beat, he adds, "Is there a reason you stopped by?" His eyes drag down my thin tank top, denim miniskirt, and slippers. "In slippers and *curlers*, might I add?"

Oh shit.

My hair.

My cheeks are on fire when he smiles and says, "Oh, did you think it was *me* fucking someone in there? Is that why you rushed over here?"

"*No*, I thought I heard someone fall, so I wanted to make sure you guys were okay." At the sound of his laughter, I know the jig is up. It's pointless to try and get myself out of this one. "Okay, fine. Maybe I thought someone was in there with you, but it was stupid. You can have sex with whoever you want. I have no right to—"

"Care to join me?" He lifts the blunt with two fingers, rolling his eyes when my lips form a thin line. "It's legal, Maya. Nothing's going to happen if you smoke a joint with me in my car."

Hanging out with Ethan has a lot more promise than going to whatever stupid party the girls upstairs convinced me to go to tonight.

"This is weird," I say. "Normally, I'm the bad influence, not you."

"Is that a no?"

Mierda, he looks good as hell right now. He makes sweatpants and a hoodie look like a thirst trap. And with him holding a blunt in his hand? He looks like a boy up to no good, even though he's the furthest thing from a rebel.

"I need to take these out first." I tug at the curlers, my heart faltering for a beat when his lips twitch, threatening a smile.

"Okay," he replies. "I'll wait."

It's been so long since he's looked at me like I'm not the person who shattered his heart. His smile gives me hope that I might have a second chance at rekindling what we had.

Well, the friendship.

Not the other stuff.

Because unfortunately, no matter how much I may want him to be, Ethan becoming anything more than a friend isn't written in the stars for us.

Nine

ETHAN

Ethan Save me. My roommate is fucking someone, and he thinks I'm asleep

Cameron Nice. Ask to join

Ethan I hate you

Cameron What? You're single, right? Why not get the real college experience?

Ethan Again, I hate you

Cameron What's the expression? Two's a crowd, and three's a party?

Ethan Ending this conversation. Forget I texted

Cameron Is that a no???

~

It's pointless trying to convince myself that staying away from Maya is for the best when she's always been the center of my universe. Even when I tried my hardest not to think about her, it never worked, and seeing her all worked up over the thought of me sleeping with someone else? I've got no chance in hell.

I don't know the reason why she ran away from us, but she said it had nothing to do with me, and where I doubted that before, now I don't. Jealousy was written across every single one of her delicate features, which means the connection between us is still there. So why did she end things? Or is she just the type of person to be possessive about someone she's had sex with?

She returns to me with curls that remind me of a '90s bombshell, and damn, is she a sight for sore eyes. Everything about Maya is perfect, but my favorite feature? Her smile. All straight and pearly white, it could make the heavens shake, and I can't take my eyes off her. Not even for a second.

"I'm still wearing my slippers," she says, as if I care what her choice of shoes is. "They're comfortable, and I don't want to change into wedges if we're just going to your car."

I glance down at the furry pink monstrosities bedazzled in tiny silver jewels. "They're cute."

"Really?"

"I mean, by themselves, they're the most awful things I've ever seen, but I think you could wear a trash bag and still look cute." It's the first time I've openly hit on her since we hooked up, and I'm more than pleased to witness her cheeks turning a bright pink.

When we're inside my car, I pull the lighter from my sweatshirt pocket and light the blunt, seeing her eyes flick down to my lips when I take a long pull from it. We're in a secluded part of the parking lot, and since it's pitch black outside, the way she's staring at my lips seems a lot more intimate than it probably should. It forces me to lean over and turn on the radio to ease the tension.

"Here." I hold it out to her, but she shakes her head. "You don't want to smoke?"

"I do, I've just never done it."

"Oh, come on. *You?* Maya, you're the biggest daredevil I know. You *live* for partying, and you mean to tell me you've never smoked weed?" Then, so I don't sound like an ass, I add, "Not that it matters if you don't want to smoke. I'm not trying to peer pressure you or anything. I can roll the windows down if you want."

"No, it's not that I've never wanted to, but my parents disapprove of it. I know it's legal, but with the tiny trailer we live in, they would have smelled it on me in a heartbeat. I didn't want to take the risk." She eyes the blunt and asks, "Is it like a cigarette? Because I've smoked one of those once but hated the way it made my chest burn."

"Kind of." An idea forms in my mind, and I shouldn't, I *really* shouldn't, but it's too tempting to pass up. "I could shotgun it to you."

"Huh?"

"Like I'll pull from the blunt and blow it into your mouth. Less impactful on your lungs that way, so it might make your chest burn less."

Her pupils dilate at the suggestion.

Fuck me.

"I guess that'd be okay. Just tell me what to do."

I shift uncomfortably in the seat, willing my dick to settle the fuck down. This shouldn't be such a turn-on, but it's not often that I get to teach *her* something. I'm a hermit who would prefer to stay indoors, and she's the adventurous girl who has way more life experience than me.

But this?

She's going to learn something new from *me.*

"You're just going to inhale when I get close to your mouth," I say.

"That's it?"

Is it just me, or does she sound breathless?

I nod and lean over the console. "Ready?"

"Yeah," she replies with a dip of her chin. Determination oozes from her, so it gives me all the reassurance I need regarding any doubts I might have when I pull a long drag from the blunt. I hover above her lips and slowly blow the smoke out, watching her mouth part to inhale what I'm giving. Our eyes lock, and my dick hardens without me being able to control it. Maya is a flirt, there's no doubt about it, and those brown eyes of hers have always been the way into her soul. Lust and desire radiate from them, taunting and teasing me to say fuck her reasons and make a move, but I've never been that kind of guy. I'd never make a move when she verbally told me she didn't want this.

The moment between us evaporates when she throws an elbow over her mouth and erupts into a fit of coughing when she's finished. *So much for it being easier on the lungs.*

Panic bubbles in my chest. "Are you okay?"

After a few more coughs she finally comes up for air, her eyes watering and leaking a few tears. "*Christ*," she mutters, and then she *laughs*. The sound is like music to my ears. "How long before it kicks in?"

I shrug. "It's your first time, so relatively quickly. Especially since we're hot boxing."

"I didn't realize you still smoked."

"Not as much as I used to, but some nights are more difficult than others."

She nods as if she understands. "Did things get better after you told Cameron the truth about everything?" *My virginity* is what she means, but I get why she's fearful about saying it aloud when she's the one who took it from me.

I think about my life now that everything is out in the open, but nothing seems to have changed. Sure, I told Cameron that to help him cope with the loss of his mom I had pretended to be someone I wasn't when we were in high school, and although that lifted a ton of bricks from my chest, it didn't improve my life any.

"Things with Cameron are better, but—" I take one last pull from the blunt before I snuff it out. "I don't know. I think I've pretended to be someone I'm not for so long that I've forgotten who I am in the process."

She blows out a harsh breath. "That's some deep shit, Ethan."

"It's the truth. Wearing all those different masks was almost like a crutch. It's easier to pretend to be someone I'm not than face the reality of who I am."

"You say that like it's a bad thing."

"Isn't it? I have no clue what I'm doing with my life, Maya. I took a gap year thinking my life aspiration would come to me, but I'm not like Maddie. I wasn't born with a passion to help others. The one passion I grew to love I couldn't hold on to because I was terrified of the pressure that came with it. It seems like everyone I graduated with is off chasing their dreams, but I got left behind. Being here? It's because it's what I *should* be doing, but there are nights that I sit in this car and wonder why I'm wasting my time." My biggest fears escape me like word vomit, but there's no one on the planet who knows me like Maya. The real me. Our ice-cream nights let me be the most vulnerable version of myself, so spilling my guts to her doesn't make me anxious. If anything, it's like falling back into an old routine. It's *natural*.

"You're not the only one who feels that way," she whispers. "I'm trying to make my parents proud because being a cosmetologist isn't enough. I hate everything about school. All I want to do is travel the world and make people feel beautiful, you know? It's so simple, and yet it isn't. My parents need help. They need to be taken care of financially. But I don't like feeling as if I'm chained to Arizona for eternity because of them." She sighs. "I'm not trying to discount what you're saying or make this about me, but you should know you're not alone in the whole *finding yourself* thing. Without my parents here to watch my every move, I have no idea who I am with all this freedom, or what that means for my future."

Who knew two people could be so different yet go through such similar struggles? Maya craves travel, whereas I would prefer to stay in Arizona, where I'm most comfortable. This is another reason why I didn't want to play professional football. Traveling every weekend to a new state sounds like getting your teeth pulled to me and isn't something I want.

She erupts into an uncontrollable fit of giggles, and it's so fucking cute that I find myself laughing too. "Oh, god. We're high, aren't we? That's why we're talking about our deepest, darkest secrets."

No. Well, maybe she is, but I'm confiding in her because she's always felt like a safe place for me to do so. It's nothing to do with the weed and everything to do with my feelings for her.

"I think *you're* high."

She bites her cheek to stop laughing, but it's no use. She's doubled over again, and it takes a minute or so to come up for air. "Maybe this is the year we find ourselves," she pants.

She doesn't realize how much effort I'm making to do just that. Since setting foot on campus, my mission has been to find myself and figure out what I want to do for the rest of my life.

"And maybe we can do it *together* if you ever answer me about being friends again," she adds.

"We're hanging out now, aren't we?"

She rolls her eyes. "Come on. Be serious."

"Says the person who can't stop laughing." When she remains straight-faced, I grip the steering wheel and rest my head back on the headrest. "I want to be friends again, Maya, but I don't want to be tentative friends. I want things to go back to the way they used to be, and I don't want you to tiptoe around my feelings or worry about my ego or anything. I'm a big boy who can handle rejection, and while it still hurts, I'll get through it. I'd rather have you in my life as my friend than not have you at all, but I want you as my *true* friend. How we were before we slept together."

"Are you sure?" she asks. "I don't want to lead you on, Ethan."

"Flirtatious comments, sexual innuendos, and a dirty mouth are who you are, Maya. I don't think you're leading me on. It'd be weird if you *weren't* like that. As I said before, I'll be fine. I want the same as you. To be friends."

Her eyes linger on mine for a beat too long. "Right. Friends."

That term doesn't feel right to label the connection we have, but it's the one she wants to use, so I'll have to accept it. Maybe she's right about finding ourselves together, and while it'll be helpful to have someone struggling with the same thing, it's also going to be difficult to remain emotionally detached and treat her as nothing more than a friend.

And when Maya reaches into her bra to pull out a ChapStick, exposing half her chest to me, I internally curse and shift my eyes to the ceiling of the car.

This is going to be so hard.

Fuck. I must have said that out loud because Maya giggles for the umpteenth time and shouts, "That's what he said!"

But just like that, things seem to return to normal.

Ten

MAYA

College has never been something I dreamed about.

Even in high school, I found the routine tedious. Homework, studying, *reading*. None of it was for me. I hated learning about history and despised mathematical equations. It never occurred to me that it was because I was a creative person who wasn't interested in becoming a lawyer, or a doctor, or any career that required an immense amount of schooling. And then I heard about the cosmetology program.

For as long as I can remember, doing hair and makeup for others was the only potential career I could see for myself. However, since it wasn't the ideal job my parents envisioned for me, I concocted this plan that I'm not even sure would work. They want me to attend school to get a business degree and become an accountant or an investor, but in the back of my mind, I plan on using my business degree to open my own salon.

It's not something I've ever mentioned to anyone because saying it aloud means I'll be following through with it, and there are a lot of things I'd need to accomplish before I can make it happen. I'd have to build up a clientele first, then obtain a loan and a piece of real estate. Not to mention convincing my parents that this could work once I graduate. I'd be going against their wishes for me, but if I build up a clientele and have the data to prove this could work, then . . .

The professor draws me from my thoughts, reminding us about an online assignment due in a few days. I file out behind everyone else, and when I enter the crowded hallway a large, muscular arm slings over my shoulder.

Xavier Santos, basketball team captain, tugs at my ponytail. "Hi, Garcia. Fancy seeing you here. Econ?" He jerks his head toward the classroom, his sculptured jawline and pristine white teeth momentarily distracting me. The guy is attractive, I'll admit it, but he gives the term *player* an entirely new meaning, which says a lot since Cameron Holden is on my list of friends.

I met Xavier on my first day here. He was with some of his frat brothers scouting the new girls moving into the dorms, and the second he laid eyes on me, he made it his mission to get into my pants. His moves didn't work, but it's not because they weren't convincing. If this was a few years ago and my feelings weren't tangled up in someone else, I'd totally fall for the six two heartthrob.

"Unfortunately," I admit. The class seemed to last an eternity, but it's necessary for a long-term goal. At least, that's what I keep telling myself. "Did you just get out of class too?"

"Accounting. It was boring as hell, but my mood is *much* better now that I ran into you." He wiggles his brows, and his thumb rubs a tiny circle on my shoulder before I slip out of his grasp.

"Watch your hands, *Santos*. I already told you I'm taken."

"Which is funny since I've *yet* to see you around campus with another guy."

My lips tilt into a grin. "Maybe I'm simply not interested in you. Have you ever considered *that*?"

I roll my eyes when he tosses his head back and laughs. He's a confident, arrogant jock who couldn't possibly fathom that a girl wouldn't be interested in him. I've had my fair share of *Xaviers* and am more than pleased to say I've learned my lesson.

With tan skin and green eyes, he's a walking wet dream, but he's the kind of guy who flaunts his status around campus. Even now, he's dressed in a white TEAM CAPTAIN T-shirt with the school's red and black bulldog logo and tight gray sweatpants that leave little to the imagination.

"Come on," he urges. "I helped you move into your dorm. The least you can do is pay me back with a date."

"*You* were the one flexing your muscles in front of half the student body, insisting you could carry my baskets with hardly any effort. You offered, and I already paid you back by allowing you to help me. Girls fawned over you the entire time, so I'm guessing you got your fair share of *payback* thanks to me."

His grin kicks up a notch—one I'm sure usually gets him what he wants. "Fair enough. I did get a lot of numbers that day. It won't stop me from shooting a final shot with you, though. Go on a date with me, Garcia. Just one."

A lump forms in my throat as he stares at me expectantly, awaiting my answer. College is supposed to be filled with hot mistakes like Xavier, but it doesn't feel right to agree to a date, especially after Ethan and I seemed to have mended things last night. We decided to be *friends* and return to our normal, flirtatious banter, but I'd be lying if I said there wasn't a sliver of hope that something more than friendship could eventually transpire between us.

And I shouldn't hold on to that hope when so many odds are stacked against us, but I can't help how I feel around him. Can't help it that—

As if fate wants to intervene, I round the corner and run smack dab into Ethan Davis. His eyes meet mine in confusion before they flick to the tall man beside me, an expression of annoyance crossing his face for a split second. He quickly feigns indifference when he says, "Hey. I didn't expect to see—"

"I was supposed to meet you for coffee. I'm so sorry. Class ran over," I finish, sending pleading eyes to my one and only savior. I'm not ready to go on a date with anyone, especially not Xavier, and I hate how well Ethan seems to know me, because he picks up on my reluctance regarding the basketball player all too quickly.

"Hey, man. I don't think we've met." Xavier sticks out a hand for him to shake, but Ethan doesn't reciprocate the gesture.

"In passing. I vaguely remember you pulling on her ponytail the first day we moved in and calling her *Garcia*." His jaw clenches as if he's reliving the memory. "Or something along those lines."

"Ah." Xavier smiles wider. "The boyfriend, I'm assuming? My bad, man. I didn't mean to overstep. She told me she was taken, but—"

I won't let Ethan become an actor for a part he's been desperate to play since we slept together. I'm not cruel, and I refuse to be a tease when I'm the reason for our falling out in the first place.

But before I can interject, Ethan takes a step closer and grabs my hand. It sends heat over every inch of skin, and my pulse skyrockets when he adds, "And yet you're still here talking to her.

Is *no* a word you haven't learned yet?" Then my pulse stops when he scans my face and asks, "Are you okay, baby?"

The nickname sends my heart into overdrive.

I'm comforted by the arm he wraps possessively around my waist. I lean into his touch and tug on my bottom lip when his fingers absently trail along the bare skin of my midriff exposed by my crop top, every nerve ending in my body seeming to short circuit in his presence.

Students headed for the next set of classes crowd the hallway, seemingly oblivious to the tension between the two men. Thankfully, Xavier throws his hands up placatingly while sporting an innocent smile. "You're right. I apologize." He gives Ethan a once-over before shifting his attention to me again. "See you around, Garcia."

"Don't count on it," Ethan tosses over his shoulder when Xavier passes us.

When Xavier disappears from view, I selfishly allow Ethan's touch to linger for a beat longer before I step out of his arms. "Thank you. He's been trying to convince me to go out with him for weeks."

"Seems like a dick."

"Eh. He's nice enough, but he's the type of guy who does everything under the moon to score you, and then, as soon as he does, he leaves you high and dry."

Ethan's brow lifts, and I almost cringe when I replay the words I just spoke. In his eyes, I must be no better than Xavier. It's what I did to him, and I've regretted it every day since.

But rather than embarrass me by calling me out, he stares down at his sneakers and asks, "So, you don't want to go out with him?"

"Ugh, *no*. He's not my type."

Ethan chuckles. "Come on, Maya. That guy is exactly your type."

"*Used* to be." Because ever since Ethan, my type has changed. The woman-eaters who chewed me up only to spit me out don't compare to the guy who's made my feelings his priority since day one. I've come to prefer the guy who loves basic sweatpants and hoodies over the jocks who flaunt their status and reputation. Down to earth, kindhearted, and shy are the qualities I find myself seeking now, but I always come up short. I know, without a shadow of a doubt, no matter how hard I search, I'll always end up here—right in front of *him*.

Ethan's baby blues bore into me, attempting to decipher the truth behind my words, but I won't allow him to discover it. We agreed to be *friends*. Nothing more. Regardless of the physical and emotional pull I feel toward him, I have to fight it.

He clears his throat, sidestepping a guy who attempts to pass. "Well, I have to get to class, but we'll talk later?"

"Right. Of course. Thanks again."

"You don't have to thank me, Maya." He hits me with a smile that shoots straight to my ovaries, and then he follows it with a *wink*. "I'll be your fake boyfriend anytime."

I shouldn't, I really shouldn't, but *he's* the one who said he wanted things to go back to the way they were between us, right? He wants my flirtatious comments, so I don't think twice when I grab his hand as he turns to leave.

"Good to know, *baby*. I'll see you soon."

And when he releases a belly-gut laugh, grinning from ear to ear, I can't shake the giddiness that floods through every vein, sparking me up from the inside out. It's a feeling that's been dormant for too long. It's *electrifying*, and I didn't realize the full extent of my misery without him until now.

Because where things with Xavier and every other guy feel wrong, Ethan is a painful reminder of just how *right* they are.

Eleven

MAYA

"Okay, but I think I like the pink better." Destiny examines each nail, one painted baby blue and the other bubble-bath pink. When my new friends found out I'd graduated from cosmetology school, I became their designated personal tech. Not that I care. It's my favorite thing to do, giving makeovers, so I'm living for this little get-together we're having in the common area of the dorm.

Thankfully, no one else is in here, so it's just us with my bucket of nail polish. I wish I had the money to buy supplies to do acrylic sets, but I'll live with just doing polish for now. It's better than nothing.

"I like the blue." Callie leans over to inspect the colors, then gives a nod of affirmation. "Yeah, definitely the blue. It goes better with your complexion."

"You think?" Destiny tilts her head to the side with her hands splayed out in front of her. "Okay, blue it is."

I'm sitting cross-legged on the uncomfortable couch while

The Bachelor plays in the background on a shitty television that sometimes loses signal. This common area doesn't include much. A few couches and chairs and some random artwork that doesn't go with the dingy blue walls whatsoever, but it has a TV. That's all I care about.

I can't miss my show.

I'm getting everything set up on the coffee table when Ethan and Leo enter the room. Their eyes quickly share the same reaction, and they make a move to bolt from the girlfest unfolding until I smile and say, "Care to join? We're watching *The Bachelor*."

It's been a week since Ethan and I agreed to be friends again, but we haven't seen much of each other since that night. We've been busy with classes, and the times we have bumped into one another, it's been in passing. Example: him pretending to be my fake boyfriend for five minutes. I don't want to miss out on an opportunity to hang out with him, even if I do have to rope him into a girl's night.

"We were going to play cards." Ethan holds up a box.

"Well, don't let us stop you. There are plenty of free tables over there." I point to the ones directly behind us. "I promise we won't be *too* loud. Unless you want us to be."

Leo immediately strides to the table. "I'm in."

Ethan rolls his eyes. "Seriously, Leo? One flirtatious comment and she has you giving in that easily?"

Leo shrugs. "I can't help it. Pretty girls are my weakness."

Ethan seems annoyed by the comment, but rather than say something, he sighs and joins Leo at the table. Leo is shuffling the cards when Ethan turns to me and says, "You aren't working at Happy Endings tonight?"

"Nope. I only work Saturday and Sunday nights."

He frowns. "You don't ever get a weekend off? How are you going to balance school and work?"

I shoot him my best puppy-dog eyes. "Aw, do you care about me?"

He smiles softly and looks at the hand Leo dealt him. "That's a stupid question, Maya."

"Because it's true?"

"Will you guys *shut up*? Ryder is about to hand out the roses!" Callie turns the volume up, eyes glued on the devastatingly handsome man in a suit. I take turns painting Destiny's nails and stealing glances at the television, muttering my disapproval when he hands a rose to the woman causing the most drama in the house.

It's not until Ryder is on the final rose that I hear Ethan scoff from behind us, "This is completely unrealistic."

Callie seems offended. "Why do you think that?"

"Because you can't know in a matter of weeks if you love someone. This show is based purely on attraction."

Callie shakes her head. "So untrue."

"Is it? Why don't they have any plus-sized people on this show? Why are all the contestants drop-dead gorgeous? The show doesn't pick anyone average looking to participate. Why do you think that is?"

"I . . ." Callie furrows her brows, attempting to think of a valid response.

"It depends on the bachelor or bachelorette," Destiny adds. "I've watched some pretty self-centered people on this show, but there are also genuine ones who don't base it on how someone looks."

Callie sighs dreamily. "Call me superficial. I don't care. I only know what's been revealed on the show about him, but Ryder's my dream man. He's perfect."

"Point proven," Ethan says.

"Someone sounds a little salty," Leo teases. "What? You don't think you could be the bachelor, Ethan?"

He tips his head back and laughs. "No way in hell would I be chosen."

I hate the way he views himself. I hate that he feels so insignificant when he's so fucking hot. He's the sexiest man I've ever laid eyes on, and I'm not kidding. He has no reason to be insecure, but it's evident in the way he's expressing his hatred for this show. He thinks he doesn't compare to those guys when that's simply not the case.

"Maya could be the bachelorette," Destiny says, then goes back to blowing on her polish. "You're the prettiest girl I've ever seen."

I roll my eyes. "Come on. Have you seen *yourself*?"

Callie switches places with Destiny and sorts through the nail polish. "She's telling the truth. You'd be perfect for the role. Guys would literally drop to their knees to get a chance with you."

Ethan grunts and shuffles the cards.

"If you could have a dream guy, what would he look like?" Callie asks.

Out of the corner of my eye, I see Ethan pause his shuffling, then flick his eyes to mine before returning to his task. Leo sits back with an amused grin, arms crossed over his stomach, as he watches the scene unfold.

I could lie and make things less awkward for everyone, but I've never been one to do the right thing. I promised I wouldn't lead Ethan on, but hearing him think so poorly of himself? Having him think he couldn't be a contestant? It bothers the hell out of me. And just like I told him to take his shirt off five months ago, I'll continue to do what I need if only for him to see himself the way I see him. Consequences be damned.

"Well." I grab the red polish from Callie and shake it. "I'm a sucker for blond hair, and I like a man with a stockier build. More to cuddle with, you know? But more than anything, my dream guy would be someone I feel safe sharing my secrets with. He'd be the kind of guy I could talk to for all hours of the night and never get tired of. He'd be . . ." I smile fondly at the memories. " . . . the kind of guy who'd give me the last bite of ice cream because he knows it's my favorite flavor."

Ethan doesn't take his eyes off me. For a heartbeat, we're the only people in this room, and if I could, I'd climb onto his lap and kiss him in front of everyone with no fucks given. I'd prove to him that he's so worthy of all the love in the world, and I'd tell him I'm sorry for ever putting more doubt in his mind when I walked away from us. I'd fix it all if I could, and I wish that could be enough, but it isn't.

It never will be.

"That's very specific," Leo says. "See, if I was the bachelor, I'd—"

"Ugh!" Destiny whines and points at the television. "It lost connection *again*! Right before the sneak peek for next week!"

This is the only downside to not having a television in my dorm room, but I can't afford to buy one, and my roommate still hasn't shown up yet. I'm starting to think I'll be living solo for the remainder of the semester, which annoys me. I miss Maddie like crazy, and although Destiny and Callie are good substitutes, they aren't *her*. I was hoping to share a bond with my roommate like the one I share with Maddie, but the older I get, the more I realize that what Maddie and I have is a once in a lifetime friendship.

It's irreplaceable.

Leo rises from the chair and inspects the back of the television. "Did you try tightening the coaxial connector?"

Ethan laughs when all three of us stare at his roommate like we're deer in headlights.

"The *what*?" Destiny asks.

"The coaxial connector," he repeats slowly. "It transmits analog signals, and—" He stops midsentence and shakes his head. "Never mind. Sorry. AV nerd coming out." Then he reaches behind the television, replugs one of the cords, and suddenly our favorite television show is back on just in time for the sneak peeks.

Destiny squeals. "Ah, thank you! You're our hero."

Leo leans against the wall and arches a brow. "What does the hero get in return?"

"All right." Ethan groans and rises from his chair with the cards in hand. "That's our cue to leave. Sorry, guys. He's new to the dating game and says things like *that* without realizing how much he sounds like a total douche."

Leo jokingly gasps. "Excuse me. I can't help the fact I had a major glow-up last Tuesday. The braces came off." I laugh at how quirky he is in his button-down shirt with flamingos on it. He's handsome in a geeky meets sexy kind of way, so I can see why the girls are flocking to him now. Especially when he flashes perfectly straight, white teeth.

"We have a lot to work on," Ethan grumbles. He towers over me behind the couch, analyzing the work I did on Callie's nails. I'm just finishing the topcoat when he bends down to whisper, "Those look beautiful, Maya." My eyes flutter shut from the feel of his lips brushing against the shell of my ear. "You're really good at this."

Fuck.

Me.

I don't have any willpower when it comes to him. Ethan Davis makes me want to continue along my path of reckless decisions, and I'm seconds away from saying fuck the inevitable heartbreak when Leo suddenly interrupts. "And you're telling me *I'm* the douchebag?"

Ethan rounds the couch. "Shut up, Leo. Let's go."

"I'm serious," he says when they disappear around the corner. "Did you hear yourself back there? We *both* have things to work on if we . . ." Their voices fade, leaving the three of us alone again.

"Holy shit." Callie fans herself dramatically. "I'm sweating for you."

"Same," Destiny agrees. "The tension was off the fucking charts."

It's suddenly sweltering in here, and all I want to do is find Ethan and drag him into my room so we can make up for lost time. But deep down I know that being friends is for the best. We have chemistry, there's no denying that, but it's not enough. It's a constant reminder that this could never work between us.

"Hey, guys?" Destiny breaks the silence, gnawing on her bottom lip before she says something that has us all breaking into hysterics. "This could be the nail polish remover giving me a contact high, but I think I want to bang the AV nerd."

88

Twelve

ETHAN

I've always been someone who prefers to stay at home. Bingeing movies or listening to music is more my thing than being stuck at some party with people who don't really care about getting to know me. Over the years of attempting to cope with anxiety, I've come to learn that protecting my peace is more important than anything else. I've learned to say no when my mind is overwhelmed, which is precisely why I told Leo I wouldn't be joining him in his attempt to sneak into a sorority party.

I don't want to run into Maya, who inevitably will attend after her shift at Happy Endings. She never misses a party, especially one that everyone on campus has been talking about for the past week.

A part of me wants to walk her back to the dorm after work, but I don't want to embarrass her if she's meeting up with friends or something. She's not mine to take care of, but whenever I'm near her, I can't help but take on that role. Being friends with her again is nice, but that yearning to pull her against my chest and kiss her doesn't fade no matter how hard I try.

I'm taking a break from my *Fast & Furious* marathon to use the bathroom, but as soon as I leave my room, I see Maya at her door with her shower caddy in hand, and . . .

Is the universe trying *to punish me?*

A thin towel is wrapped around her very naked body. Her hair is wet, and droplets of water trickle down her neck and over the delicate curve of her collarbone. My eyes flick to the spot, wondering what her skin would taste like if I lapped up that droplet with my tongue.

Christ.

I need to get a grip.

"Sorry," she says in a breathless, little voice that shoots straight to my cock. "I thought I packed a change of clothes in my toiletry bag, but I must've forgotten."

"You don't have to apologize." She never has to apologize for looking like *that*. All barefaced and fucking perfect. "I'm surprised you're back. I assumed you'd be at that sorority thing happening tonight."

Her lips tilt into a grin. "It was my first shift since I finished my training, and I'm exhausted. It's a *lot* busier at night than it is in the afternoon." She looks behind me into my empty dorm room, and I swear the temperature rises about ten degrees. "No Leo tonight?"

I swallow thickly. "Nope. He went to the sorority thing to try and get lucky. He's an idiot, though. Those places are hard to get into."

Maya waves her hand. "Trust me. If he waits until they're all plastered, no one will care. Anyone will be allowed in at that point." Silence falls between us, but it's not awkward. We're both alone tonight, and it's like one of us is waiting for the other to extend an invitation, but it never comes. "Well, I should get changed."

No, I think to myself. *You should come into my room, drop the towel, and finish what you started five months ago.*

"Right." I exhale heavily through my nose because I'm a nervous fucking bastard when it comes to her. "Have a nice night, Maya."

"You too. Oh, and I'm sorry in advance for the thin walls."

What the fuck does that *mean?*

She closes the door before I have the chance to ask, and now I'm furious when I storm into my room. It's an effort not to slam the door. Is she having someone over tonight? Is that why she apologized for the thin walls?

I have no right to be a jealous man, especially when she was never mine to begin with. She's had way more experience than me, so it'd be reasonable for her to move on faster. I can't even think of starting something with another girl. It's going to take a hell of a lot longer for me to get over our night together when the reality of the situation is our night of fucking was just that to her. *Fucking* and nothing more.

My mood turns sour and I plop down on my bed and grab the remote. I'm just about to press Play on the movie when I hear it.

A buzzing.

My body stills on the mattress, my cock raging when I realize why she was apologizing for the thin walls. It wasn't because she was inviting a man over. Maya is *masturbating*, and now that's all I can think about.

This woman.

I have no right to jack off. None. Not when she didn't mean

for me to hear this. However, she apologized in advance, so maybe she *did* intend for me to hear.

Moans filter in a minute later, and they're not muffled. They aren't the moans of a woman who's trying to be quiet, and dammit, I'm not strong enough for this. I'm a weak man when it comes to her; I always have been. Shame fills me when I slip my sweatpants and boxers down to my knees, release my cock, wrap my hand around it, and give it a hard tug. A bead of liquid has already formed at the tip, a representation that I never had a chance at overcoming this torturous situation in the first place.

Even though it's wrong, I can't help but wonder what toy she's using. Is it a vibrator? A dildo? What does she need to bring herself a mind-blowing orgasm? I'd like to think I know her, so I imagine it's a vibrator that's pink and girly. I wonder if she likes it on her clit or if she'd prefer it inside her. I wonder if she likes to finger herself at the same time.

I'm panting while I continue to stroke. My release is seconds away, but that's not surprising since it's been a long fucking time since I've done this. Sharing a bedroom with a roommate and showering with other dudes will do that to a person.

I want her in here with me while she does this. I want to watch her use that toy, or better yet, *join* her while she uses that toy. I wonder if she'd like to use it on her pretty little clit while my fingers curl deep inside of her. Or would she like my tongue? I've never done that with a girl before, but I'd like to try with her.

Fucking hell.

I stroke myself harder and throw my head back on the pillow.

Her face when she came on my cock fills my head. It's an image I'll never forget, and right now, I use that as my motivation to fuck my hand over the edge of no return. The hottest fucking squeal echoes from the other side of the wall, and that's my det-onator. I shouldn't be coming with her, but that's exactly what I do. I fist my cock and let the ropes of come stain my sweatpants and the sheets beneath me, groaning and working myself until I feel completely empty. The sound of the vibrator shuts off a moment later, almost as if she was waiting for me to finish. I don't doubt she heard me. I wasn't quiet the first time and don't plan on starting now.

But it still makes me feel *gross* to have gotten off listening to her when, despite what I assume, she never verbally told me she'd be okay with it. And why *would* she be okay with it? She ended things and has yet to explain her reasoning. For all I know, she was asking for privacy, and I just invaded a very intimate moment for her.

One by one, the thoughts barrel in.

You're not good enough.

You're worthless.

She didn't want you then, and she doesn't want you now.

Maya Garcia has always been unattainable, and this is noth-ing but a painstakingly brutal reminder.

Thirteen

ETHAN

I told myself I wouldn't enjoy coming to this youth football practice. Mark wanted me here, so that's the only reason I'm striding through the grass toward the field where a bunch of kids are stretching in a circle.

Mark is standing beside an older man who is holding a clipboard—Ronnie Wilson, the coach for State. I only know this because he attended our games in high school not only to watch Mark play, since he took Mark in, but also to get a feel for the other players. He had his eye on me for a scholarship. At least, that was what my coach told me. It only makes this situation even more awkward when I approach Mark's side.

"Hey, you made it!" Mark claps me on the back, which damn near knocks me over. The strength of this guy is insane. I'm starting to believe he really *is* Thor. He turns to the group of kids, who have all suddenly grown silent as they stare at the newcomer. "Guys, I'd like you to meet—"

"Ethan Davis," Ronnie finishes, eyeing me in a scrutinizing way. "One of the best linebackers I've ever seen."

The kids all *ooooh* like I'm a newfound specimen.

"Where do you play now?" one asks.

"Do you go to school here?"

"Do you want to go to the NFL?"

Jesus. This is the worst interrogation of my life.

"*Used* to be," I correct, shifting my weight from one foot to the other. "I don't play anymore, but thank you."

The kids' faces drop, but before the punch to the gut can sink in, Mark says, "He's here to watch you guys play today, and maybe, if you're lucky, he'll have some pointers to give. Drills. Let's go." Mark jerks his head for me to follow, and, together, we walk to the opposite side of the field, allowing the kids to race ahead. "They can be blunt."

"You don't say?"

He laughs. "They're really great once you get to know them."

"How old are they?"

"Thirteen. Right in their prime."

"So, the worst is what you mean."

Mark grins wider. "Oh, come on. Don't you remember middle school? When we were all awkward and trying to adjust to our new voices after our balls finally dropped?"

"You know, I can't say I do. My brain probably did me a solid and blacked those years out."

Mark blows his whistle, getting the kids' attention again. "All right, Ethan's going to take over defensive line drills. Offense, you're with me."

My eyes bug out of my head. "*Excuse me?*" I thought I'd be

watching today, not fucking coaching. This isn't my job. And why is Ronnie on the opposite side of the field mean-mugging me? Is that supposed to be intimidating?

"What? You can't help? Don't act like you don't know how to do drills. We used to practice that shit in our sleep. Just tell them what to do. All the props you need are behind us by the bleachers."

Mark is a sly motherfucker.

"You're going to pay for this," I say, but his back is already facing me as he walks away.

"Next round at Happy Endings is on me!" he calls over his shoulder.

Suddenly, a group of kids surround me, waiting for instructions, and it feels so fucking wrong to have them look up to me right now. What do I have to offer them? I'm not good enough to be a coach to *anyone*, let alone these eager kids who are jumping from foot to foot like they're so excited they can't sit still.

My chest clenches at the sight.

I don't want to do this, but I'm also not going to break these kids' hearts. I know how to do drills. I've done them thousands of times. If I have to suck it up for an hour, then so be it. After today, I never have to come back again.

"Mark!" I call, then watch his head whip around. "I need to borrow an offensive player."

Something akin to pride lines his features before he dips his chin and sends over a boy named Sam. They look so small in their helmets, and yet the determination and willpower to play is oozing off them. I can *feel* their passion, and we haven't even started yet.

Walking over to the bleachers, I swipe a sweat towel before I return to them. "All right, I'm going to try and keep this simple. The goal of a defensive lineman is to get to the quarterback, right?" They all nod, watching when I turn Sam to face me and drop into stance, instructing Sam to do the same. "The key to achieving this is to ensure you're low and letting your shoulder drop." I put the towel behind Sam's heel and glance over at the kids. "You want to find that gap, and by staying low and dropping that shoulder . . ." I spring into action, ripping the towel from the ground behind Sam before I jog into the backfield. "It allows you to find that gap," I say once I'm finished. "Easy enough?"

All the boys nod enthusiastically.

"Who wants to go first?"

When all their hands shoot up, I start to understand what Mark means. I forgot why I fell in love with football all those years ago, but after ten minutes of being here, I'm starting to remember.

~

"Jake needs to work on his stance." I ramble while we pick up the cones. "And Devonte? Your offensive player? He's your star in the group. The speed and agility on that kid . . ." I shake my head in disbelief. "He's going to be good. Really good."

Mark hums a happy tune, and shoves one of the footballs into a mesh sack. "So, same time next week?"

My lips form a thin line while I contemplate my answer. I can't lie and say I didn't enjoy myself today. There's something satisfying about watching a kid use your advice and nail the following drill or play after a few attempts. But to take on a coaching job? One I'm not even sure exists? That's a lot of pressure, and it's one I don't know if I want to take on yet.

"I might be all right being a guest for a few more practices, but I'm not accepting a position or anything. I don't want to let the kids down."

Mark nods and passes me a bottle of water, and we take a seat on the bleachers. "I can respect that."

"*¡Apresúrate!*" Ronnie blows his whistle, signaling for the kids to wrap up their post-workout stretching.

"Ronnie speaks Spanish?" I ask.

"Oh, yeah. For a lot of kids, Spanish is their first language, so Ronnie mixes it up to include everyone and make them feel more comfortable here." Mark stares blankly at the now-empty field. "He's one of the best guys I know. If it wasn't for him, I wouldn't be playing college ball. I'd be . . . I don't know. Somewhere in the system, I guess. My schedule can be hectic, but Ronnie has a hectic schedule as the coach for State, too, and he still comes out here and dedicates time to teaching kids twice a week. Helping out is healing for me too. I can be the role model for these kids that I never had growing up. Well, until I met Ronnie, that is."

"I can see why," I add. "You were right about it being a reminder of why we started playing in the first place, but I think playing college ball or playing football professionally is out of the cards for me. And it's not because it's not my passion. I don't like the pressure that comes with it. I'm not a center of attention type of person. Never have been. But you are, Mark, and despite what you went through growing up, I hope you make it out of here and make your dreams come true."

He takes a swig from his water bottle. "I've accepted that getting drafted probably won't happen. I didn't have the money to attend all those fancy camps and get scouts' attention. Ronnie makes a good living, but not enough to house me and send me to those places. I never expected it. Does it help Ronnie is the coach for State? Sure, but that's not enough when it comes down to it."

I realize how much I've taken for granted over the years. My parents sent me to those camps in high school simply because I wanted to go. I never stopped to think about people like Mark, who dedicate their entire lives to the sport but can't attend camps because their families don't make enough money.

"It's happened before," I say. "People get drafted all the time and have these incredible stories to tell about their background and the struggles it took to play professionally. Those people are inspirations to others. Don't sell yourself short, dude. You're killer at what you do."

"Thanks, man. I'll—" He stops abruptly when his gaze catches something in the distance. Tabi, the girl from Happy Endings (also Ronnie's daughter), is walking hand in hand with a young girl in a ladybug sundress. Tabi seems upset, swiping at her face as she approaches her dad on the field, but Mark is already standing with his hands balled into fists at his sides. "I'm going to *kill* that motherfucker."

I'm lost, unable to do anything but follow him to the other side of the field. The little girl is smiling, seemingly oblivious to Tabi's distraught state as she races for the field and heads straight to the mesh bag filled with footballs.

". . . and I told him I had a shift today, but he showed up early with her and claimed he had to *meet up with friends*." She flings her arms into the air. "He hasn't seen her in two fucking weeks! He gets her for *one* weekend and is already sick of her after a day. I don't get it. How could he not?" Her voice breaks as she stares at the little girl in the distance. "How can he not love his own daughter?"

"Because he's a piece of shit." Mark steps up to her side, his hand flexing like it's taking everything in him not to console her.

Ronnie lets out a *huff.* "Can't say I disagree. So, what did you tell your boss?"

"I told him I'd figure something out and hopefully I'd be back, but I didn't know you had a meeting after this." She inhales deeply through her nose. "It's fine. Hopefully he'll understand that I won't be back to work the rest of my shift. It just sucks because I needed the money. Rent is due on the first, and—"

"Leave her with me," Mark says.

Tabi's mouth snaps shut, and hazel eyes swing to his. "Why would I leave her with *you*?"

"I don't see anyone else offering."

"I'd feel more comfortable leaving her with a pack of monkeys, but thanks," she replies dryly.

"Oh, come on. I changed the girl's diapers and fed her bottles when we all lived under the same roof. Annie loves me."

"Because you're the *fun* guy who throws parties and is so irresponsible that of *course* your personality would appeal to children." She sniffles and swipes away more tears, cursing under her breath.

"Tabi." Mark's tone is soft, dragging her attention to his. "Let me take her for the day. No funny business, all right? We'll go to the park, grab some ice cream, and we'll meet you at Happy Endings when your shift is over."

A long stretch of silence follows, their eyes never leaving each other's, and I start to feel like this is a conversation I shouldn't be overhearing at all.

"Fine," she mutters in defeat. "But if anything happens, you call me the *second*—"

"—something goes wrong," he finishes. "You have my word."

Ronnie smiles at the two of them. "See? It isn't *so* hard to get along, is it?"

Tabi rolls her eyes. "Don't push it, Dad."

"Well, I'm gonna get out of here." I clear my throat and stick a thumb over my shoulder. "Thanks for having me at practice today. It was fun."

"We enjoyed having you," Ronnie replies. "I could use a second assistant, you know. If you're interested."

Mark laughs. "I already tried. Ethan's going to take a while to come around, but we'll wear him down eventually. He's agreed to be a *guest* at a few more practices."

"Well, I hope you change your mind." Ronnie claps me on the back. "Because, kid? I've never seen Jake work that hard during any practice we've held. You've got a knack for this." Then, as if he didn't just give me one of the best compliments of my life, he blows his whistle and shouts, "Annie Rose! Pick those balls up. You're going to go have some fun with Uncle Mark!"

"Uncle Mark?" She squeals and jumps up and down. "This is the best day *ever*!"

"I'm *not* her uncle," Mark mutters.

Ronnie waves a hand. "You might as well be."

But when Mark's eyes slide to Tabi, who isn't paying attention to the conversation at all, I don't think it was *Ronnie* he was trying to remind, but rather a woman who couldn't care less about his affection.

Fourteen

ETHAN

Now that it's October, the scorching heat has begun to subside. It's in the low eighties during the day, which still isn't ideal for me, but it'll have to do. Other guys hang around campus in tank tops and shorts that end at their midthigh, but me? I'm in sweatpants and a sweatshirt year-round. Needless to say, summer is my least favorite season, and I have no complaints about it ending.

I'm not sweating my balls off now on my walk back to the dorm. Leo and I got done eating at the dining hall, and with the sun already setting in the distance, the temperature is actually *chilly*. It's enough to make me downright giddy.

"They need to work on their menu," Leo says as we walk down the hall together. "I mean, come on. We're college students, not prisoners."

I roll my eyes. "The food was good, Leo. You're being dramatic." Because the more time I spend in his company, the more I realize he's kind of extra. We've grown close over the past month, but with growing closer comes recognizing each other's quirks and bad habits. He's funny as hell, but when something doesn't go his way? He acts like he's a trust-fund baby cast into the wilderness for the first time.

We're passing by Maya's door when a flash of yellow catches my eye. It's a note taped to her door that reads: READY FOR A NIGHT OUT? BOOK ME FOR THE SERVICES BELOW! A list of prices follows for a variety of services from manicures and pedicures to hair and makeup. Her socials are listed for examples of her work, and the only thing I can do is smile at the note like an idiot. I'm fucking proud of her for being such a go-getter. She's already working at Happy Endings on the weekends, and now she's doing this as a side hustle? Where does she find the time?

Leo chuckles when he opens our door. "You're a goner, buddy."

"Leo, ninety percent of the time, I have no clue what the fuck you're saying."

He points at the note. "For her. It's all over your face."

"It is not."

Maya opens the door, freezing when she sees us standing out here. "Oh, hey. What are you up to?" She's wearing a pair of tight leggings and a sports bra, and has a mat tucked beneath her arm. It seems she's still doing yoga, and I do *not* need to think about just how many positions she's mastered. Neither of us has spoken about that night a few weeks ago when we shared a moment of intimacy on opposite sides of a wall. I don't know what the hell I'm supposed to call it, but I'm certainly not going to bring it up if she didn't intend for me to listen to her. I won't be a *creep*.

"Just looking at your door," I reply, like a goddamn idiot.

Fucking hell.

You already are *a creep.*

"The note," I quickly correct. "About your makeup services and stuff."

Her lips twitch. "Do you want to book me?"

"What? No, I just—"

She laughs, and at the sound, words stall in my throat. "I'm joking, Ethan. A lot of the girls around campus have been asking if I charge, so I figured, why not? Make a few extra bucks while I'm at it." She bites her lip, seeming to contemplate before she continues. "Truthfully, it's been a while since I've done anyone's makeup. I'm nervous I'm going to fuck it up."

Leo leans against our doorway with a grin I'm itching to smack off him. "I'm sure Ethan would be your test dummy. He's got skin like a baby's bottom."

Maya furrows her brows. "Really?"

"Oh, totally. I caught him researching how to make home-made facials the other day."

I'm going to kill him.

Slowly.

Painfully.

"I didn't know you had such an interest in skincare," she replies, with a sly grin of her own—a grin that lets me know she's aware Leo's lying. "But I wouldn't ask that of you. Fragile masculinity and all."

"You think I care about cultural standards?" I say it without thinking, and dammit, I hate how she makes me so quick at the mouth when I'm around her. I want to be the guy who thinks rationally, but I'm beginning to slip more and more in her presence, which is why I'm following her into her room thirty seconds later, a cackling Leo in the background as she closes the door behind us.

"I can't believe you're offering to do this," she says, setting the yoga mat on the floor. I watch her go to her desk and get everything set up, loving how energetic and excited she is. I'd do anything she asked me. That's what she fails to realize. Painting my face with makeup only scratches the surface of the things I'd gladly sign up for if it meant putting that smile on her face.

"I've got nothing better to do," I lie. I've got three papers due by the end of next week, but this is better than sitting in a library for hours, that's for sure.

She instructs me to sit on her bed, and after she squeezes some lotion into her hands, she steps between my legs and tilts my chin up. My eyes meet hers, but only for a second. The connection is too strong, too insufferable. I have to close my eyes to avoid it.

She wants to be friends.

Just friends.

Her fingers gently apply the product to my skin, and I hadn't realized just how good her touch would feel. I'm buzzing from the attention, tilting my head back to grant her more access. It takes everything not to moan at her caress.

"You look good in a backward cap," she says. Her voice is nearly a whisper. Almost as if she can sense the intimacy of this moment too.

"Bad hair day." It's supposed to be a joke, but I can hardly get the sentence out. Not when she's standing between my thighs. Not when I can smell her intoxicating scent, and her lips are mere inches from mine.

If I'd known it'd feel like this to get my makeup done by her, I would have offered to be her test subject a long damn time ago.

"So, when are you going to open your own salon?" I ask. "After you graduate, I'm assuming?"

She freezes for a split second before she uses a weird sponge to dab a thicker cream into my skin. "That's the dream, but it's not what my parents want for me."

"What do you mean? Why else would you be getting a degree in business?"

She shrugs. "Become a CEO, work in marketing, be an accountant. . . . Starting my own salon isn't guaranteed success, and they'd rather I had a job that'd give me a stable income instead of taking a risk on something that might not."

"Even if it's what you love to do? What you're passionate about?" I don't know her parents, but I can't help the anger that surfaces. "What was the point of going to cosmetology school, then?"

"To feed my interests. I can work a job on the side with it, but owning my own salon one day? Making it my full-time career? I'd have to convince my parents that owning my own salon would prove to be a success, and—" She shakes her head, darkness entering her eyes. "It can't happen. At least, not right now."

"But that's not—"

"It is what it is, Ethan." Her tone is firm; no room for discussion on this.

The last thing I want is to upset her, so I drop the subject and allow her to do as she pleases with my face. I love watching her so focused and in her zone. I love watching her do what she was *born* to do. Cosmetology is her life. Running her own salon has been her dream since we met, and I know this because it was one of the first things she ever said to me. She braided Maddie's hair one day and I complimented it in front of her, and then she rambled about the different styles of braids she could do. How becoming a cosmetologist so she could do everything under the sun was her goal.

And now she's accomplished that goal, but it was all for nothing.

It doesn't sit right with me.

"Has anyone booked yet?" I ask.

She grins while applying some sort of tan powder. "Actually, yeah! I've had three sign-ups already."

"That's incredible, Maya. I'm really proud of you." I avert my gaze when her eyes soften, because the last thing I need is to start assuming things. Just because she's giving me *that look* doesn't mean she wants to be more than friends. She created a boundary, and I refuse to cross it.

I lean back on my hands to put more space between us, but all it does is expose my body to her. She's still standing between my legs, and her eyes dart to my chest before she clears her throat and grabs an assortment of colored tubes from her desk. "Which color do you want?"

I tilt my head to the side, studying them. "For my lips?"

She nods.

"Pick whichever one you think will look best."

With a decisive nod, she twists the cap off a dark red. "I know you're going to kill me, but red is the hardest to apply. If I have you as my test subject, I'm going to make the most of it."

"Have at it."

I'm the perfect model for her. I sit still and don't move a muscle until her task is complete. When she's finished, she takes a step back with her arms crossed over her chest and studies her work.

Then, she tugs on her lip to in an attempt to stop laughing, but it's no use. She erupts into a fit of giggles, and shakes her head in disbelief. "I didn't think you'd actually let me do it."

I can't help but laugh with her. "Was it worth it, at least? How do I look?"

She grabs her phone from the band of her leggings. "You look so pretty, Ethan."

"Oh god. That bad, huh?"

"I mean, I guess the only thing left to do is take a picture of my work."

Before she has the chance, I grab her and flip her onto the mattress, laughing hysterically as she clutches the phone in her hand with a death grip. I try to pry it away from her, but whatever yoga exercises she's doing are paying off. She flips me onto my back instead, and it isn't until she snaps the picture that I realize she's straddling me.

She looks perfect like this.

And it's not even her body (which also looks extraordinarily perfect), but it's the way she's staring at me. Her pupils dilate and her chest heaves, and for a second, we're transported back to that hot tub, with locked gazes that reveal more to each other than our mouths ever could.

"I'm—" She inhales sharply at my hardness between her thighs. I'm a man who respects boundaries, but I *am* a man, and this position isn't exactly innocent. "Fuck. I'm sorry, Ethan." I'm a bundle of mixed emotions as she scrambles off my lap and passes me a wipe to take the makeup off. Upset because I want her back on me, but relieved because if she had stayed on me another second longer, I would have done something reckless. "Thank you," she adds in a rushed voice. "For letting me practice on you."

And because I'd do it all over again despite the agonizing throb this encounter brought to my chest, I reply, "You don't have to apologize. I'll be your test subject anytime."

Fifteen

MAYA

Maddie So . . . do you have something to tell me?

Maya About what?

Maddie A little birdie told me you and my brother almost had a make-out sesh

Maya Is that little birdie your horny boyfriend who thinks every interaction with a woman should result in a "make-out sesh"? I hate that term, by the way

Maddie Deflecting with anger. Yep. Something definitely happened

Maya If there was something for you to know, you'd know. Trust me. And tell your little birdie to stay in his nest from now on!

Maya Also, I miss you. Sorry for being a bitch. It's my time of the month

Maddie I miss you more. On the plus side, at least it'll be over before your birthday next week. Who wants to party with a tampon?

~

Friday nights at Happy Endings are always busy.

It's a college town, so it's unsurprising that it's packed in here. Music blares all around me, and I have to lean into every booth to hear their drink orders. It's rare people order food here, because it's only frozen garbage, but at the last call around midnight, lots of orders pile in from drunk people who aren't thinking clearly.

Stray pieces of hair are stuck to my forehead from sweat. Putting my hair up in a ponytail did nothing to erase the humidity flooding in from the outdoors. It's still eighty degrees out tonight, and since it's practically a mosh pit in here, it's useless to try and stay cool. I gave up on looking cute an hour after my shift started.

I'm approaching the bartender to slide him another order when I spot Tabi beside me, dressed in uniform. "What are you doing here?" I ask.

She heaves a sigh. "I had to pick up Friday nights. It's complicated. My baby daddy is an actual piece of shit. Claims to want to see his daughter but is ready to give her back after the first night. I had to leave early from work again because of him, so now I'm working the night shift to improve my attendance. This is the third time it's happened in the past month."

"Damn. That sucks, Tabi. I'm sorry."

The bartender delivers her drinks and she shrugs. "It is what it is. I can't change it, you know? When you have a kid, you don't have time to dwell on how shitty it is. You just find a way to make it better and do it."

"That's true, but that doesn't mean you can't have people empathize with you. Lean on those you have in your circle, you know?"

She scoffs. "You'd be the first one to offer. Well, aside from my dad, but he doesn't count. All my friends are off doing college things. As soon as I had a baby, they wanted nothing to do with me."

"Well, I'll gladly be part of your circle if you let me," I say. "I happen to *love* kids."

A genuine smile falls onto her face. "Thanks, Maya. I needed to hear that tonight. It's been a rough few days."

"Anytime, I—" A tap on my shoulder interrupts me. When I turn around, a tall, muscular man is smirking at me in a creepy-ass way. I can tell by his outfit that he's part of a frat—dockers, loafers, and a polo that's a size too small. "Can I help you?" I ask.

"Yeah," he shouts over the music. "My friend thinks you're hot. I told him I'd ask you for your number." He points behind him to a group of guys in almost identical outfits. Unfortunately, it's not the first time I've been hit on since I started working here, and it won't be the last either.

"I don't date where I work," I reply with a smile.

"Oh, come on. He's *really* into you. Give him a chance." His hand lands on my elbow. "I'll introduce you."

"I'm working." My voice carries more grit to it now, but the drunken idiot doesn't get the hint. He's swaying where he stands, his eyes dropping to my cleavage, which is exposed by the tight-ass tank top. I'm not exactly a fan of the uniform here, but I'll put up with it for the good tips it brings.

"Just let—"

Tabi steps up to the guy and props one hand on her hip. She snaps her fingers at him with the other like he's a dog and says, "Did you not hear her the first time? Need your ears checked? Go back to your trust fund table or I'll call security."

My jaw drops, but I snap it shut when the man rolls his eyes but does as he's told. Not that I can blame him. With her fiery red hair and right arm covered by a full sleeve of tattoos, I wouldn't mess with her either. She's the kind of woman to walk a man on a leash and have him thank her for it.

When he returns to his friends, the bartender passes me the

shots my table ordered. "You need to be more firm," Tabi says. "Don't let these idiots walk all over you. That's what Doug is for." She glances over her shoulder at where the hefty security guard stands at the entrance.

"Trust me, I have no problems putting douchebags in their place, but this is also where I work, and I have to be professional, so . . ."

"The owner doesn't give a shit about professionalism when it comes to our safety. When we say no, and they don't listen? All bets are off. Now, let's finish this last hour and go the fuck home, yeah?"

I breathe a sigh of relief. "*Please*. My feet are killing me."

~

After our shifts are over, Tabi and I finish wiping down the tables and flipping the chairs. It's close to three in the morning, and honestly? All I want to do is go to sleep. My plans tomorrow include lying in bed for the entire day.

Knocks on the door make us jump, but when Tabi squints out the glass windows, she heaves an annoyed sigh and flips the lock. "What the fuck are you doing here, Mark?"

He ignores her and strides into the empty bar, irritation rolling off of him in thick waves. "Your dad mentioned you were picking up the night shift. You don't work nights."

"So? I do now."

"Is this because of *Andrew*?"

"What if it is? You aren't my father, Mark. You don't control what I do." She plops the towel she was holding onto her shoulder. "What are you even doing here? It's three in the morning."

"I set an alarm so I could drive you home."

My heart flutters for her, but Tabi doesn't seem to be swooning like me. Instead, she throws her head back and laughs. "You've got to be kidding. I drove here! I'll be just fine getting home."

His nostrils flare in irritation. "You don't know what creeps could be lingering outside of here at night. It's not safe. Especially when you two are the only ones here. What would you do if—" He stops midsentence when his eyes drop to the Taser Tabi's now holding against his stomach.

"I can handle myself," she says sweetly—like she isn't holding a weapon that could bring him down in seconds. "Take your big, doofus self out of this bar. I don't need your protection. Never have, never will."

"*Tabi*—"

"Or would you rather I pepper spray you? Pocketknife, maybe? Your choice. The options are endless." She holds up her key ring, which houses an abundance of different threats, for emphasis. I make a mental note to buy some form of protection. I walk home at night, and although nothing has ever happened, it doesn't mean it couldn't.

Mark's jaw ticks. "Has anyone ever told you that you're stubborn as hell?"

She smiles brightly, as if his insult is actually a compliment, and wiggles her fingers for him to leave. "All the time. Bye, Mark."

When the door slams shut behind him, she twists the lock again and says, "Sorry about him. He's so fucking extra."

"I think it was really sweet. He seems into you."

Her nose wrinkles in disgust. "*Mark?* God, no. He just likes to feel useful with his hulk-like body. Showing up to drive me home was for him, not for me."

"Didn't seem that way."

"Trust me," she says. "It's not like that."

"Then what is it like? You need to clarify that statement."

She sighs like this is her thousandth time telling this story. "My dad took him in when he was a freshman in high school. At the time, Mark didn't have anyone to raise him, so my dad made our home a place Mark could call his own. It was sweet of him, but . . ." She shakes her head. "It doesn't matter. I don't need Mark acting like my knight in shining armor. Or *any* man, for that matter."

I shrug as we head down the hallway to the office. "All I'm saying is I wish a man would show up to make sure I got home okay. It's thoughtful."

"Oh god. Don't tell me you're into the romantic, sappy shit."

Is it so wrong to want to be treated like a princess? Love notes, outlandish displays of affection, gifts for no reason. Some girls say they *aren't like other girls*, but me? I'm a cookie cutter for what some people define as a *cliché* woman. I love Starbucks. Makeup and designer bags call to the depths of my soul. I'm obsessed with the color pink and think rom-coms are the greatest thing to ever exist. I'm naive when it comes to self-protection.

And sue me if a man showing up to take someone home has my knees buckling in response.

"Let's just say Lifetime movies are my favorite pastime. Still want me in your circle?"

Tabi grabs her purse off the desk. "I'll deal with it. You don't have a car, right?"

"No. It's only a ten-minute walk to the dorm, though. I'll be fine."

With a roll of her eyes, she flings an arm over my shoulder as we walk to the exit. "You're in luck tonight. I'll be the man of your dreams and drive you home."

It's only when Tabi starts her car that I have a chance to look at my phone. I have three unread text messages, all from the same person.

Ethan Hey, do you need a ride home? I just thought I'd offer since you don't have a car. It's dark outside, and I don't feel comfortable with you walking home alone

Ethan Not that you're mine or anything to look after. I'd feel that way about any woman walking home alone downtown

Ethan Please ignore the previous texts. Just let me know when you make it back safely

I'm smiling like a downright idiot on the way back to the dorm, and it's at this moment that I realize my dream man has always existed. Ethan Davis is the one for me, and with every sweet gesture, it's becoming increasingly difficult to ignore.

Sixteen

ETHAN

Cameron Who needs Vogue when I have this gem?

Ethan How the hell did you get that picture?

Cameron Maya sent it to Maddie, who, of course, sent it to me

Ethan DON'T SHOW IT TO ANYONE

Cameron Why not? You look hot with makeup. I'd bang you

Ethan Tell Maddie she's a brat for sending it to you

Cameron Sorry, but that word will never leave my lips when it comes to your sister. I can think of some other ones she enjoys, though . . . ;)

Ethan Fuck me. Why? Just why?

Cameron I might after seeing you all dolled up <3

~

On the night of Maya's birthday, which also happens to fall on Halloween, the dormitories are buzzing with excitement. Halloween is the one holiday a year that has almost everyone getting dressed up and joining in on some party or other festivity on campus. I'm not a fan of Halloween because I absolutely hate dressing up, but this year Leo didn't give me a chance to decline when he slapped a cowboy hat on my head. It's the shittiest costume of all time, but Happy Endings is throwing a party that requires one for admission, and since Leo isn't letting me stay inside tonight, I'll suck it up for a few hours to make him happy before I come back to the comfort of my bed.

But first, I have a gift to deliver.

I rap my knuckles against Maya's door, a bag with pink tissue paper clutched tightly in one hand. I'm trying to catch her before she leaves, and since it's only eight, I assume she's still getting ready.

The door swings open, and my world stands still.

Maya is an angel.

Literally.

But she's not an angel I'd find in heaven. The way that tight miniskirt is hugging her curves is downright sinful. She's temptation wrapped in a white corset that pushes her breasts up, and a pair of white wings are splayed behind her back.

"Jesus."

It's ironic since *Jesus* doesn't seem to be in the room with us at all, but it's the only thing I can think of to say.

"That good, huh?" She spins to give me the full view, and my mouth dries out at the sight of a white thong peeking out of the top of her skirt. Long, sleek hair falls to the middle of her spine, and her makeup is done just like her outfit—light but radiant. Her skin is glowing almost as brightly as her smile.

Whatever rope that's been holding me back from her is fraying second by second, and it takes *everything* in me not to push her onto her bed and have my way with her. I'm so tired of running from this attraction to her. Tired of trying to convince myself my infatuation will pass.

She's it for me.

Always has been, always will be.

"I have a gift for you," I say, holding the bag out to her. "Happy birthday, Maya."

Pink tinges her cheeks and she holds the door open wider for me to enter. She takes the bag and sits on her bed, fumbling with the tissue paper until she sees what's inside. I hold my breath, scared she'll take the gift the wrong way after our conversation a few weeks ago, but the same breath *whoosh*es out of my lungs when she releases a choked sob and *smiles*.

The box encasing the latest hairstyling tool sits in her trembling hands. "Ethan . . ."

"Is it the one you wanted?"

"Yes, but—" She shakes her head in disbelief. "How did you remember that?"

I remember everything you say, is what I want to reply, but I refrain from doing so and shift my weight from one foot to the other. "It was all you could talk about for a month when it first came out. You were saying you wanted to try it on Maddie's hair, and now with you starting up this side business at school . . ." I shrug as if it isn't a big deal. "You should have it."

"I can't accept this." A sheen coats her eyes when they lift to mine. "It's too expensive, Ethan."

My lips tilt into a grin. "Consider it an investment. I believe in you, Maya. If no one else does, just know that I do." I swallow thickly and add, "I always will."

A tear slips onto her cheek before she curses and swipes it away. "You know, you're the first person who makes me think I really can succeed at the salon thing. I mean, Maddie is support-ive, don't get me wrong, but you've always made me believe in myself in a way that no one else can. Not even my own *parents*, and I—" She inhales deeply. "I'm so sorry it took me so long to realize it."

My brows lift. "What does that mean?"

"It means—" Knocks interrupt us, and I want to tell whoever is on the other side to fuck off, but it's her dorm room, not mine.

Maya opens the door, only to be bombarded by a set of thick, bouncy blond curls. "SURPRISE!" My *sister* grips her with a force that nearly knocks her over, and Maya squeals before she recip-rocates the gesture.

"Oh my god, what are you doing here?"

"I wouldn't miss your birthday for the world. Are you kid-ding? And, boy, do I know you well. I'm glad I came prepared." She gestures to her nurse outfit, which makes me nauseated. She shouldn't be wearing *that* if she's going to party with Maya alone, and—

"Hey, do you know where—" Cameron, who is too tall for the damn door, dips his head to enter the room. He freezes when he notices me standing behind Maya, his notorious grin coming out in full force. "Oh, I'm sorry. Did we interrupt something?"

Maddie, who finally notices I'm in the room too, cringes before taking a step back from Maya. "Shit. Sorry. I didn't know . . ."

"You weren't interrupting anything," I blurt, turning to my best friend before he embarrasses me. He may be a dick at times, but I missed the hell out of him. He's my brother, and without him, I don't feel as complete. "How the hell did you guys plan this?"

Cameron pulls me in for a hug and claps me on the back. "I

had a weekend off from football, and Maddie cleared her schedule. You actually have my dad to thank. He paid for the tickets."

"Oh, shit. I'll have to text him. I'm so fucking happy you're here. Where are you staying? Do you need to crash with us?"

He shakes his head, shifting his eyes to my sister. "Nah. We got a hotel a few minutes away from here." And it's only then that I notice his costume. He's dressed in a hospital gown, and with Maddie being a nurse . . .

I wave a finger between them. "This is sickening."

Maddie rolls her eyes. "Get used to it already, Ethan."

I have gotten used to it. If I'm being honest, I'm *happy* for them. It's been years since I've seen my best friend the way he used to be. He laughs and smiles more, and his relationship with his dad is getting better every day. If it wasn't for my sister, who knows where he'd be right now? They found solace in each other, and the way my sister stares at Cameron like he hangs the moon for her is enough validation for me. He's good to her. That's all that matters.

"I can't wait for you to meet Destiny and Callie," Maya gushes. "You'll love them. We were just heading to Happy Endings! It's the bar closest to campus. The one I work at. I tried to work tonight, but my boss refused since it's my birthday, so . . ." She wiggles her ass in the miniskirt, and I shoot my eyes up to the ceiling as Cameron stifles a laugh. "We're partying, bitch!"

"Is that where we're heading?" Cameron asks me. "If not, can we tag along with the girls? I can't be without my nurse." His hand lands on Maddie's waist before he tucks her into his side.

"Do you do this on purpose?" I ask, but fail to hide my grin.

"What?" He fake coughs and places the back of his hand on

his forehead. "I'm *sick*, Ethan, and there's only one person who has the cure."

"Fucking hell," I mutter, and Maddie and Maya erupt into giggles. "But, yeah, I was heading there anyway with my roommate, Leo."

"Sweet. Can't wait to meet him."

The thought of Leo and Cameron together?

Lord help us all.

"I'm glad to know you've changed your mind about country music," Cameron continues, waving a hand over my outfit. I changed into jeans, a white T-shirt, and cowboy boots (courtesy of Leo). The man seems to have an outfit for everything, and although I feel out of my comfort zone, Maya can't take her eyes off of me. Leo's accessories were worth it. "It's not so bad, is it?"

"Please," I scoff. "I still think that genre is garbage."

"Same," Maddie adds. "Something Cam and I will never agree on."

Cameron opens the door, and as we all file out he adds, "Well, you certainly look the part, Ethan. Now all you need is a lasso so you can wrangle in a cowgirl tonight."

Or an angel.

Maya glances over her shoulder with a devilish smile. "Ethan doesn't need a cowgirl. He just needs to find someone who can ride that cowboy hat right off of him."

Well, I'll be damned.

Her words act as scissors, cutting the last strand of rope holding me back, and now all I can do is pray I can keep my sanity for the rest of the night.

Seventeen

ETHAN

As expected, Leo and Cameron hit it off. It took them less than five minutes to jump into a deep conversation about whether or not aliens are real. I'm pretty sure Leo was the one who broached the subject, and Cameron is tipsy enough by now to start entertaining conspiracy theories.

Mark came to Happy Endings dressed as Fred Flintstone, his muscular body on display like a Greek statue in the scrap of fabric that barely reaches his thighs. It's an effort not to roll my eyes, but it's very Mark. He's never cared what anyone thinks.

We've all been occupying the edge of the dance floor, and it's not because we're trying to get lucky. Maddie and Maya have been dancing their asses off for the past hour, and with men swarming around them like vultures, we decided to stay close just in case one of them got too handsy. I'm not Maya's protector, and I have full confidence she'd be able to tell these douchebags where to stick it, but selfishly, watching her hips move to the sultry beat has me glued right where I stand.

"When are you going to make a move?" Cameron shouts in my ear. The light from the DJ booth casts his face in an orange and red hue.

"I've been asking him the same thing," Leo interjects. "She's clearly into him."

I heave a sigh of frustration. "You guys don't *know* her. That's just how she is! She's flirtatious. It's her personality." Cameron whacks me upside the head. "Ow! Fuck was that for?"

"You're being an idiot," he says, taking a swig from his beer. "Dude, she asked you about sailing over spring break. *She* asked *you* to kiss her. She's made every fucking move so far, and you're questioning whether or not she's into you?"

"That was *before* she fucking ghosted me. Or did you forget that part?"

"Look." He throws an arm over my shoulder. "I've had my fair share of experience with women, and I don't know what happened to make her ghost you, but she's not over you in the slightest. It's obvious."

"It is *not* obvious."

"She told you to find someone who would ride this cowboy hat off of you," Cameron says slowly, as if I'm too dense to understand him. "Who do you think she meant?"

Mark slaps a hand over his mouth to keep from laughing while Leo, who's dressed as a hot dog, blatantly chuckles.

"I don't know!" I toss my hands up in frustration. "Maybe she wants me to find someone else so I can finally move on from her. Maybe she thinks I'm too obsessed with her, so she—" All three of my friends whack me on the head now. "Jesus!" I hiss. "What is *wrong* with you guys? That fucking hurt."

"Good," Mark replies. "Maybe we knocked some sense into

you, then. We wouldn't be pushing you to do this—all *three* of us—if we thought there was even a chance that she'd reject you again. She's into you, man, and it's time you do something about it before someone else swoops her out from under you."

"Girls think it's hot when a man takes charge," Cameron adds.

Mark scoffs. "Not all of them."

Leo's eyes snag on a girl dressed as Little Bo Peep, and with full confidence he strides toward her. "I need to find my buns for the night!" he shouts over his shoulder. "I hope you do the same, Ethan!"

Mark tilts his head to the side. "Is he always like this?"

"Dorky and embarrassing? Yeah. He got his braces off and is trying to fuck everything with a pulse. Emphasis on *trying*."

"Didn't you say you woke up to him screwing someone?" Cameron asks.

"Thanks for reminding me of that, but, yeah. I guess his moves worked *once*. Although he hasn't gotten lucky since. And I haven't seen that girl come around again, so . . ."

"I like him," Mark says. "He knows exactly who he is."

I wonder what that must be like.

Before I can respond, two girls with obvious intentions saunter up to Cameron. A girl with red hair and freckles dotting her nose and cheeks reaches him first. I'm used to girls hitting on Cameron over me, so when the blond wedges between Cameron and me and attempts to strike up a conversation, I know it's to pass the time until she can shoot her shot with the six three football star. I got used to it a long time ago.

"Let me get your number," the girl with freckles suggests. She blinks up at him with innocent baby blues, but Cameron keeps his eyes locked on the dance floor where my sister is having the time of her life.

"I'm taken," he replies. He doesn't give her the time of day, which seems to deflate the redhead's ego. And now that Cameron is off-limits, she shifts her eyes to Mark, who seems oblivious to the interaction. He's staring at the bar where Tabi waits for a round of drinks, and his lips twitch into a smile when he sees that along with the Happy Endings uniform, she's wearing cat ears and has painted black whiskers on her face.

"I'm going to go irritate the Tabi cat," he says with a wicked grin, abandoning the redhead before she even had a chance.

This leaves me, the last option on the table, but the girl doesn't have an opportunity because Maya grabs me by the hand and tugs me toward her instead. My sister has found Cameron again, and he pulls her in for a kiss before sliding his hands down her back. I was an idiot for thinking he couldn't change, when he's clearly so obsessed with Maddie.

His gleaming eyes meet mine. "I think we're going to head back to the hotel. I'll see you tomorrow? Mark said you guys are coaching youth football."

Of course he did.

"*He* is coaching. I'm just a guest."

"Cam." Maddie childishly tugs on his arm, and when he stares down at her, it's clear how strong of a hold she has on him. His entire face melts as he kisses her forehead.

"Sorry, baby. Let's go. Do you need me to carry you?"

"Yes." Maya responds for her. "She's had three shots tonight."

For Maddie, that's more like six.

Cameron nods in understanding. "Got it. Thanks. See you tomorrow, Ethan."

Maya turns to me with pleading eyes as he carries Maddie out of the bar. "Dance with me."

I don't have a chance to refuse before I'm pulled onto the dance floor during a Bad Bunny song, which happens to be her favorite artist. The beat is sensual. *Sexy.* And I'm completely unprepared when she spins around and presses her ass up against me. I have no idea where to put my hands. No idea if she wants me to touch her. I mean, she's dancing on me, but that doesn't mean . . .

Cameron, Mark, and Leo's remarks a few minutes ago make me cringe.

Okay, so maybe she *does* want this.

The question is, what am I going to do about it?

Maya puts her hands on her knees, and her hips take control. I'm hard as a fucking rock as I stare at one of my biggest weaknesses bouncing in circles on the crotch of my jeans. I know she can feel it, yet she doesn't pull away. The music takes over, and with the crowded dance floor, the heat is getting to be too much. My control is slipping, and the sanity I've tried so desperately to hang on to crumbles when she stands upright again and presses the full length of her back against my chest.

I groan when she reaches behind me to grab the cowboy hat off my head and places it on hers instead. Then she interlocks our fingers and drags our hands to her thigh. I'm panting heavily as she grinds against me and moves our hands a little higher every few seconds. If we get any higher, I'll touch the thong that's been teasing the fuck out of me all night.

"Are you drunk?" I pant into her ear.

Please say no.

She twists her head to the side, that devious smile returning to her pink lips. "No. I stayed sober in case I needed to ride the hat off a certain cowboy tonight."

The rope has already snapped.

My sanity is gone.

And before I let myself overthink it, my lips meet hers in a ferocious hunger that consumes every ounce of my being.

I don't care that we're in a bar with our friends. I don't care that it's ninety degrees in here when I spin her around so I can push her against the wall and slide my hands down her waist. All I can think about is her lips on mine. I can't get enough of her. My lips can't kiss her fast enough.

I want to *devour* her.

Who cares if I don't know the reason that she ghosted me? It doesn't matter when she wants this. She wants *me*, and we'll figure out the rest as we go.

She gasps when my tongue runs up the column of her neck, and when I bite her earlobe, she slumps against the wall and tilts her head to the side.

Just like the first time, lust seems to be a blanket for my anxiety. It overpowers my nerves, and adrenaline takes its place, making me the most confident version of myself. I suddenly know exactly where I want my mouth. I know exactly what I want to do with her.

And I can't do those things in a crowd full of people.

"We need to leave," I growl. "Right now."

She nods while attempting to catch her breath.

"Your room or mine?"

"I—" She closes her eyes as my hands skate down her sides. "What if I told you I had a place closer than the dorm? A place we could go right now?"

My eyes darken at the thought. "I'd say what are we waiting for, then? I'd tell you to take me there so I can give you your *real* birthday present."

I don't have to tell her twice. Maya laces our fingers again, and drags me through the bar to a hallway in the back, and the entire time, I can't fight the smile on my face.

Happy Endings might live up to its name after all.

Eighteen

MAYA

What am I doing?
    What am I doing?
    What
    Am
    I
    Doing?

It's the only coherent thought in my head when I shut the door to the office and twist the lock behind me. It's soundproof in here, so the bass only beats quietly from the other side of the wall. Ethan's chest is heaving as he looks around the small space. From the desk in the center of the room to the old hardwood floors and scratched-up walls, it's not much, but it's a place where we can be alone, which seems to be enough for him.

Flirting with Ethan was inevitable when I saw that girl almost make her move. Does it make me selfish? Entirely. But when have I *ever* been selfish? Every decision I've made, I've put others before me. I planned *my* life around my parents, but when I'm with Ethan, I question all of it. How can someone who makes me feel this good not be suitable for me? My parents will have to see that at some point, right? The man wears his heart on his sleeve. Even now, every ounce of passion he has for me is displayed on his face. His eyes, which keep scanning my body from head to toe. His jaw, which is set in a firm line as if it's taking everything in him to hold himself back from me.

I don't want him to.

For once, I want to be selfish and have something for myself.

I've never had a thing for cowboys, but damn if Ethan doesn't change my mind. He makes jeans and cowboy boots look criminally attractive. It should be against the law to look this fuckable.

Ethan takes a step closer and backs us up until my ass hits the edge of the desk. My knees threaten to buckle under the grip he has on my hips, and despite every warning alarm going off in my head telling me to stop this, I ignore each one. I'll handle my parents later. Tonight, I'm taking control of my life and taking what I want.

And I want Ethan Davis.

"Should I be worried about cameras?" he whispers against the shell of my ear. Every section of skin his breath hits is ultrasensitive.

"Not in here." I gasp when he nips my collarbone. *"Ethan."*

His chest rumbles with a moan, and then he does something I've only imagined in my wildest fantasies. He drops to his knees on the hardwood floor, his eyes *ravenous* when they lock with mine. I'm speechless as he runs his hands up the backs of my thighs, stopping beneath the hem of my skirt. "Your friends were right," he says. "Men would get on their knees for a chance to be with you."

"*Ethan—*"

"I would kiss the ground you fucking walk on, Maya." His lips meet my knee, nearing my inner thigh, and I can't help it when I run my fingers through his hair. I love the way his eyes flutter shut from the feeling. It's like he melts from my touch and affection. "You're the most stunning woman on the planet, inside and out, and if anyone has ever made you feel differently, I want to show you why they were so . . ." He parts my thighs with his hand, his entire face softening at what he sees. "*So* wrong."

I *whimper*.

I fucking whimper.

"But I've never done this before, so I need you to show me what you like."

The thought of going another second longer without teaching him this is unbearable. I flip my skirt up to sit around my waist while simultaneously taking my thong off. My pussy is bare and throbbing before him, and when he darts his tongue out to lick his lips as if *preparing* to have the best meal of his life, I think I might faint.

"You can't do this wrong," I pant.

"Bullshit," he scoffs. "I may have been a virgin when I met you, but that doesn't mean I haven't heard things. Guys can be bad at this."

"You're right, but I'm saying *you* can't do this wrong. The second your tongue hits my clit I'm going to be a fucking goner, Ethan. You have no idea how many times I've—"

"You've thought about it?" he asks. "Me, doing this?"

"All the time."

I'm breathless when he moves closer and hooks one of my legs over his shoulder. My comment seems to have instilled more confidence, because he doesn't look nervous when he kisses my inner thighs. "Are you wet?"

Using two fingers, I slide them between my legs and spread my pussy, and then I dip one into my core to show him just how wet I am. Arousal is evident when I pull it out. "What do you think?"

He leans forward and takes my fingers into his mouth, sucking while maintaining eye contact with me. My mouth drops at the sensation, and I can see how his eyes darken when my taste hits his tongue.

Ethan Davis, who has worn so many different masks, isn't wearing one at all when he runs his tongue tentatively along my slit. The wind is knocked from my lungs the second he delves inside, and my hand remains wrapped in his hair to try and hold on to *something* to keep me tethered to this world.

"Oh my *god*." His moaned words are muffled between my thighs.

His grip on my hips tightens as he drags me more onto his mouth. I'm worried I'm suffocating him, but he makes no complaints as he continues to experiment with his tongue.

I splay one hand out behind me on the desk, knocking over a pen holder in the process. I couldn't give two shits about the pens rolling on the floor. Not when Ethan is seconds away from tasting precisely what he's striving for.

But then he rips his mouth from between my thighs, eyeing the mess. "Are you okay?" He pants. "Does it feel good for you?"

"Ethan, don't fucking stop." I tighten my hold on his hair and drag him back exactly where he was. The tentative, nervous, shy boy is nowhere to be found when he flicks his tongue against my clit and *smiles*. I throw my head back, my hips voluntarily bucking to grind against his tongue. I can feel the pressure building. I can feel the dip in my lower stomach, letting me know I'm close, and Ethan seems to sense that. My motions have grown frantic, *desperate*. "You're doing *so* good," I practically moan. "There's no way this is your first time. Fuck, I'm gonna come."

"*Please*." His voice vibrates against my clit, and it's all I need to make me come so hard that light bursts behind my eyelids. Stars erupt everywhere in the room as I shatter against his tongue. Nothing has ever felt so right. So *good*. Ethan's tongue is ecstasy in its purest form, and so is his voice when he moans against me, his tongue licking and tasting everything I have to offer.

He sits back on his knees, his mouth glistening with my arousal, and I don't think twice before I bend down to kiss him. His tongue entwines with mine, and where we were borderline animalistic a second ago, this kiss is slower. Calculated. *Intimate*.

My hands caress his cheeks when I pull back and ask, "How was it?"

He licks his lips as if he's already reminiscing. "I think I like doing that. A *lot*, actually."

"Well, I think you'll enjoy having it done to *you* a lot more." I flick my eyes down to the pitched tent in his jeans. It sends a rush of heat down my spine knowing I affect him so much. "Trade places with me."

I'm about to kneel when he shakes his head and rises from the hardwood floor. "It's your birthday. Let's have tonight be about you."

"Are you kidding?" No man has ever not expected something in return from me. I don't feel right being devoured like a five-star meal only to leave him starving. I'm a giver, not a taker. I've been that way my whole life.

And yet, so has he.

"You haven't had sex since—" I shake my head, not wanting to know if he's slept with someone else aside from me.

He grips my chin and forces my gaze to his. "There's been no one since you. I've waited this long. I can wait a bit longer."

It's horrifying how much relief blossoms in my chest at his confession. I shouldn't care this deeply about him when my parents aren't going to be easy to convince. But thinking things through isn't my forte, and now that the lust cloud has faded, I'm left with the potential repercussions of my decision.

But I can't find it in myself to regret it.

When we get back to the dorm an hour later, Ethan kisses me goodbye before I shut the door, but I don't even have the chance to twist the lock before he pushes it open again, his hands landing on my hips.

"Can I taste you again?" he asks between kisses. "Please?"

I land on my mattress and tug him on top of me, nodding eagerly as Ethan hikes my skirt up and slides down my body. He settles himself between my thighs, and since I didn't bother to put the thong back on earlier, it gives him perfect access.

It's ironic I'm still wearing this angel costume because as Ethan performs the most sinful acts between my thighs with vulgar words spilling from his tongue, I'm the furthest thing from pure.

And I still don't regret it.

Nineteen

MAYA

Since Maddie is only in town for the weekend, she wanted to split her time between me and her parents, so I agreed to grab coffee with her in the morning before she drove to Wickenburg with Cameron. The coffee shop on campus is closed since it's the weekend, so we choose the closest place that offered caffeine, which happens to be Happy Endings.

When it's not alive with nightlife, the daytime menu offers brunch on the weekends, but I didn't come here for the food, and I suggested Maddie avoid it as well. It's a recipe for food poisoning.

Maddie is still perusing the menu when Tabi approaches the table. Since Tabi and I are co-workers, she doesn't hesitate to say, "I hope you aren't ordering any food."

Maddie arches a brow. "Is it really that bad?"

"*Yes.*" We reply in unison.

"Fine, fine." She sets the menu down, wincing at the stickiness of the booth. It doesn't matter how many times we wipe the tables down, it's like beer is forever coated on the cheap wood. "I'll just get a coffee with cream and sugar."

"Same. Thanks, Tabi."

"No problem. Be back in a few." She grabs our menus and disappears, leaving my best friend and me alone again. Maddie stares at me unnervingly, her chin resting in her palms.

"What?" I ask.

"Oh, nothing." She sighs dramatically. "Just waiting for you to tell me what happened last night." Fuck. I try my hardest, but I can feel the heat prick along my neck and cheeks. I know the redness is giving me away, and Maddie grins. "So something *did* happen. Did Ethan make a move? Ugh! I wish I didn't get so drunk. I would have witnessed it myself."

"There was nothing to witness."

"And you expect me to believe that?"

"Maddie." I didn't come to have coffee and talk about her brother. Despite what happened, Ethan is still her *brother*. I'm not one to be shy when it comes to sex, but it feels awkward when the man who went down on me last night is related to her. She may act like it doesn't give her the creeps, but I know better. "Let's talk about other things, shall we? How's school?"

"Good. I'm still at the top of my class." She waves her hand like she's shooing a fly. "It's all boring stuff. I want to talk about something *exciting*. Now, are you with Ethan or not?"

Tabi picks the perfect time to deliver our coffees. She catches the tail end of the conversation and says, "Ooh. Are we discussing the man who gave you *three* orgasms last night?"

Oh god.

Maddie blows out a harsh breath. "Wow. Go Ethan."

I'm too mortified to speak. Yes, I texted Tabi this morning

after I woke up to an empty bed because who the fuck else would I text? Certainly not Maddie when she'd blow things out of proportion and probably cuss her brother out before I could ask him myself. Tabi isn't emotional. She'll give it to me straight, which is why I confided in her about last night.

Quickly regretting my choices.

"Erm." I clear my throat, feeling the burning on my cheeks only worsen. "Tabi, this is Maddie. Ethan's *sister*."

She winces. "Oh, shit. Sorry."

"Don't be," Maddie says. "I've known about them for a while now. It's nothing new."

"There's nothing to know, Maddie." Slumping back in the booth, all my efforts to hide this from her dissolve. She'll figure it out eventually, either by sleuthing or by breaking me down until I finally cave. "He wasn't there when I woke up this morning, so . . ."

Tabi gives me a stern look. "Stop assuming the worst. Maybe he had an assignment to do. Or maybe he had plans with that guy he was with. You said his friend was visiting, yeah? The one the girls were drooling over?"

"That's my boyfriend." Maddie seems proud, sitting up a little straighter. "His name is Cameron."

"He wasn't supposed to meet up with Cameron until later today at the football practice," I admit. "And I *know* Ethan. He wouldn't—" He wouldn't just *leave*. He thinks everything through. He plans five steps ahead before deciding something. Irrational decisions aren't his thing, and if something came up, he would have told me. Which means . . . "He regrets it, and I can't say I blame him. Not when I treated him like shit after spring break."

"Do you want me to text Cam?" Maddie suggests. "Or I could text Mark. Either of them would snoop for more details."

Tabi suddenly stills, paying a lot more attention to my best friend. "You know Mark?"

"Um." Maddie chews on her bottom lip as she tries to find an answer. "Sort of? It's complicated."

"Complicated *how*?" Tabi props a hand on her hip, her eyes narrowing slightly. It's obvious she would *not* be okay if something had transpired between Maddie and Mark, and my best friend suddenly looks like a deer in headlights. Not that I can blame her. Tabi is intimidating.

So I help her out and come to her rescue. "Mark asked her out over spring break, but when the day of their date arrived she chose to be with Cameron instead and basically stood him up."

"Wow." Maddie hums. "Way to make me sound like a bitch."

"I'm not trying to make you sound like a bitch! It's over and done with, right? Mark was fine with it, and there wasn't any awkwardness when we were around each other last night." My focus shifts to Tabi. "Nothing happened between them."

Tabi fidgets with her apron and rolls her eyes. "It doesn't matter if anything did. We're not a thing."

I arch a brow. "And yet you let him linger by your side like a lost puppy all night while you delivered drinks."

Maddie squeals at this new information. "You guys would make such a cute couple! I could totally see it. Opposites attract, you know? You're like a badass biker chick, and Mark's the golden retriever who sneaks into your life whether you want him to or not."

"We are *not* together," Tabi reiterates.

"You also dressed up like a cat. Is it a coincidence that Mark calls you Tabi cat? I think not."

Tabi *huffs* at the ceiling, her cheeks turning bright pink. "All right. Enough about me. Aren't we talking about *your* shit show of a love life?"

Maddie, who takes the hint, sighs and takes a sip of her coffee. "Ethan doesn't regret it, Maya. He's been pining for you since, well, since *forever.*"

"Then why would he leave?" I've been fighting the ball lodged in my throat all morning, but tears prick the backs of my eyes before I can stop them. I'm not a crier, but Ethan leaving without a word is one of the most hurtful things that has happened to me in a long time. I shouldn't be surprised when I basically did the same thing to him after we first slept together, but I am. I thought we were past that, but maybe he wasn't. Maybe he was seeking his revenge, and . . .

No.

Ethan wouldn't do that.

"I already told you what you need to do," Tabi says. "Just talk to the guy. Communication is simple. Straight up ask him why he left, and you'll have your answer."

And get my heart broken again in the process? The thought of embarrassing myself is horrifying when I have so much to lose. Ethan is the guy I want to be with, and last night was the eye-opener I needed. I was set on visiting home as soon as I could get the time off work to see my parents. I was going to do whatever it took to get them to come around to the idea of Ethan and me, but waking up alone ripped both those ideas and my heart into tiny little pieces.

How can a night so memorable turn into such a nightmare?

I wish I had woken up to him leaving so I could have asked where he was going. I wish he hadn't given me so many orgasms so I could have kept my eyes open once he was finished. The last thing I remember is him holding me against his chest and then *nothing*. The blinding sunlight woke me up to dirty sheets and empty promises.

"I agree with Tabi," Maddie says, mulling it over. "My brother is a lot of things, but he's not a dick. He wouldn't leave you after doing something like that without good reason. You still haven't told me why you ghosted him in the first place, though, so I don't exactly know the whole story."

Because admitting to Maddie that my parents don't approve of her brother is hard for me to confess. My parents are nice people who only want the best for me, and I'm sure if they got to know Ethan, they'd love him. They just wouldn't love him for *me*.

"It doesn't matter," I reply. "Honestly, I think my ego is taking the biggest hit. Waking up alone was . . . new. I'm normally kicking guys out of my bed, not the other way around."

I'm not used to fighting for anyone. Guys would do all the work, get what they were after, and then I'd go on with my life with no strings attached. My feelings were never invested, but they are with Ethan, and knowing he's the first guy to ever truly hold my heart is terrifying.

"What if I'm afraid of the reason?" I continue. "I know communication is the best idea. I could call and get it over with, but what if he says something I'm not prepared to hear?"

Maddie reaches over to squeeze my hand. "Then I'll be here to pick up the pieces."

"Me too," Tabi adds. "Inner circle, remember?"

My heart swells at the potential of having not one true friend but *two*.

"Thanks, guys. I'll think about it. In the *meantime*, I'd like to chug some caffeine after my lack of sleep last night." I can't do anything without a clear head. I've been irrational regarding all my decisions about Ethan, so I'm trying to do better. *Be* better. I want to be someone he deserves. Although I don't know why he left me in the middle of the night, Ethan's heart is too big to intentionally do something so cruel. There's a logical explanation for it.

I just have to grow a pair and get the courage to ask.

Twenty

ETHAN

Having *the* Cameron Holden as a guest at practice had the kids acting like they'd had an overload of sugar. None of them could sit still, *thrilled* to show the NFL-bound quarterback their moves. It didn't bother me any, since I'm used to living in his shadow. Cameron is taller. Funnier. More talented. He's always been the person I've looked up to because I knew I'd never match his potential.

Throughout practice, he ran drills with Mark on the offense while I worked on defense again. I hate to admit it, but I look forward to these practices now. When I'm not working on papers or a presentation for school, I'm researching new drills to introduce to the kids.

I've formed a close relationship with Jake. He reminds me of myself, with his shyness and hesitancy around the others, but his love for the game shines through. I'm pushing him because I know there's a beast on the field buried beneath his layers of insecurities, and maybe it's partly because I couldn't find the one everyone claimed was in me too.

"I can't do it," he grumbles, his chest heaving. "It spins out from beneath me whenever I aim for the tackle. It doesn't make sense. I'm pushing as hard as I can."

"Strength isn't the only important part of a tackle," I instruct from the sideline. Practice ended ten minutes ago, but Jake pleaded for a few extra minutes. Two dummies are in front of him to represent a blocker and the ball carrier. The object is for Jake to create separation for the blocker so he can tackle the carrier, but he's having difficulty with it. "You're lowering your head before the impact, so you're connecting off-center with the dummy. Your shoulder needs to hit dead center. Try again. This time, maintain eye contact with your target. You've got this."

His eyes narrow behind his helmet before he dips his chin and retakes his stance. At the sound of my whistle, he launches at the dummy with enough brute force to probably knock *me* over. The dummy goes flying, but it slides out from beneath him again since he didn't drive through the tackle with his feet.

"Fuck!" He slams his fist on the turf. The kid is thirteen, so he shouldn't be cussing, but it's my job to coach. Not parent.

"You're tired. We'll try again next week."

He slowly rises to his feet, defeated and exhausted. "It's impossible."

"It's not. You're a powerhouse, Jake. It's just the technique we need to work on. I'll take some videos at the next practice and show you exactly what I'm talking about. Film will really help open your eyes to what you need to improve on."

"You'd do that? Stay a few minutes late again with me?"

"Of course. It's my—" It's *not* my job, but damn, if it almost slipped off my tongue. "I can feel your dedication to nail this, Jake, so of course I'll help. But you know what *won't* help?" I wait for him to guess, but he keeps his mouth shut. "Talking negatively about yourself. With practice, you'll get it in no time. Now go meet your mom. She's been waiting for a while over there." I wave at the woman in sunglasses and a visor with a book sprawled on her lap. She isn't reading, though. She stopped when Cameron sat at the opposite end, sweating and shirtless after running around with the kids for the past hour. Her book has long since been forgotten.

"Thanks," he says. "I'll see you next week."

When he jogs off to meet his mom, Cameron strides over to take his place. "Mark was right," he muses. "You're a damn good coach."

I roll my eyes. "Please. Don't tell me he roped you into his plan too."

"He didn't have to rope me into anything. It's clear that you're attached to these kids, Ethan. Why are you so hesitant to accept a position?"

We don't have enough time in the world to open this can of worms. Telling him about my constant comparison to him and everyone around me, the stress of performing during a game, and the random bursts of anxiety, it's all too much. There's a time and place for that conversation, and today isn't it.

"I just don't know if it's something I want to fully commit to. Being a coach is a lot of pressure, and I don't know if I can live up to that."

He cocks his head to the side. "You're already doing it."

"I'm a *guest*. It's different."

"*Riiight*," he says, clearly not believing me. "Sure."

We walk back to the bleachers together so I can grab my water. I chug half of it before I say, "I'm thinking about it, all right? It's a big decision to make. I just, I feel like it's a downgrade after turning down a scholarship to play, you know?"

"You think coaching is a downgrade?"

"*No*, but it's embarrassing to refuse to play in college and resort to coaching years later. I don't want people to talk."

Cameron sits on the bleachers and releases a heavy sigh. "You've always cared too much about what other people think, Ethan. Who the fuck cares? If coaching is something you love to do, then do it. You're good at it. *Great* at it. It'd be stupid not to explore it."

I know he's right, but it's not something I'm ready to battle. I'll cross that bridge when I get to it. For now, I have bigger fish to fry than agreeing to become the assistant coach. I fucked up painfully last night, and my only hope is that Cameron, the previous womanizer, can give me the advice I desperately need.

"I need to talk to you about something else," I say, switching the subject. I sit next to him and hang my head in my hands. "I'm the biggest idiot alive."

"I assumed as much since I haven't heard anything about what happened with Maya. What'd you do? Lay it on me."

Leaving the more intimate details out, I give him the gist of our night. "She fell asleep on my chest, but I didn't know if she wanted me to sleep over. I don't want to speak negatively about her, but you know her past as well as I do. Staying the night with a guy isn't her thing, but holding her? It felt so fucking right. Too right. And doubts crept into my head about what our time together meant, so before she could shatter my ego again, I left."

Cameron turns to stare at me open-mouthed. "You *left*?"

"I didn't know what else to do!" Going into a full-blown

anxiety attack next to the girl I've wanted for years didn't seem like the best option. I'm petrified of her telling me she's changed her mind. "I ghosted her before she could do it to me again." I groan. "And that's so fucking stupid, but I let my fears get the best of me. What do I do? How do I fix it?"

"Christ, Ethan. You need to go and tell her that you regret it. *Now*. She's probably confiding in her friends and coming up with a revenge plan as we speak. Women who've been wronged can be downright brutal." He shudders at the thought. "I understand your fear of things turning into a repeat, but by leaving her without an explanation, especially after your night together, you just lost any chance at it going *right*. Does that make sense?"

"It does, I just—" I palm a hand over my face in frustration. "I'm not *you*, man. I can't show up and let my body do the talking. I'm not confident. I'll stumble over my words and look like an idiot. She's like the girl version of you, and it's intimidating as fuck. I'm surprised the two of *you* haven't hooked up." The thought has the bile rising in my throat, and it only worsens when Cameron arches a brow.

"You think I didn't try to hook up with her back in the day?" At the murderous expression on my face, he winces. "Look, I'm not proud of who I was in high school, but to be fair, you never told me you were into her, and I wasn't in a place to consider Maddie's feelings either. I was drunk at a party and flirting with anyone with a pulse." I still feel like tackling him until he adds, "The point I'm trying to make is she turned me down. She said she was interested in someone else." He *huff*s out a laugh. "I didn't understand it back then, but I do now. Whether you want to believe it or not, Maya's waited for you too. You don't need to be me; you need to be you because *you're* the guy she's head over heels for. Now, will you let your fears get in the way of making things official, or will you finally claim your girl?"

My hands are already shaking at the thought of laying it all out in the open for her and putting my heart on the line, but Cameron is right. There's always a risk that she won't feel the same, but I'll definitely lose her if I don't tell her and run away.

I guess there's only one way to find out.

Twenty-one

ETHAN

After a much-needed shower, three nervous breakdowns, and a self-pep talk, I rap my knuckles against Maya's door and hold my breath in fear that I'll hyperventilate if I don't.

How are guys good at this stuff? I don't have *game*. Not at all. I'm as shy as they come, so doing this? Seconds away from groveling at Maya's feet? I'm surprised I haven't upchucked all over the hallway linoleum.

The door swings open, and one look at Maya brings a swift punch to the gut. Her eyes are red-rimmed and puffy, and she isn't wearing makeup. Her hair is piled up on her head in a bun, and she's wearing an oversized T-shirt and pajama pants. This woman is never *not* done up. Even her pajamas are silky and fancy. Knowing she's more than likely in this state because of me doesn't make me feel better. I *hurt* her, and yeah, she may have hurt me in the past, but two wrongs don't make a right. Not in my eyes.

Still, she looks surprised to see me. I'm still holding my breath while she quickly recovers and clears her throat, darting her eyes to a box of tissues and her laptop on her bed. "What are you doing here?"

"Can I come in?" My voice wavers, a clear indication of how fucking nervous I am, but she doesn't seem to notice. "Please?"

With a heavy sigh, she moves over to allow me to pass. I take a few steps into the room, inhaling deeply through my nose to try and get control of my anxiety. It doesn't work. This shouldn't be so fucking hard, but a simple task such as telling the truth feels like the world is pressing in around me. My chest feels tight. My lungs feel constricted. And I can't help thinking how *weak* this makes me. It's fucking embarrassing.

"Are you okay?" Her eyebrows furrow before they dart down to my chest, which is currently heaving. My heart is racing, my hands are shaking, and fucking hell, I genuinely think I'm going to pass out. I've been on medicine for over a year now. I've gone through therapy to learn coping mechanisms, but no breathing exercise is going to help me with this situation. Not when this girl means everything to me. There's a chance she could walk away again, and it scares the living shit out of me. "Ethan, what's going on?"

"Just give me a minute," I plead, waving my hand as if it's nothing. "Anxiety. It sucks."

"Oh my god. Are you having an anxiety attack? Sit down." She pulls on my arm and forces me to sit on her bed. I've been a complete dick to her, and yet here she is, sitting beside me and rubbing my back in gentle strokes. I don't deserve it. "Does this happen often?" she whispers.

I shake my head. "It used to in high school, but after therapy and medication, not so much anymore. Just, stressful situations seem to trigger it."

She rolls her lips together before she says, "I get it, Ethan. I understand if you regret what happened last night. I haven't treated you fairly, so if you're nervous about breaking the news, don't be. I'll be hurt, but I'll get over it."

Like someone taking a needle to a balloon, my anxiety bubble pops, allowing me clarity again. "You think that's what I'm here to do? To end things?"

"Um, yes? Why else would you have left in the middle of the night and proceeded to avoid me all day?" She didn't reach out to me, either, but now isn't the time to point that out.

"I'm sorry," I blurt. "For everything, Maya. What happened last night was everything I've waited for, but I got scared that you'd wake up and change your mind. It hurt like hell when you left the first time, so knowing there was a possibility you'd wake up and regret it scared the fuck out of me. It didn't give me the right to leave without an explanation, and I hate miscommunication, so even though it's difficult for me to do this with the whole—" I lift my hands to show her how badly they're shaking. "I'm powering through it because you're worth it, and if there's a chance you *don't* regret what happened last night, then . . ."

She arches a brow. "Then what?"

"I'm not like those guys you watch on the Lifetime movies. I can't pull off big gestures in front of crowds or embarrass myself by holding a boom box outside your window, but I can be honest even if it's hard for me to be. I'm scared you don't feel the same and that you'll change your mind about us, but if you tell me that you don't regret last night, then I'll show you just how sorry I fucking am, Maya, until you aren't left with any doubts. That I can promise you."

With it all out in the open, I can hardly look at her, afraid of what I'll see. Instead, I focus on the empty wall where her room-mates' stuff should be, but no one has arrived yet. I feel the bed dip, and the breath stalls in my lungs when she sinks to her knees between my legs. "What are you doing?"

She places her hands on my thigh, her nails leaving goose bumps in their wake. "If I'm being honest, there is one thing I regret about last night." I curse under my breath when she tugs at the band of my sweatpants. Her eyes are wild and devious and so *her*. "Stand up, Ethan."

An order, not a suggestion.

My legs are shaking when I rise to my feet, and not because of anxiety. No. They're shaking because I have a feeling that I know what's about to come next, and nothing in my wildest dreams compares to the way she's staring up at me right now.

"What do you think I regret about last night?" she asks sweetly, tugging the last barrier of clothing down. My cock springs free and bobs in front of her, and she greedily rakes her gaze over me while watching a bead of liquid drip onto the hardwood floor.

"Fuck," I pant. "I don't know."

She wraps a perfectly manicured hand around my length and bats her eyes up at me, feigning innocence. "The *only* thing I regret about last night is not reciprocating, Ethan, and my prom-ise to you?" I almost fall to my knees when she darts her tongue out to lick the tip. "You're not going to leave this room with any doubts either."

"*Maya.*"

"Hmm?" She strokes me leisurely, which is ironic since her touch is nothing but sensational, even when she's not trying. "I figured you're in my head so damn much I might as well give you some, right? Have you gotten head before?"

"No," I growl.

"Were you waiting for me?"

"Fuck, yes." My head falls back before one of my hands instinctively slides into her hair. I tug the hair tie free to replace it with my fingers instead. "Always you."

Maya hums in approval, licking me from base to tip. "Then I'm only going to tell you this once, Ethan Davis. Don't ask me if I like it; the answer is *yes*. Don't ask me if I want to do this; the answer is *yes*. You think of everyone but yourself, so right now, I want you to let *me* apologize for ghosting you the first time. I want you to *take*, not give. And lastly?" I'm not breathing when she smiles and says, "Don't ask me if I want you to come down my throat because the answer is *yes*."

The wind is knocked out of me when she wraps her mouth around my cock and takes me to the back of her throat. The sensation is . . . fuck. It's otherworldly. She's holding me hostage with her eyes, which remain glued to mine, and my fingers tighten on her scalp in response. She moans around my cock and presses her thighs together.

She releases me with a *pop*, her lips glistening with my arousal. "I said *take*, Ethan. We both know there's a beast inside of you. I saw him last night, and I saw him the night of the hot tub. Let him out. Stop letting anxiety win."

"What you're doing is enough," I groan. "I don't need—*fuck*." Maya rubs my balls with one hand while working my shaft with the other. She continues to suck the tip, her hips moving back and forth to try and gain friction that isn't there. Sucking me off turns her on, and hell if that doesn't make me let my reservations go.

My hips jut forward, experimenting and seeing just how far

she can take me. Maya *smiles* around my cock, opening wider for me, and when she gags, a chortled curse echoes into the room.

"You like that?" She gasps when she comes up for air. "When I gag on your cock?"

With one hand holding her hair away from her face, I use my free one to trace her bottom lip with my thumb. Maya's always been perfect, but with her lips all swollen and pink, she's irresistible. My breathing returns to normal, and all I want, all I'm *focused* on is enjoying her. She wanted the beast? Well, now she's going to get him.

"Such a dirty girl," I mutter. "Do it again."

Her eyes darken in response when I push inside, and when I find a rhythm, Maya doesn't falter. She keeps up with the speed I desire, wrapping her hands around my ass to push me as far as I can go. With one glance at her watery eyes and mouth full of my cock, I shatter into a million pieces.

I come with a shout, stilling in her mouth and coming down her throat as requested. My legs shake when she continues to suck, getting every last drop. She sits back on her knees, tongue darting out to lick her lip. "That might just be my new favorite flavor."

"Take your clothes off," I instruct. "Hands on the bed. I'm not finished with you yet." Because she won't swallow me whole and not get anything in return. We're both givers, but intimacy allows us to be in control. We have such a lack of it in our lives that we both enjoy being dominant, which is why I let her steal the show while she went down on me. But now?

I enjoy watching her remove her clothes, and just like before, seeing her naked makes me feel unworthy. I don't hide my perusal of her perky tits with perfect brown nipples or her thick thighs with a tiny gap between them. She's every man's dream, yet she wants me. Wants *this*.

She's more than her body, so much more, but have I envisioned what she'd look like bent over for me while she takes my cock *countless* times? Yeah. Her ass is unreal, and she knows it's my weakness, which is why she senses precisely what to do when she bends over her bed and gets into position.

"You weren't slick, you know," I say as I step up behind her. "In high school when you'd wear those yoga pants." My fingers trace down her spine, and a laugh rumbles in my chest when she shivers. "I knew what you were doing."

"And what was that?" She's breathless.

"You *wanted* me to imagine you bent over for me like this. Did you touch your clit at night while you thought of me touching you *here*?" It takes everything in me not to groan at how soaking wet she is when my fingers brush her center.

"All the fucking time." She gasps.

I lean over her until my chest is entirely against her back. Then I dip my mouth to the shell of her ear and whisper, "Where are your condoms, Maya?"

"Top drawer," she whimpers. "In my dresser."

I step away to grab what I need, more than pleased to see the condom box stashed in with her underwear. Neon and cheetah print thongs greet me, and thankfully, they make my cock rage to go again for round two.

"Show me how you touched yourself." I stand behind her, and while I rip the condom packet open with my teeth, she obliges without complaint and reaches between her thighs to circle her clit. Her ass is distracting the hell out of me, but the sound of her wetness is enough to make me come without touching her at all. She's aroused because of *me.*

"Ethan, *please*," she begs.

I ignore her, laying the palm of my hand flat on her back. "Arch."

One word and she instantly complies.

"Do you want to know what *I* thought of when I saw you in those tight pants?" Her ass is up in the air now, and her pussy is drenched when I slide my cock along her slit. It's been less than a year since I lost my virginity to her, and yet it feels like a lifetime. I'll come in less than two minutes, so I want to make this worth it. Foreplay is essential, so getting her riled up first means she'll come quicker. At least, I hope. "Give me your hands, Maya, and turn your head to breathe."

"*Fuck.*" A mixture between a laugh and disbelief echoes through the room, but she does as she's told. With her hands secured behind her back, I take in the sight just for a second. Black hair fanned out around her and her cheeks a rosy pink.

My voice drops deeper when I lean over to kiss her neck. "I'm going to make another promise."

She nods, unable to speak.

"When I'm done with you"—I reach between us to grab my sheathed cock, using my free hand to keep hers hostage—"you're never going to belong to anyone else."

I relish the way she gasps when I fill her. Her pussy grips me in a way that nearly pushes me over the edge, but I regain control. Our first time was special and intimate, but my only goal *this* time is to ensure she doesn't have the ability to change her mind. I want to tattoo myself on her heart. Mark my territory. Claim what's *mine.*

My thrusts are forceful but Maya doesn't complain. She's moaning so loud I wouldn't be surprised if the entire hall heard, but I could give two shits about that. I was tentative the first time, but now I want to explore.

I want to take control.

"You look so fucking pretty taking my cock like this," I say. "Look at you. *Stunning*."

"Ethan!" With her cheek pressed against the mattress, I can see how close she is. I watch her eyes roll to the back of her head before they flutter shut. Her mouth is ajar, and a puddle of drool has already formed on the comforter. "*God*. I'm already so fucking close."

"You're mine," I seethe between thrusts. "All. Fucking. *Mine*. Say it."

"I'm yours," she gasps. "I . . . always have been. Fuck, I'm—"

A wave of release sends a zing of electricity racing down my spine, and while I feel her thighs quiver against mine, I do the one thing I've held back from to get me to finish with her. I glance down between us and watch her ass recoil against my cock with every thrust, and that's all it takes to have my release barrel through me like a bull fresh out of his cage. I release her hands and sink my fingers into her hips instead while I jerk inside her, cursing and ignoring the people who have started banging on her door, telling us to keep it down.

I've never felt so complete when my body collapses on top of hers, both of us sweaty and out of breath. Maya is *mine* in every sense of the word, and I'm never going to let her go or let my insecurities come between us again. She's hot as fuck, but for whatever reason, she chose *me*. I can't keep searching for reasons why this won't work when there are reasons why it should.

It takes me a second to come back down to reality, but I finally get the ability to roll off of her and onto my back. Maya grins from ear to ear as she scoots closer and rests her head on my chest. I'm still wearing my hoodie, and she twirls the strings before giggling to herself.

"What?" I ask.

"Nothing. I just. . . . Well, I knew the sex would be good, but that was *wow*."

"A good wow?"

"A *very* good wow."

Pride surges within me. "I aim to please. Well, I'm trying to. Not exactly the most experienced at this."

"Could've fooled me. It didn't seem like it was your second time at all."

"That's because I've thought about exactly what I'd do, what I'd say, and how I'd do it if we ever slept together again, Maya. It was basically preplanned."

She snorts. "Did I live up to your expectations?"

"And then some." As I bend down to kiss the crown of her head, she runs her fingers down my chest, and the feeling of contentment I felt with her the night I lost my virginity comes back like an overwhelming force. I've been searching for this feeling ever since she left. I thought it was my bruised ego that wouldn't allow me to find it again, but it turns out it wasn't a feeling at all.

The source of my contentment is *her*.

Twenty-two

MAYA

Waking up next to Ethan stirred up a flurry of emotions I'm still trying to sort through. Grateful because he stayed, nervous because my parents won't approve, and elated from the amount of warmth his body provides.

I was cold in the middle of the night, so Ethan didn't think twice before giving me his sweatshirt. The fabric engulfs me, but it smells like *him*. I'm warm and cozy, and with the sun beaming through the window, the rays cast Ethan's face in a golden hue. He's still sleeping with one of his arms holding me to his chest and the other propped behind his head, and with his long eyelashes and the perfect slope of his nose, he looks like an angel.

Why can't I have him in my life? I should be able to choose my happiness, and if Ethan is the reason for it, why should my parents dictate who I end up with? If I explained our situation and forced them to meet him, there's no way they could refuse. Not when Ethan cares about me so much. Right?

With a sigh, I brush the stubble on his chin and rub my

thumb beneath his eyes. He slowly blinks them open, and the tiny smile on his face sends my heart racing. "Sorry," I whisper. "I didn't mean to wake you."

"You have nothing to apologize for." His gravelly voice is much sexier than it should be.

"Please. You're not a morning person, Ethan. Everyone knows that."

"No man in their right mind could wake up in a bad mood when you're wearing nothing but their sweatshirt." He snakes his hand beneath the hem and rubs circles on my thigh. "If I wake up to this view from now on? I'll start to *love* mornings."

I roll my eyes, giggling softly when he nuzzles his face into my neck. "I want to stay here all day. Seriously. I don't want to move."

"Neither do I." He groans, smacking his hand on my night-stand for his phone. "I guarantee I have a million texts from Cameron asking how our conversation went."

Maddie probably also blew up my phone, but I don't feel like talking to her about this right now. I don't want to talk to *anyone* about it. It doesn't make this real between us if my parents don't know. At least not in my eyes. First, I need to call my job and find a weekend to take off so I can go home and visit. Then, when my parents hopefully change their minds, I can shout from the rooftops that Ethan is all mine. Until then, this feels like we're playing house, and I hate that feeling. It makes me want to stay in a bubble with just the two of us. In this room, we're together, and no outside factors can sway us.

"How about we don't get on our phones today?" I take the phone out of his hand and lean over to return it to the nightstand. "Let's spend time together. Enjoy *us*." Then I place my lips against his, moaning when he rolls me on top of him and slides his hands down to my ass.

"Fine with me. However, we'll have to tell them eventually. You know, about what happened. They'll figure it out if we don't."

"I know, but . . ." I sit up to straddle him and trail my fingers down his bare chest, loving that he doesn't seem to mind me ogling his body the way he did before. He feels comfortable with me, and he should. Ethan doesn't have a reason to be insecure when he's so damn *hot*. "For the first time in my life, you make me want to be selfish. I want to keep you to myself for just a bit longer."

His grin kicks up a notch. "It's about time you start thinking about yourself and what *you* want. We're supposed to be finding ourselves this year, right?"

"Right. Speaking of finding ourselves, I heard you're coaching youth football with Mark."

"I'm not—" He *huff*s a breath, his hands finding my hips. "I don't know. At first I thought I was helping as a guest, but the more time I spend with the kids, the more I think coaching is something I enjoy doing. I haven't accepted a position yet or anything, but I was offered one."

"I think you should do it," I say. "If it's something you enjoy, then why not?"

"Because what happens if I fail at this too?" Almost as if he didn't mean to say that, he scoffs and adds, "Never mind. It's stupid."

"It's *not* stupid, Ethan. Talk to me." I grab his hands off my hips and interlace our fingers, squeezing them for encouragement.

"I don't have the greatest track record, you know? I was good at football, and that didn't pan out. My anxiety got the best of me, and although I've worked really fucking hard to overcome it, I'm worried that going back into the field of football, even if it's just as a coach, will reignite it again and become a stressor I don't need. These kids . . . they need guidance. Someone who can dedicate themselves to making their lives better and help them become the athletes they dream of becoming. It's a lot of pressure. I don't know if I can handle it."

Some might view Ethan as weak, but I think his way of thinking is one of his most attractive and strongest qualities. He doesn't jump into something before he's fully ready, and I wish I had that much control over my emotions. It makes me confident in *us* after last night because I know with complete certainty that Ethan has been thinking about making a move for a while. It's how he's wired.

"Everyone keeps pestering me about it," he continues. "It's nice knowing my friends think I can do this, but accepting that coaching is what I'm meant to do is life changing. I'd have to change my major and commit to these kids for the rest of the season. I'd have to be a role model for them, so until I'm certain, I won't take that risk."

His confession sparks a pang of jealousy inside of me, and maybe it's because he's doing what I can't and contemplating all of these life moves to get to where he wants to be. I've thought about where I'd like my life to be if my parents approved of me being a cosmetologist. I'd open up my own salon and maybe even a spa. I'd already be in the process of building my clientele and portfolio.

The difference between Ethan and me is he's gaining the courage to do something to achieve his dreams whether he sees it or not, and I'll always be stuck in the same place because the need to please my parents has *always* outweighed my aspirations. Planning to use my business degree to open a salon is one thing, but *acting* on it is a different story.

"I think you're brave," I admit.

He lifts a brow. "How? I haven't accepted the position yet."

"But you're thinking about it, and even if you have an *inkling* that coaching is what you're supposed to do in life, that's an improvement from where you started, right? You're already considering the next steps."

"Guess I've never thought about it like that." His eyes smolder when he dips his eyes down to my legs, which are still straddling him. His sweatshirt has ridden up to sit around my hips, and in seconds, I feel his erection between my thighs. "Enough about the future. We're enjoying *ourselves* today, and it'd be a crime if I didn't show you how good you look in my clothes."

I've never been more thankful for a subject change.

"Well, we *should* eat first, considering the strenuous workout we put ourselves through last night, but—"

I squeal when he flips me onto my back and parts my thighs with his knee. Ethan's body is bulky and dominating, and his thigh is the size of both of mine combined. The sheer force they're capable of puts a shiver down my spine when I remember how he took me against the bed yesterday, how everything around us seemed to cease the second he slipped inside.

"Oh, I fully intend to *eat*, Maya." He grins wickedly before throwing my legs over his shoulders, and then he bends down to give my slit a long lick. "Never say I'm not a morning person again. This is going to be my new favorite morning tradition."

And after the multiple mind-blowing orgasms he brings me, when he leaves to get us breakfast, I call my job and figure out the soonest weekend I can take off from work. I need to come clean to my parents and convince them that Ethan is what's best for me. He's on his way to finding himself, and even though it's not a profession my parents dreamed about for my partner to have, it's important to him, and that's the only thing that matters to me.

If Ethan can be brave, then so can I.

Twenty-three

ETHAN

"I'm trying to decide what's louder." Leo hums as he sorts through his clothes. A towel is wrapped low around his hips, but no matter how many times I beg for him to change in the showers like a normal human, he claims it draws more attention from the girls in the hall. "A stadium full of fans who just won the Super Bowl or you having sex."

I snort. "Wow. I'm surprised you even know what the Super Bowl *is*."

"Just because I don't watch sports doesn't mean I haven't attended it."

My eyes snap to his. "Attended? The *Super Bowl*? When?"

"Arizona versus Baltimore three years ago in Vegas. Sat in the box."

"*What?* Did you win a contest or something?" Leo is speaking about this like it's an afternoon picnic at the park, not the fucking Super Bowl. It's the one event I've always wanted to attend, but I've had to accept that I won't be able to. Not at the price those tickets go for anyway.

"Nah, my dad is . . ." He shrugs, tugging a button-up shirt with planets on it from a hanger. "He's into tech. He's one of the main reasons I know so much about it."

"And by into tech, you mean . . . ?"

"Meaning he may or may not be the CEO of one of the largest tech companies on the East Coast." I avert my gaze while he puts his clothes on, but he must see the confusion written on my face because he sighs and says, "I didn't want to tell you when I first got here. I'm used to being treated like royalty or being used because of my family's wealth. It was nice just to be normal, you know? I've been able to be a regular guy here."

I think Leo and I know each other well enough by now for him to realize I'd never use him for his money. I'm not that kind of person. It's probably why he's confiding in me about it now, and I don't take that kind of trust for granted.

"Well, your secret is safe with me. However, your upturned nose at the menu makes a lot more sense. You're used to butlers with serving trays, huh?"

"Fuck you." He laughs. "At least I don't sound like I'm using a megaphone when I come."

"At least the woman I slept with came back for seconds. What's your excuse?" Making fun of each other is our friendship, so we don't take the insults to heart.

Leo acts as if I shot him by placing a hand on his chest. "Funny, but she knew it was a one-night stand when it happened. I'm playing the field a bit, you know? After I got my braces off, women started flocking to me left and right, and the AV nerd in me who was a wallflower at the prom is eating the attention up. I'm not afraid to admit it."

"So, you don't plan on settling down anytime soon?"

He shakes his head. "No way. I'm not ready for that yet. A

few girls showed interest in me in high school, but it was for the wrong reasons. Being elusive and enjoying my life as a single man for the next two years sounds like a solid plan. I'm totally supportive of you locking things down with Maya, though. Just buy me a pair of noise-canceling headphones for Christmas."

I abandon the textbook on my lap and look over at him in exasperation. "You remind me *way* too much of—"

"Cameron?" he guesses. "How's he doing, by the way? I miss him."

"I'm sure you do," I mutter.

Leo's brown eyes twinkle with amusement. "I'm going to see what gruel they're serving us today in the dining hall. Want me to bring you back anything?"

"Nah, I'm good. Trying to finish up this paper. Thanks, though."

When Leo swings the door open, Maya is holding her fist in the air as if she was about to knock. I inwardly groan at the tight workout set she has on. It's neon pink, her favorite color, and all I want to know is who I have to thank for creating those shorts. She's a fucking knockout.

"Hi, guys," she says cheerily, peeking around Leo's shoulder to give me a little wave. "Can I steal you for an hour or two, Ethan?"

In that set?

She can have me for more than an hour or two.

"Absolutely. What's the occasion?"

Leo excuses himself after a quick goodbye, and with him out of the doorway, I can see an exercise mat tucked beneath her arm.

"I thought you might want to join me for yoga today."

Oh god. I am by no means athletic. I haven't played football in years, so to say I'm out of shape is an understatement.

"To help your anxiety," she adds. "You had an attack the other day, and studies have proven that incorporating a morning yoga session can help."

"You researched this?"

The pink that tinges her cheeks has me falling even harder for her. "Yeah. It's not a big deal or anything. I just thought it might be worth a try."

Well, how am I supposed to refuse *that*?

"Uh, sure. Let me change real quick."

I throw on my usual sweatpants and a sweatshirt, and then we trek across campus to the gym. It's the beginning of November, and with the sun rising in the distance, the air is growing warmer by the second. "Do you come here every day?"

"Not on the weekends when I work, but during the week I do. It's a nice way to start my mornings." She swipes her card at the gym door, and I follow after her. It's a shame this is my first time going to the gym on campus. Not working out isn't a bad thing, to each their own, but it makes me feel like shit because I used to live and breathe the weight room when I played football. Then anxiety struck, I went into a depression, and I felt like there wasn't a way out of it until therapy and medication came along.

Cameron has attempted to help me with a few sessions in the gym whenever he's home from school, but I never get inspired to keep going. Now I'm just waiting, I guess, for the exercise part of my life to work itself out.

Maya chooses a secluded corner in the back and rolls her mat out. She instructs me to grab one from the set they keep in the gym, so I follow suit and roll mine out beside hers.

I have no idea what I'm doing regarding yoga or even where to begin, but thankfully, Maya starts with something simple. I'm sitting cross-legged across from her when she passes me a pair of headphones. "This is my meditation routine," she explains. "I'll let you listen to it today. It'll tell you when to breathe in and out and all that jazz."

"So, I don't have to do any weird poses?"

She giggles, and the sound makes my heart soar. "No, no weird poses. That's what *I'm* doing. Meditation is mainly to connect with yourself, and I'm not talking about your brain. It's supposed to build awareness within and bring you *away* from your thoughts."

Wouldn't that be nice? I can't remember the last time I was just me without racing thoughts. My brain doesn't shut off. Ever. I'm always thinking five steps ahead, never enjoying the present moment, and worried about anything and everything. Medication helps, but it's not a cure.

Living in my head can be exhausting.

Maya presses Play on her phone and gives me a thumbs-up. Soon, bells start chiming, and a soft, melodic voice thrums through my ears. I'm instructed to close my eyes, and although I don't believe this will work, I give it a shot for Maya, because I don't want to disappoint her. She went out of her way to research this for me, so the least I can do is try.

I follow the woman's breathing instructions, inhaling deeply through my nose and exhaling. I'm not sure how much time has passed, but eventually, a faint buzzing hums beneath my skin, and an overwhelming sense of *relaxation* hits me out of nowhere. It feels like I'm in the greatest sleep of my life, one I don't want to ever wake up from. All I can hear are the bells and the gentle humming of the music. My thoughts are nonexistent, and it's strange. I'm not a crier, but this feeling makes me want to burst into tears.

Could I have felt like this the entire time simply by *meditating*?

It's unfair to myself how much time I've wasted letting my anxiety take the forefront. It's taken up so much of my life, controlled every decision I've made, and I feel like by taking a chance on this, I'm standing up to my biggest bully and telling him *fuck you.*

The music ends, and a glance at Maya's phone beside me when I open my eyes says I've been sitting here for thirty minutes.

"Well?" she asks. "How was it?"

"It was—" My mouth dries out at the sight of her. She's on her yoga mat with her legs behind her head. *Literally.*

She smirks when she sees the expression on my face. "The formal term for this particular pose is Dwi Pada Sirsasana."

"Pada Sira *what*? Is that Spanish?" I'm too distracted even to attempt to repeat what she just said.

"You're acting surprised." She hums. "I told you I was flexible."

"Yeah, but I didn't. . . . Christ, I didn't think you meant like *this.*"

She unfolds herself from the pretzel-like state before leaning over to grip the bottoms of her feet. "You never answered my question. How was the meditation?"

"Honestly? It was probably the only thing that's ever truly worked to silence my thoughts. I zoned out. Didn't even feel like five minutes, let alone thirty."

A genuine smile appears on her face that nearly knocks me off-kilter. I don't know why she ghosted me, but the more we continue what we're doing, the less I care. Her smile says it all, just how much I mean to her. I don't have to question if this is real. She wouldn't have googled how to help my anxiety if she wasn't serious about me.

"I'm glad it worked for you, then. Maybe this can be something we can do together from now on?"

I blow out a breath. "Damn. Things are moving pretty fast for us, huh? Two morning traditions made in the span of a few days?"

"What morning—*oh my god.* You were serious about that?"

"About having my prebreakfast before breakfast?" I tilt my head to the side, letting her feel the heat of my attention. "Hell, yeah, I was. If I didn't have plans later, I'd suggest we head back to the dorm and explore that pose you did without clothes on."

Maya's growing smile tells me she wishes we could do the same. "And these plans of yours can't be postponed?"

"Afraid not. It's a secret."

"Oh, come on!" She sits up on her knees and does her best impression of begging. I hate to admit it, but her expression almost makes me cave. *Almost.*

"It wouldn't be a secret if I told you, now, would it?"

"Fine." She *huffs* in defeat. "Can we grab some food at the dining hall when I'm done stretching at least?"

"We can, but first, I want you to show me how to do the sira thing. How did you do it again? Like this?" I roll onto my back while attempting to get my feet behind my head, which results in an epic fail. My legs barely swing past my torso, but her endless laughter doesn't make me feel like a loser at all.

It makes me feel like the luckiest guy there is.

Twenty-four

ETHAN

Five years earlier

"I can't believe you forced me to do this." Tugging at the sleeves of my sweatshirt, I curse under my breath because the fabric feels too hot. Cameron continues trying to set me up with random girls because the one he's trying to hook up with always has a friend she wants to bring.

"I didn't force you to do anything," Cameron replies. "I asked, and you said yes."

Because if I didn't, he would have asked someone else. He's still coping with the loss of his mom, and the thought of him choosing a new best friend doesn't sit right with me. Even though I don't want to be here, I'm doing it for him.

We're standing outside the local movie theater, and I feel Cameron grow tense beside me. I do what I do best, filtering through the different facades in my brain before choosing the correct one to prepare to face the girl I'll have to charm tonight, but my sister is the *one who greets us instead. Maya is with her, and behind them is a guy twice her size. I don't recognize him from school, so he must be from another one nearby.*

"What are you guys doing here?" Maddie asks.

"I could ask you the same question," I reply. "Who dropped you guys off? Mom?"

Maddie points to the guy behind Maya. "Emmanuel drove us."

I don't bother looking in his direction. It hurts enough to see his hand on Maya's ass out of the corner of my eye. I know Maya is off-limits, but her choice of men is awful. She deserves someone who'll treat her right, and the douchebag currently glued to his phone rather than her isn't it.

"We're just waiting for Ryan to get here," Maya admits, her eyes sliding to mine. I'd think there was a hint of regret there if I didn't know any better. "He's one of Emmanuel's friends. They play soccer together."

"And what movie are you guys seeing?" Cameron's voice is different now, but I can't understand why.

Maya swoons when she says, "The new romance. You know, the one about the baker and the chef." The interest she has in clichéd rom-coms is comical. If I ever had a shot with her, I'd have to up my game and surpass all her high standards. Emmanuel seems to be doing a fantastic job feeding her need for romance by texting, utterly disinterested in the conversation.

Sarcasm intended.

"I'm assuming it was your choice," Cameron muses.

"What makes you think that?"

"Because Maddie hates clichéd movies. She's more of a fantasy or horror-flick fanatic." His eyes flit to her, but Maddie fixes her gaze on the parking lot instead. The two had a falling out after Cameron's

mom passed and haven't been friends since, and whenever I ask about it, neither of them feels like sharing what happened. I gave up trying after a year, and now it is what it is. So much has changed in such a short amount of time that if I think about it too much, it gives me a fucking headache.

"He's here." Emmanuel finally speaks and scans the crowd. "Let's go get our tickets. He'll meet us in line." Without acknowledging us, he stuffs his hand in the back pocket of Maya's jeans and leads her to the booth at the front of the theater. My jaw ticks as I watch his hand explore. I'm silent when Maya goes to enter the theater, pausing by the door because she's expecting him to open it for her, but Emmanuel stands there and waits for her to open it instead, like a fucking idiot. I clench my hands into fists at my sides when our dates for the night finally arrive.

I barely pay attention to the lame greeting I give, not when fury burns in my veins and threatens to destroy me from the inside out.

What is Maya doing with a guy like that? Sure, he's tall, dark, and handsome, but looks don't mean everything, do they? Emmanuel acted like a total tool. He—

"So, what movie are we watching?" Cameron's date asks.

Cameron grins. "I thought we'd see the new romance that just came out. Apparently, it's about a chef and a baker."

I whip my head to look at him. "I thought we were seeing the action movie?"

Smooth as ever, Cameron wraps his arm around his date's shoulder. "Change of plans. I think the girls would prefer the romance, right? We should give them what they want."

Complaining about sitting through an hour and a half of a romance movie sounds appealing, but if I did that, I wouldn't get to watch Maya's date unfold, and curiosity gets the better of me.

~

"*You started without me.*" Maya joins me in the kitchen later that night. I've already scooped some cookies and cream into a bowl and pause mid-spoonful to my mouth when she reaches my side.

Truthfully, I didn't know if she'd want to continue our tradition with Emmanuel in the picture. From the row behind them, my eyes were glued on them the entire movie, and although she didn't reciprocate the kiss when he leaned in, she still went on a date with the guy. It must mean there's some interest there.

"How was your date?"

I clear my throat. "Fine. How was yours?"

"Fine."

She usually grabs her own spoon, but now she takes mine and scoops some ice cream out of the bowl then brings it to her mouth. I dip my eyes to her lips and how they wrap so perfectly around the spoon, internally groaning at the thought of her mouth on mine.

I look forward to these intimate nights between us. These secret ice-cream sessions have allowed us to become vulnerable on top of having a friendship. It gives me a confidence that I don't have with anyone else. It allows me to be honest, which is why I say, "I don't like him for you."

Maya seems taken aback by my boldness. "Emmanuel? Why?"

"Come on. You mean to tell me he's the guy for you? He tried to make out with you ten minutes into the movie."

She tilts her head to the side. "I didn't realize you were analyzing my date."

Fuck. I need to be more careful with my words. While I've never said I'm interested in Maya, it's hard to deny the chemistry, and the *more we have these conversations, the more it's becoming impossible to stay away from her. It won't be much longer until I break.*

"You deserve better than him," I say after another bite of ice cream.

She lifts a brow. "And who do you think I deserve?"

"Someone with the decency to open the goddamn door for you."

Christ. Way to be subtle, Ethan.

When I have my emotions back under control, I add, "You're a hopeless romantic, Maya. Anyone close to you knows that, and being a hopeless romantic means you have high standards."

She huffs a breath. "Unrealistic standards."

"No, you just choose guys who don't have the desire to meet them. Where do you think the ideas for those movies stemmed from? When a man is genuinely in love and wants to pursue something with you, you'll know it. You won't have to question it. You won't have to beg them to do better. You won't have to lower your bar because he'll do everything fucking possible to surpass it and then some." *My chest is heaving by the time I'm finished.* That guy should be me *is what sits on the tip of my tongue, but I swallow it back down instead. I know there are guys willing to put in the effort because, if given the chance, she'd never have to second-guess with me.*

"Ethan—" *Her voice catches.* "I don't know what to say."

"You don't have to say anything at all. Just know that your standards aren't too high. You deserve someone better than Emmanuel."

When she reaches for the spoon to fill the silence, she frowns. "There's only one bite left."

I nudge the bowl with two fingers toward her. "Go for it."

"Really?" *Her brown eyes twinkle, and a genuine smile appears for the first time of the night.* "Thanks, Ethan."

"Anytime." And because I'm a selfish bastard who can't leave without dropping some sort of hint, I add, "Unlike Emmanuel, I'm a gentleman. It's the least I can do."

~

I wish I was a confident guy.

And it's not necessarily that I think I'm unattractive, but when I'm out with friends, I compare my personality without realizing it. Other guys are funnier. More outgoing. More intelligent. I thought it had gotten better after Cameron left. All of these insecurities started when we got into high school, but since this semester began and I've had a chance to just be *me* in college, I haven't felt any of those doubts creep in.

Until now.

Maya wanted to go to a party with her friends but refused to go unless I joined her. I wasn't going to leave her hanging, so I came out despite my distaste for partying. I did it too much in high school with Cameron, and it got old pretty quickly. Maya didn't get a chance to experience these types of things as much as she would have liked, what with her parents being so strict, so I sucked it up for her and plastered a smile on my face.

Luckily, it's in another dorm, and it's low-key. There are only about fifteen people max, but I'm unsurprised that Maya is the center of attention. She lights up every room she walks into. She's the life of the party, always has been, and although I'd never change that about her, it's difficult *not* to compare myself to all the guys discreetly checking her out. None of them know I'm her boyfriend. Well, I think that's what I am. Fuck. How could I have forgotten to clarify a title?

Shifting uncomfortably, I take a swig of my beer and internally groan. Maya is playing a game of suck and blow, and every now and then she'll smile over at me before Destiny or Callie grabs her attention again. In tight leather pants, heels, and a baby-pink corset, she's mouth watering tonight, but it's her laugh and her ability to work a room that keeps my eyes glued to hers and her nearby surroundings. I don't trust any of the guys here simply because I don't know them, and after the situation at the frat party, I'm not taking any chances.

"It's Ethan, right?" A random girl calls my name from the circle and waves me over. "Join us! You haven't played one round."

"Nah, I'm good here. Thanks, though."

"Come on," she says and scoots over. "There's plenty of room next to me."

"I'm—"

Maya cuts me off before I can finish. "He said he's fine." Her smile is sweet. *Too* sweet. She looks downright murderous when her attention shifts from me to the brown-haired girl in the circle. Guilt creeps through my veins, but what do I have to be guilty about? I was saying no. Maya isn't mad at *me*, is she?

The girl shrugs, twirling a card from the deck between her fingertips. "Sorry, why can't he sit next to me? Are you guys—"

"It doesn't matter *what* we are. He said no, so he clearly doesn't want to play. Now, can we continue the game?" In this scenario, the last thing I expected was for *Maya* to get jealous. She has no reason to be worried, but I have to admit, seeing her acting possessive brings me the reassurance I didn't realize I needed until now. Her voice carries a hint of her accent, which only comes out when she's angry, and it's doing dangerous things to me. "Actually, play this round without me. I'm going to grab a drink." She rises from the couch and heads for the counter in the kitchen, where the liquor bottles are displayed. This is a shared suite between three people, so it's a lot bigger than our dorm rooms.

"You okay?" I ask when I reach her side.

She pours vodka in silence.

"She was only trying to be nice," I add. "She didn't mean anything by it."

"Ethan, you're so oblivious. She was hitting on you."

"Okay, let's say she was. That doesn't mean I want her. I want nothing to do with her."

"I *know* that, it's just—" I'm utterly confused when she knocks back half of her drink. "You could do so much better than me."

What the hell is she talking about?

She's been drinking, this much I know, but what's the saying? Drunk words are sober thoughts?

"I think you're wrong." The sad expression on her face nearly breaks my heart in two, so I tilt her chin up so she can look me in the eyes. "You're the perfect girl for me, Maya, and I'm sorry if I haven't given you the reassurance you need. We never clarified what we are, so I didn't want to make a move on you around your friends if you didn't want them to know, and—"

"I'm going to stop you right there." She sets her drink down and steps closer until we're chest to chest. "I'm not embarrassed by you, Ethan. Not now, not ever. You're not the only one with doubts going into this. I'll admit it's terrifying to try again after we crashed and burned before, but one thing you'll never have to worry about? Me wanting you. I've *always* wanted you." She hooks her arms around my neck, and I instinctively tug her against my chest.

"And I've always wanted *you*. You don't have to worry about other girls, Maya."

She shrugs. "It wouldn't be the first time a guy has chosen someone else over me. A lot can happen when people get to drinking, Ethan."

Sometimes, I forget Maya has a lot more experience. I remember the guys she brought around in high school, and all of them pissed me off. Not only because I wanted Maya for myself, but they genuinely didn't treat her right, and I told her as much. It doesn't surprise me that she's gone through some duds, and especially since we've both been drinking, I can see why it's a trigger for her.

"I'm not trying to compare you to guys from my past," she blurts. "I'm tipsy and not thinking clearly. Ignore me."

"I'm not going to ignore you. I want to put your worries to rest." I cup her cheek, stroking the pad of my thumb along her perfect contour line (something she taught me about last week). We're more similar than I imagined us to be. Beneath her mask of confidence is a girl who's as lost and insecure as I am, but there's no one else I'd rather go on this journey to discover ourselves with. No one else I'd rather be vulnerable with. No one else I'd rather share a bowl of ice cream with at three in the morning.

We may both be a mess right now, but we'll figure ourselves out.

Together.

"It doesn't matter how drunk I get, Maya Garcia. Do you want to know why?" I press my lips against the shell of her ear, loving the tiny inhale of breath she takes when I whisper, "Because no amount of liquor could make me forget who I belong to."

She pulls back to stare up at me in a lust-filled daze. "Ethan?"

"Hmm?"

"I want you to kiss me and show everyone who *I* belong to. Can you do that for me?"

A laugh rumbles in my chest. "Gladly."

My lips meld with hers in front of a room full of people, and in this moment, when her body shudders against me, something solidifies between us. The insecurity that I'm not good enough for her no longer exists as we kiss in perfect synchrony. We both want this *equally*, and I'm done holding on to this last reservation about us.

In the tunnel I've hidden myself in for years, Maya glows like the sun at the opening, and it feels like I just stepped into her light.

It makes me never want to go into the dark again.

Twenty-five

ETHAN

At my first home game of the season, I told myself I wouldn't act like a coach. I haven't accepted an official position, yet I'm standing on the sidelines with my fist pressed against my mouth as the clock winds down. It's the fourth quarter, and it all comes down to a single field goal. Marco is a decent kicker, but his track record isn't stellar. Not that *any* thirteen-year-old's would be.

Ronnie approaches my side when Marco runs out to the field. "Have you decided yet about being my assistant?" Over the past month or so, Ronnie and I have gotten closer, and at every practice he asks me the same question.

My jaw ticks when I reply. "No."

He exhales heavily through his nose. "All right."

"Is that all you're ever going to say in response? You aren't going to push?" He never says anything *but* "all right."

"Why would I push?" He shrugs and points at the field. "You're right about this being a big decision. I didn't start this program to have people come into these kids' lives and not stick around. When you know, you'll know, and I'll hand you over a whistle when you do."

Marco aligns himself with the ball, and all of us, including those on the bleachers, hold our breath when he makes the kick. The ball soars into the air, and it's an automatic no-brainer. It strikes dead center through the end zone, and the boys go wild. They run onto the field to hoist Marco into the air, carrying him on their shoulders while they chant his name. It brings me back to when Cameron and I won the state championship in high school. Even though I knew it would be the last game I played, it was the best day of my life. Confetti. Dumping the water cooler on our coach. The roaring of the crowd.

I snap out of the flashback to find Ronnie smirking at me. The opposing team heads off to the other side of the field with sad faces and broken hearts, and I can't help but notice they don't have official uniforms. "Why are they only wearing those jerseys?" They're made of basic red and blue mesh material and remind me of the ones we used to wear while playing capture the flag in gym class.

"They're a team without many sponsors," Ronnie explains. "Some programs lack funding. Possibly because they live in a bad section of town, or simply because the coach isn't dedicated enough to raise the money."

My eyes linger on the kids with the tattered jerseys. I try to fight the pinch in my chest, but it's useless. My mind immediately strays to how I can get their team better jerseys.

Ronnie claps me on the shoulder. "Let me know when you're ready," he repeats. "In the meantime, let's go celebrate with these lunatics."

The boys are crowding Mark a few feet away, hooting, hollering, and giving him multiple high fives when Ronnie and I join them. The breath stalls in my lungs when the kids swarm me next, nearly tackling me to the damn ground in their excitement. Pride surges through me. It has me thinking that there might be a sliver of potential that I'm good at this, even if there's still a lingering fear that I'm not.

"Congratulations."

I spin around to find Maya, her eyes softening at the hold the kids currently have on me. She looks cute dressed down in sneakers, shorts, and a T-shirt. It's the simplest I've ever seen her look, and she's still the most beautiful woman I've laid eyes on. Her hair is tied up in a ponytail and she's not wearing any makeup.

"Thought you could use this," she says, passing me a water bottle.

"I didn't think you'd come." I mentioned it briefly over dinner last night but never asked her to meet me here.

"Why would you think that?"

"Because the outdoors is your least favorite thing. You hate mosquitos and everything to do with sports."

"True, but this is important to you, Ethan, which makes it important to me too. Although, the *orange* jerseys might be a little much. Don't know if I'll be able to pull that color off."

She'd pull off *any* color, but before I can say that, Derrick, one of the players, interrupts.

"Who is she?" he asks.

"I'm his girlfriend," Maya replies with a smile. "Congrats on winning, by the way."

I'm so stunned by her use of the official term that I don't see Derrick's hand shoot out to whack me on the chest.

"*She* is your girlfriend?" He grabs the other boys' attention and shouts, "Guys, this is Ethan's *girlfriend*!"

The collection of their surprised gasps makes me roll my eyes. Leave it to a bunch of thirteen-year-olds to take a hit at my ego, but I can't blame them for foaming at their mouths when she looks like *that*.

"What's your name?" one asks.

"Has he kissed you yet?"

"Does he do that weird gargling thing with his water bottle in front of you too?"

"All right," I groan. "That was *one* time. I'm pretty sure a bug flew in my mouth."

"I, for one, am glad you two finally made it official," Mark interjects. He sighs dramatically while batting his eyes. "It's a dream come true, isn't it?"

I scowl at him. "Please don't tell me Cameron rubbed off on you during his visit."

"Cameron? Nah. *Leo*, however . . ."

Whose idea was it to create a friend circle with a bunch of jackasses?

Oh, right.

Mine.

"So, how are we celebrating?" Maya asks, thankfully changing the subject.

"We typically go to the pizzeria on Main Street after practices. That's the place the kids like best." The fact that I know which pizzeria they prefer shows how much I care about them. Obviously, I'm no longer a guest here, but to say I'm an assistant coach aloud means it's true, and that means my entire life trajectory changes.

It's a huge step, but the more time I spend around these boys, the less daunting the step becomes.

"I could go for some pizza," she says.

The boys stare at her with wide eyes. "Is she going to eat with us?"

"*Maybe* if you can keep your tongues to yourselves. She's taken, boys." I drag my eyes down the length of her, wishing we were in bed rather than on a football field. Maya shifts her weight from one foot to another in response.

The knockout with toned legs, a heart of gold, and a smile that could light up an entire stadium is now off-limits. She did something out of her comfort zone by coming here tonight. Extracurricular activities aren't her thing, but she still made an effort because this team means something to *me*.

And I'm officially the luckiest guy alive.

"We'll meet you guys there!" I shout at Ronnie and the boys.

Maya links her arm through mine. "Lead the way, *boyfriend*. I'll hitch a ride with you."

I pick her up to wrap her legs around my waist, grinning uncontrollably when she squeals and tosses her head back with laughter. She's a sight for sore eyes. That's for sure. "Of course, I'll let my girlfriend hitch a ride with me." Then, when we're halfway to the parking lot, I add, "You can hitch a ride on something else if you'd like too."

"Oh my god!" She swats the back of my head. "Cameron is rubbing off on *you*, not Mark."

I pinch her ass, and as we erupt into another fit of laughter, I can't remember the last time I've been this happy. And not fake happiness, like the times I had to act it with all my different masks on, but *real*, genuine happiness. The type where my stomach dips and laughter is the only thing I can produce to absorb the foreign emotion.

My life is starting to fall into place, and although the puzzle pieces seem to be slowly coming together, I can't shake the nagging fear that all of this is too good to be true.

Twenty-six

MAYA

My side hustle has completely taken off. What started as one or two girls has become a full-blown client list, and my room is packed with girls waiting their turn. Ethan and Leo helped me move a few chairs in from the common area, and with Bad Bunny playing in the background of my tiny salon, I've never felt more whole.

I'm a machine powering through a multitude of different looks, treating each face as my personal canvas. I'm so busy that when Ethan offered to help sort the payments from each client, I couldn't refuse him. He's been a trooper for the past four hours, sitting on my bed and handling the cash when I'm finished, and if he wasn't handling payments, he was keeping the clients distracted during the wait by chatting to them about their time at school and what they plan on doing with their degree.

On my last client of the night, I'm holding a comb between my teeth while putting the finishing touches on a gelled-back ponytail. My client, Samantha, is still gushing over her makeup, and Ethan has been smiling at me strangely for the past half hour now that everyone else is gone. Him looking at me like that has my throat tightening and warmth bubbling in my chest. That look could kill a girl if he tried hard enough.

"Thank you, again," Sam says when she glances in the mirror. "I've never seen myself look this hot."

Pride surges through me, a sense of accomplishment forcing its way into my heart before I can tell it to stop.

Silence echoes in the room after Sam leaves. Ethan passes me a thick envelope before he clears his throat and says, "I've never been more proud of you."

Damn him and his nice words.

Does he have to be Prince Charming *all* of the time?

"It's nothing." I shake my head and clutch the envelope with white knuckles, but it's useless to hold back my tears despite how hard I try. Tonight was everything I wanted it to be and more. It's what I've always dreamed of, and yet I feel like I can't celebrate it.

My lip wobbles, but Ethan gently clasps my chin and swipes his thumb to gather the falling tears. "It's not nothing, Maya. This is what you were *born* to do. Tonight proved that."

"It may be what I was born to do, but it'll never work out when my parents disapprove of it. Running a salon and having a clientele will always be a hobby, not how I make a living."

Ethan holds my stare before he purses his lips. "Can I be honest?"

Oh, god. That's never good.

But I can't help it when I nod, letting my curiosity get the best of me.

"You say you're trying to find yourself, but I think you already have. You know exactly what it is you want to do in life, and you're damn good at it, but you're scared to stand up to your parents."

I open my mouth to defend myself, but he continues before I can interrupt.

"I understand I may not know what it's like to be in your shoes and to have had my parents sacrifice so much for me, but wasn't the point of coming to the States to give you a better life and allow you to be whatever you wanted to become? If your parents saw how much you love this and could see your passion like I do, I'm sure they'd change their minds. I mean, come on, can you tell me you honestly plan on using this business degree once you graduate for anything else but this? Can you look me in my eyes and tell me being an accountant will be fulfilling?"

"You know I can't do that," I whisper.

"Then tell me what would. For once, be honest with yourself. If your parents weren't a factor, what would make *you* happy?"

It's sickening that I don't have to think hard about it at all. At night, I've allowed my thoughts to stray to what *could* be, which is how I concocted this secret future plan in the first place. Maybe Ethan is right. Maybe I have already found myself but I'm too nervous to stand up to my parents to do something about it.

I'm a coward.

But for the first time, I'm going to share my plans for the future with someone. My *real* plans.

"I'd like to start my own salon with the business degree," I tell him firmly. "Then, I want to travel to clients all over the world. I'd make sure my salon was successful and hire a few other stylists to work there, too, before I started hopping on flights and stuff, but I want to see the world and all it has to offer. I've only ever been on this side of the country, so to see the rest of it and then some would be a dream come true." Saying it out loud makes it real. Being this honest about what I want my future to become proves how afraid I am of being true to myself.

Ethan may hide behind his masks, but I'm the biggest fraud in this room.

"Then *that* is what you need to tell your parents," he says.

I laugh up at the ceiling. "You make it sound so easy when it's a lot more complicated than that."

"It's not, though. You're just making it complicated."

"What happens if my parents listen to me and still tell me they don't approve? What will I do then?" They've already shot my dreams down once before, and although I didn't fight them on it then, it's hard to imagine they'd react differently now.

Ethan shrugs. "Then we figure it out together."

His unwavering confidence in our future makes my heart both race and plummet at the same time. I'm going home in a few weeks to fight for this, for *us*, but to fight for my future too? That's another battle, and I don't know if I'm ready yet. Ethan is dead set on us being together for the long term, and although I want to be on the same page, I can't until my parents approve.

But what if they didn't, and I chose Ethan anyway? What if I confide in them about us and my future without caring about their opinions? I admire them more than anyone, and I appreciate everything they've sacrificed for me, but what good were all those sacrifices if I end up miserable?

What if Ethan is right, and we figure it out together, no matter what happens?

"You'd be okay with me traveling a lot?" I ask with a tiny grin. "You'd travel the world with me?"

"I'd support you doing whatever makes you happiest, but

traveling for me is…" He winces before blowing out a breath. "I don't know. Staying in Arizona has always been my comfort, and it's one of the main reasons I didn't want to go pro with football. Traveling to places I know nothing about can be a lot. It's a trigger, I guess."

I nod thoughtfully and wrap my arms around his neck. "I can understand that. I'll be sure to keep my trips short, then. Three days max so I can hurry up and come home to you." The thought slips out before I can stop it, but Ethan doesn't seem disturbed.

Instead, his eyes darken when he pulls me closer. "Good. I wouldn't want you to be away from *home* for too long anyway."

He presses his lips against mine for a blistering kiss, and all those fears from my mind are replaced with the prospect of living with Ethan. Sure, we live next door to each other, but we're in college. I wonder what it would be like to make coffee with him in the morning in our kitchen or stay up late on our couch bingeing movies.

A life with him is one I want, and I have a few weeks to gather the courage to make it happen.

"What are you doing?" I squeal when he lifts me into his arms. My legs instinctively wrap around his waist, and I love how comfortable the action is becoming. "It's a mess in here! I have to clean up."

A laugh rumbles in his chest when he tosses me onto my bed. Hairbrushes and lipsticks tumble to the floor, but I'm only focused on Ethan staring down at me in that primal way of his.

Mierda.

I'm utter putty when it comes to him.

"*We* will clean up together." He crawls on top of me and parts my thighs with his knee, a piece of his dirty-blond hair falling away from the rest. "But first, we're going to make it a little dirtier in here."

Twenty-seven

MAYA

I don't know how long I've been holed up in this library staring at a blank computer screen, but judging by the strain on my eyes, I'd guess it's been a while.

Writing a paper isn't how I want to spend my Wednesday. I could have been working on Ashley's makeup for her date tonight—a new client I had to cancel because of this looming due date. But when it comes to schoolwork, I've always pushed it off to the last minute. I make procrastinators seem like they've got their shit together.

I prop my chin on my hand, staring at the line flashing on the document, waiting for me to write something. Nothing comes. All I can think about is how I'll have to endure two more years of papers, reading, and online quizzes that make my head hurt. I've known from a young age that school isn't for me, but *today* is making it painstakingly obvious.

It could be worse, though. The library is surprisingly quiet in the late afternoon. The whispers of others at surrounding tables and the homey ambiance the dark mahogany bookshelves provide would kick the average student into gear. It's a place designed for focus, and with others zoned in on their laptops with headphones over their ears, it seems to be working for them. Apparently, I'm the exception.

Suddenly, a coffee cup lands in front of me, and I lift my eyes to see Ethan smirking down at me. "Destiny said you were here writing a paper for business administration." He eyes the screen entirely void of writing before giving me a sheepish look. "No luck, huh?"

"None." I groan. "I'm not cut out for this."

"Sure you are." I'm speechless when he pulls over a wooden chair and sits beside me. He picks up the sheet of paper that's been sitting on the desk and gives it a quick read. "International supply chain and inventory management." He hums with a hint of amusement. His eyes are lit with humor when he looks at me again and adds, "Sounds *riveting*."

"My point exactly," I mutter. I lift the Styrofoam cup to my lips and sigh when espresso hits my tongue. "You're my knight in shining armor. Thank you for this."

Sitting this close to him gives me something to focus on for the first time today, but it sure as hell isn't my paper. He smells so *good*. I want to crawl onto his lap and snuggle my nose into his sweatshirt, but then that would lead to other things, and I *really* have to finish this paper. It's due tomorrow.

"I find that starting a paper is always the worst part," he says. "Have you looked at any textbooks here on the subjects?"

"Nope. I've just been sitting here. Hoping inspiration will come to me, I guess."

Ethan doesn't make me feel stupid or reprimand me for

waiting until the last minute to write my paper. In a situation where he could tell me to get my shit together, he rises from his seat instead and heads for the business section of the library.

I'm dumbfounded as I watch him scan through the rows, grabbing books he thinks might help, and when he sets them in front of me, I have the biggest grin on my face.

"What?" he asks.

"Nothing." I shake my head, biting my lip, as he sits beside me again. "You're just a real Lifetime boyfriend."

"Lifetime boyfriend?" He scrunches his brows. "What does that mean?"

"Like, you don't seem real. Guys don't just stick around the library to help their girlfriend with her paper. Most guys would ask to meet up later and leave her to it."

"Oh, you thought I was sticking around? I just dropped off the books." He laughs when I swat his arm. "Okay, but in all seriousness, helping my girlfriend write a paper shouldn't be something girls rave about. The bar is really fucking low, huh?"

"You have *no* idea." The little things mean the most to me, and that's what he doesn't realize. I don't need fancy jewelry, designer bags, or a luxurious car. Having him go out of his way to bring me a coffee and help me with my paper matters more than all those things combined.

"Well, let's get started," he says, flipping one of the texts to the first page. "This paper isn't going to write itself."

～

Three hours later, I'm walking hand in hand with Ethan back to the dorm after submitting my completed assignment.

Now that the deadline isn't hanging over my head anymore, I feel light and carefree, and so fucking giddy that I get to call him my boyfriend. We knocked the paper out in three hours, a record time for me. I'm on cloud nine as I huddle closer to his side, relishing in his warmth. It's a shame he's so self-conscious about his body because I wouldn't change a damn thing about it. I like him exactly the way he is.

It's getting colder, and my choice of a T-shirt and shorts wasn't the brightest. Then again, I didn't expect to be at the library all day either. Ethan notices and strips his sweatshirt off and passes it over to me. I make no complaints when I slide the fabric over my head, his scent and warmth causing my chest to become warm and fuzzy.

I lift the sleeve to my nose and inhale deeply. "It smells like your cologne."

"Is that a good thing?"

"A *very* good thing. On the nights we don't sleep together, I miss it. I mean, my sheets carry a hint of it, but nothing like this."

His eyes soften a fraction. "Keep it. I have plenty more of them."

"Really?"

"Yeah." He briefly glances down at my bare legs, his lips twitching at whatever he sees. "It looks adorable on you."

The fabric swallows me whole. I highly doubt I look *adorable*, but before I can offer a rebuttal, he tugs at my hand and leads me through the quad, my favorite spot on campus.

I guess I appreciate it so much because it's a constant reminder that everyone is unique in their own way. Some kids are lying on a picnic blanket reading textbooks while some jocks are passing a football by the science building. One girl has her back against a tree with a sketchpad tabled on her knees, deep in thought, as she scribbles away with charcoal. We all have different interests and hobbies, and college is the place where we try to turn those hobbies into the rest of our lives.

It's as clear as day who these people want to become.

And it gives me hope that my time here will clarify that for me as well.

We pass the statute of Pete the Bulldog—the school's mascot—and continue walking until the dining hall comes into view. Our dorm is just over the hill, the building Ethan keeps heading for until I pull out of his grasp.

"I'm starving," I admit. "Let's eat something first."

He draws up short, sending me a sympathetic grin. "I can't stop today. I've got a meeting I can't miss."

"*Ooooh*," I taunt. "Is this a follow-up meeting to the one you were so secretive about during yoga?" When he doesn't answer right away, I bounce from foot to foot impatiently. "Come on! Tell me. What is it?"

He rolls his eyes. "Remember what I told you before? It wouldn't be a surprise if I told you, now would it?"

"Well, *no*, but it'd make me happy."

"And you *will* be happy once I feel confident enough to share it with you."

What the hell is he up to? Over the past few weeks we've fallen into a comfortable routine with each other, but every Wednesday night he mysteriously disappears to whatever *meeting* he has scheduled.

The old me, the one who is used to dealing with toxic guys, wants to question him further about it, but deep down, I know Ethan is nothing like the boys from my past. He wouldn't screw me over or mess with other girls. Whatever he's hiding from me, he has a reason for it, and I trust him implicitly.

Leaning up on my tiptoes, I kiss him quickly. "Okay, fine. You'll come over after, though, right?" My hand drags down his chest, covered only by a T-shirt, and I love how his pupils dilate from the slight touch. "I've been thinking of a *lot* of ways to say thank you for helping me with that paper . . ."

"Maya." He groans, knowing precisely what I'm referring to. "Come on. Don't make me walk back to the dorm with a raging hard-on. Leo already teases me enough."

"I have no idea what you're talking about." Batting my eyelashes innocently at him, I continue to act oblivious. "All I'm offering is to wrap my lips right around your thick—"

He throws his head back and laughs, slowly backing away from me. "Nuh-uh. You're trouble! I'm not falling for it."

"But you'll come over later?" I call.

"Are you kidding me? I'd be an idiot not to cash in on that offer. Oh, and save me one of those muffins! The—"

"Strawberry," I finish, waving him off with my hands. "I know your favorite. Now *go*. Don't be late."

His smile is brighter than the sunset behind him, and the more comfortable we become with each other, the more I realize that I never had a chance at fighting this connection we share.

Ethan Davis makes it impossible not to fall head over heels for him, and the truth is? Out of the both of us, I'm not the one who's trouble.

He is.

Twenty-eight

ETHAN

"How am I *not* supposed to feel offended? *Mark* found out you were dating Maya before me. Are you kidding?"

Cameron called about two minutes ago and has been ripping me a new asshole ever since, not letting me get a word in edgewise. Mark mentioned something over text to him, and since I hadn't told Mark to keep it quiet, he didn't realize he was supposed to keep the news to himself.

If this is anyone's fault, it's mine.

Cameron's animosity radiates through the phone as I flop onto my bed, and finally, he takes a breath. I use the moment of silence to say, "Maya wanted to keep it between us at first. I would have told you if I could."

"And yet Mark found out before me. Interesting."

"Only because she made things official in front of him! Everything is still new. I don't even think Maddie knows." *And I don't want to jinx it.* Things didn't exactly work out for us the last time, and I don't want to be embarrassed if things end up crashing and burning to the ground before we even get the chance to start again.

He scoffs. "Oh, she definitely doesn't. I would know by now if she did."

"Because you both just tell each other everything?"

"Um, yeah. That's kind of how relationships work, asshole."

The door opens and Leo strides in with a bundle of food in his hands. I swear, I don't know where he puts it all. He's always at the cafeteria, which is ironic, considering he thinks the food is trash.

"Whatever," Cameron continues. "All I'm saying is your best friend should have known first."

My brows fly to my forehead. "Are you really lecturing *me* on keeping my relationship a secret?" He's the one who hid the fact he was dating my sister, allowing it to happen right beneath my nose. "I forgave you a long time ago for that, so you should extend the same olive branch to me."

Leo leans over my bed, not allowing me a lick of privacy. "Hey, man. Good to see you."

"Oh. Hey, Leo. Did you know about Ethan and Maya, or am I the last to find out?"

"For fuck's sake, Cameron. He's my *roommate*. Of course, he knows!"

"This is some bullshit," Cameron mutters. "I'm missing everything in Pennsylvania."

"Since when do you care about my love life? What do you need to come here for? So we can paint each other's nails and gossip all night? You're making it a bigger deal than it needs to be."

Leo chuckles. "Trust me, man, it's better you're finding out now. You wouldn't want to be here. I'm barely surviving their lovefest as it is."

"Only because you want one," I shoot back.

"Hardly. You know what I *do* want?" His grin grows wider when he notices the impatience on my face. "A full night of sleep. It hasn't happened since you and Maya started fucking like animals."

Cameron throws his head back and laughs. "All right, maybe I'll stay in Pennsylvania a little longer."

"Good choice," Leo says. "Seriously. If you combined a howler monkey and a rocket launch, you'd get Ethan when he—"

"Hey, just a quick thought here, but can you both go fuck yourselves?" The two of them together are insufferable. A part of me wishes I'd never introduced them, but I also appreciate that they care so much about my relationship. It means they care about *me*, and it's rare to find friends with good intentions nowadays.

Cameron stops laughing and takes a few deep breaths to calm down. "Bullshit aside, I'm happy you're happy, man. You've wanted her for a long-ass time, and it's good to see you like this."

"You don't think it's too premature of me to celebrate, right? After what happened previously?"

He shrugs. "Any relationship is a risk, but after what I witnessed on Halloween, I'd say she's just as obsessed with you as you are with her. You should enjoy it, Ethan. You deserve this."

Maybe he's right. Maybe I deserve this, but as much as I thought I let my reservations go, there's still a lingering worry that she'll ghost me again, leaving me high and dry. It's like I'm waiting for the other shoe to drop. *Something* has to go wrong because what we have between us is too perfect. Too right.

I'm growing used to our yoga sessions and forming a domesticated routine with her. We spend our mornings in the gym, then study in the library for a few hours or go to the common area to binge a new reality series she's obsessed with. Our conversations are never dull. There hasn't been a moment when I've wondered if I'm with the right person because, in my bones, I know she's the one for me. I've always known it. There may have been times I didn't want to admit it and times I tried to deny it, but at the end of the day? She's the center of my fucking universe, and I'll always be stuck in her orbit.

"In that case, things are good, then. *Really* good."

Leo snorts with a mouthful of burger. "You can say that again."

"Oh, shit. I gotta go. Maddie's calling," Cameron says.

"And you can't tell my sister to wait a damn minute?"

He gives me a look as if to say, *What kind of idiot do you take me for?* "Part of making a long-distance relationship work is comparing schedules to find available times to talk. Hate to break it to you, but your sister is more important. Bye."

My mouth is hanging open when the call disconnects, and Leo doesn't help by throwing a french fry at my head. "That look really isn't becoming on you. Close your mouth."

I blow a breath up at the ceiling. "Fuck me," I mutter to myself.

"Couldn't even if I wanted to. Maya doesn't give me an opportunity."

"Oh my god. If you're going to be annoying, at least give me some of your fries." I want to be upset, but truthfully, I fight a smile the entire time. This is exactly what I wanted my college experience to be like. I found the girl I'm meant to be with, made more friendships along the way, and on top of it all, I'm accomplishing what I set out to do. I wanted to find myself, and isn't that what I'm doing?

The realization sends a sensation of warmth shooting through my chest.

"Thought you'd never ask," Leo says, reaching across the tiny space between us with a carton of fries. "I know you're hungry from all the calories you're burning now."

This time, rather than roll my eyes, I tip my head back and release a full-blown belly laugh. For the first time, I'm loving my life, and I refuse to let anxiety get the best of me anymore. I'm going to enjoy myself to the fullest and focus on the present, not the future or my past.

I'm *happy*, and it's about time I start living like it.

Twenty-nine

ETHAN

Afternoon sunlight filters through the window behind my bed, streaks of golden hues passing across Maya's face. She's lying between my legs with her chin propped on my chest, her hair mussed and lipstick smeared after a couple's yoga position got a little too personal and led us back to my dorm. Leo was in biology class, and my door came before hers, so . . .

"Your bed is more comfortable than mine." She rolls onto her side, tucked beneath my arm now. "It's not fair."

"You're welcome to sleep with me anytime, you know."

She scoffs. "And listen to Leo's snoring all night? He sounds like a bear."

Good point.

Her soft breasts press against my abdomen, and when she rubs her fingers along my small line of chest hair, I grab her wrist and inspect a tiny heart tattoo. "What's this for?" My thumb brushes against the black ink, causing a shiver to run through her body.

"I got it on my eighteenth birthday just because I could do something for myself for once without my parent's permission." She shrugs, inspecting the design. "I guess because I wear my heart on my sleeve?"

I bend down to kiss it and inspect her other tattoo—a tiny cross on the other arm. "And this one?"

We just got finished having sex, but my lips on her skin have already made her breathless again. I shouldn't find it such a turn on, but I do. "My family is Catholic. It's a tribute to my faith."

I kiss that one, too, before I roll on top of her.

"Why do you want to know?" she asks.

"Why wouldn't I?" I counter. My lips connect with her collarbone, and I trail kisses down her chest, stopping to suck on one of her nipples before I add, "I want to know everything about you, Maya Garcia. Every square inch of you. Even the parts you hate."

Down, down, down I go until I'm met with the slickness between her thighs. She's soft and wet when my tongue hits her center, and I smile at the moan my action elicits. I'm certain the entire hall is tired of our shenanigans, but I can't find it in me to give a damn when she sounds like *that*.

I'm about to add my fingers when the door suddenly swings open. Thankfully, I'm underneath my comforter, but with the way my body is hunched over, it's obvious what we're in here doing.

"What the hell?" Leo groans. "Maya doesn't have a roommate! Why are you fucking in here?"

I pop my head above the comforter, ensuring Maya's still covered. "I don't recall you giving me the same respect with *Casey* while we were all in the same room together."

"You were sleeping!"

"And you were supposed to be in class."

He *huffs* a defeated sigh and throws his book bag onto his bed. "I left early because I have an English paper due in two days and I need to finish it. Text messages exist for a reason, you know. Next time you want the room to yourself, *tell me*. I would have walked the long way back or stopped for something to eat."

"Didn't think I needed to when you were supposed to be in *class*."

Maya, who's been silent until now, pulls the comforter around her body as she rises to her feet. Thankfully, I changed back into briefs after our last round. "As fun as this is watching you two hash it out, I have to get ready for my shift at Happy Endings. I just . . ." She scans the floor for her articles of clothing, bending down with the comforter clutched in her hand to scoop them off the floor.

"Forgot something." Leo grins wickedly as he points to her bright-red thong. "Cute color."

"Stop looking at my girlfriend's underwear," I shoot back.

Maya laughs, utterly unbothered by Leo walking in on us. She doesn't even seem embarrassed, but that's one of the qualities I find most attractive about her. Confidence exudes from every pore. Not an ounce of shyness. And where I used to think I'd be mortified if I ever found myself in this situation, I'm not.

Staring at her flushed cheeks, sweaty skin, and rumpled hair? I did that to her, and it has my inner caveman beating his chest with a club. It feels like I've marked my territory, so, no, I'm not embarrassed.

She scoops up her thong, dangling it on one of her fingertips. "I'll return your comforter before I leave for work. Thanks for the orgasms." With a wink, she hurries out the door, leaving me on my sheets in awe while Leo falls back onto his bed.

"Multiple orgasms, huh? Wow. I'm impressed."

"We are *not* discussing this," I mutter.

"Fine." Snatching his laptop from his side table, he sprawls on his comforter and starts it up. "I'm thrilled for you, though. You guys seem happy."

"Thanks, man. We are." I scroll through my phone for a few minutes before I ask, "Are you *sure* you don't want a girlfriend?"

Leo, the usually laid-back, easygoing AV nerd, grows as still as a statue. It's as if he's debating whether or not to tell me, but after a few seconds, he sighs and says, "I did have one in high school. We dated for about two years. I lost my virginity to her, and then I found out she was only in it for the money." A dark expression passes across his face. "I should have known. I had a face full of braces and chunkier glasses than I wear now, and she was a cheerleader and way out of my league. It was obvious to everyone around me but *me*."

"Damn." I set my phone beside me at the serious turn this conversation took. "I'm sorry, Leo. That's shitty."

He shrugs like it doesn't bother him, but his eyes tell a different story. "A lot of people don't realize that being a trust fund kid isn't all it's cracked up to be. Sure, it has its highs, but it has its downfalls too." Then he shakes himself out of his stupor and adds, "It was a long time ago, but trusting another girl enough to let her in? To tell her about my money? I'll pass on that. I'm good playing the field for now."

There's not much I can say to try and persuade him otherwise. I will never understand that kind of betrayal, so who am I to tell him his reluctance about relationships isn't valid?

Leo shifts uncomfortably. Clearly, he doesn't enjoy talking about his feelings, so I help him out and get us back on familiar ground. "So, asking you for Super Bowl tickets now would be bad timing, right?"

I erupt into laughter when he chucks a pillow at me from across the room. "You're a fucking dick," he says, but he's laughing too. "I hate you."

My smile grows wider because this is how our friendship is, and I wouldn't change it for the world. He's quickly becoming one of my best friends. "Love you, too, man."

And with him returning to finishing his paper and me scrolling on my phone, we fall into a comfortable silence.

Thirty

MAYA

After another closing shift at Happy Endings, I'm exhausted. My head hurts from five hours of straight bass rattling my brain, and my clothes are sticking to my body because two girls crashed into me and spilled their drinks all over my uniform. I'm a sweaty mess who reeks of vodka, and my only desire is to go home and pretend tonight never happened.

"That was a shit shift," Tabi mutters. It's the first time we've spoken all night because of how busy it was. We should've known the fair downtown would drive more customers than usual to the bar, and we were tremendously outnumbered tonight because of it. I didn't have a second to *breathe*, let alone take a break. "I think I have four new blisters on my feet. I shouldn't have worn these new sneakers without breaking them in first."

"Tell me about it. It feels like someone dumped an entire bottle of maple syrup on me."

Tabi snorts. "Those girls were plastered. I'm surprised they weren't thrown out after the first hour."

We make quick work of wiping down the tables and flipping the chairs. Tabi's curly red hair is frizzy and untamed in a messy bun, and she frustratingly pushes the falling pieces behind her ears as we grab our purses and coats from the office. "I would talk more before I leave, but honestly, I'm beat," she admits. "Annie comes home tomorrow from her dad's, so I need all the sleep I can get."

I arch a brow. "He's watching her for an entire night?"

"Trust me, he's not watching her long. I dropped her off before my shift started, and I won't be surprised if he shows up with her before ten tomorrow morning. He can't watch her for more than three hours when she's awake because that would mean he'd have to put in effort." She rolls her eyes. "He's the laziest fucker I know."

We head down the hallway together, only to stop dead in our tracks when we see Mark and Ethan standing outside the front door.

Tabi goes rigid beside me before balling her fists at her sides. "I don't have time for his bullshit today," she sneers. She flips the lock and throws the door open. "What the hell, Mark? I told you I don't need anyone walking me home at night. I can handle myself for Christ's sake."

Mark pulls a pink lamb from behind his back, and the object looks so tiny compared to his massive body that I would have laughed if it wasn't for Tabi's face paling. "Annie left this in my car this morning. I know the Asshole has her tonight, so I wanted to talk to you first to figure out what you want me to do with it."

"What do you mean?" she asks, her eyes darting to the lamb again.

"Do you want me to drive it over to his house? You and I both know she can't fall asleep without it. He's likely losing his fucking mind. If she doesn't have Lamby tonight, he'll probably drive her back to your house before sunrise."

"Why didn't you text me earlier about this?"

Mark sticks a thumb over his shoulder at Ethan. "I found it about an hour ago after convincing this one to go out to shoot some pool. You never answer your texts at work, so we drove here to meet you after your shift."

Tabi, who is usually so witty and quick with comebacks, has no words. She stares motionless at the lamb for a solid ten seconds before she says, "You'd drive it over there for her? He lives across town."

Mark shrugs as if he's not doing her a huge favor. "I had a nap earlier. You didn't. Go home and get some sleep."

"She can probably manage for one night without it."

"But she shouldn't have to. It was my fault for not checking the car when we came back from getting ice cream. She's probably crying as we speak, and—" He clears his throat. "She needs it."

I'm so caught up in their conversation that I haven't even had time to process Ethan coming along with Mark. Was he just getting a ride home from playing pool? *No.* That can't be all when his gaze roams from my head to my toes. His stare produces an electric current that zaps me awake. I'm suddenly not tired at all.

"I need the Asshole's address," Mark continues.

"He has a name, you know."

"And he doesn't deserve to be called it. He'll always be the Asshole to me. Now, can you give me the address so I can put your child out of her misery, please? Lamby needs to be returned to his owner." A sound short of a gasp works its way from his throat. "Well, I'll be damned. Did you just *smile*, Tabi cat?"

Her lips, which had slightly twitched at the sides turn into an immediate frown. "You're seeing things. Add hallucinations to the list of injuries football has caused you."

"I know what I saw."

"Mmm," she hums. "I'll give you his address, but this changes nothing. You're still . . ."

He arches a brow, awaiting her answer.

" . . . a pain in my ass," she finishes.

He throws his head back and laughs. "Hey, I'll take that over something that crawled out of the pits of hell. You called me that yesterday, in case you forgot."

She smiles wickedly now, nothing short of devious. "Trust me, I didn't."

For whatever reason, I feel like I'm invading an intimate moment, judging from how these two stare each other down. Ethan must think the same because he steps around Mark's body and jerks his head for the door. "Are you done for the night? I was going to walk you home."

Butterflies erupt everywhere in my stomach. "You were?"

"Is that all right with you?"

"Yeah. I was going to ride with Tabi, but . . ."

"Please." Tabi scoffs, ending whatever stare down she was having with Mark. "I'm three sheets to the wind. I won't be offended if you walk home with him instead. We'll have time to catch up on girl talk another day." Her eyes linger on mine as if to say, *We'll have a lot to talk about.*

"Cool. Thanks, Tabi. I'll see you next weekend?"

With a subtle nod from her, I follow Ethan into the chilly November air. Goose bumps pepper my skin, so I slip on the puffer jacket I brought and stay close to his side. Ethan's hand brushes mine, tentatively seeking to see if I'll hold it. It's ridiculous since we've already slept together, but something so simple seems to hold more intimacy than him being inside of me.

I intertwine my fingers with his, loving the red that stains his cheeks in response.

"I should have had Mark drop me off at the dorm so I could grab my car," he admits. "It's cold out here tonight."

I press my side fully against his and rest my head on his shoulder. "It's okay. You're doing a great job at being warm." But as soon as the sentence leaves my lips, water droplets from the night sky above slowly hit my skin. I blink at the stars, cursing when the few plops become a drizzle.

"Damn," Ethan mutters. "We can go back to Happy Endings. I'm sure Tabi and Mark haven't left yet."

"No, it's fine. Annie needs her lamb or whatever. I don't want to get in the way of that." This damn jacket doesn't have a hood on it, but hoods aren't a necessity in Arizona. It hardly *ever* rains.

"You hate the rain," he says.

"I do not."

"You do, or are you forgetting when you wailed like a child during lunch in the courtyard when there was a downpour? When was that, your sophomore year?"

I swing my head to give him an open-mouthed stare. "You saw that?"

"More like I *heard* that. It was impossible not to hear you scream."

I *huff* and cross my arms over my chest. "Well, maybe I love it now."

"Do you?"

I cringe when the water trails down my scalp. Although it's not a downpour, it's a steady trickle that has me breaking down and forgetting the front I put up. "Okay, I hate it, but in my defense, I have a thick head of hair! It takes hours to straighten it. By the time we get back to the dorm, it'll be a frizzy, disgusting mess."

Ethan chuckles, and I'm speechless when he strips off his jacket and passes it over to me. The rain is picking up its intensity, so Ethan pulls me under an awning on a side street to prevent me from getting drenched. The action makes my heart pound, and all I want to do is make the rom-com movies I love come to life and kiss him stupid in the middle of a rare downpour in Arizona.

"You're going to catch a cold in this weather if you don't wear your jacket," I tell him. "It's freezing, Ethan."

"It's a good thing I'll have my girlfriend to nurse me back to health, then, huh?"

The sigh I give makes his brows furrow. "What?"

"Nothing." I laugh at the absurdity of the weather and the perfect man standing before me. "You just surpass my wildest expectations. If I could have curated the ideal guy for me, you'd meet the criteria and then some." I smile softly when he drapes his jacket over my head to cover my hair, ever the gentleman. "I used to think my standards were too high, but—"

He cuts me off before I can finish. "Your standards were never too high, Maya. You were just asking the wrong person."

Dammit to hell. I don't care if it's the corniest move in existence, but I kiss him senseless beneath this awning with rain crashing down around us. He cradles the back of my head before pressing me against the brick wall of some random shop. I'm clutching his jacket over my head while trying to keep up with his lips, which leave a burning path from my mouth to my jaw and then to the column of my throat.

Ethan has embedded himself in my heart, and I'm afraid he's staying there for good. I've never been in love, but if I had to take a wild guess, I imagine I am with him. It's the only explanation for my frantic need to get his clothes off and show him how much I appreciate him. It's the only reason I feel completely myself with him in a way I don't with anyone else.

We're both panting when we rip our mouths apart. Ethan stares out at the rain bordering on a monsoon before he grabs my hand with both eyebrows raised and says, "Well? Are we doing this or what?"

I nod, clutching his jacket over my head for dear life.

"All right, ready? Three, two, one, *go!*" He pulls me into the storm, and with us laughing like lunatics and our shoes getting soaked, I realize I didn't put up a front after all.

I'm learning to *love* the rain.

Thirty-one

ETHAN

I'm drenched from head to toe when we get back to the dorm. I hardly notice because the second we enter the building, Maya's lips are back on mine. My mind is hazy and in a lust-filled daze as we stumble into the elevator, hitting random buttons that will hopefully take us to our floor.

The only woman I want is *her*. The only woman I've ever seen is her. Maya has always been the greatest thing to ever come into my life, and I plan on cherishing her for every second I have with her.

"Take this off," she pants when the door shuts to her room. I've never been more grateful she still doesn't have a roommate.

She pries off the T-shirt stuck to my body and flings the wet garment on the floor before making quick work of my pants. Lightning flashes outside, and rain pelts against the window. It's pitch black in here, but neither of us bothers with the lights. We have one thing on our minds, and we don't need to see each other to accomplish it.

In the dark, I can focus on my auditory senses, and in a way, it's more sensual than visual. Her labored breathing when I strip off her skimpy uniform top and bra. Her moans when I kiss her collarbone and blindly back her up to her mattress. The tiny inhale of breath she gives when I peel her shorts and underwear off and toss them to the side with the remainder of my clothes.

Maya's skin is cold when we land on the bed together, but I hope to change that in the next five minutes.

"*Ethan.*" My cock thickens at the sound of my name spilling off her tongue. It reminds me of what other talents her tongue is capable of, but her pleasure comes first. I've recently discovered that doing this is one of my new favorite hobbies.

I sink between her thighs and don't bother teasing her when she's shivering. I wrap my mouth around her clit and grin at the cry of bliss that fills the room. Thunder rumbles in its wake, acting as a muffler that I'm sure Leo will be thankful for next door.

Her hips buck against my face, grinding in a greedy, possessive way that makes me groan against her, begging for more. I'm suffocating between her thighs, but if I had to die, this would be the perfect way to go out.

"Come for me," I growl when she releases her hold. I slip two fingers inside of her and pump until my forearm aches. The best part about sleeping with Maya is I'm learning all of her ticks and what pushes her over the edge. I realize now that she likes to be fingered soft but fast. And she especially likes when I tongue her clit at the same time, which is precisely what I do.

She comes immediately, her hands latching onto my soaking wet hair and tugging on the strands as she rides out her high.

Just as suspected, her skin is warm to the touch when I crawl back on top of her, but then she flips us over and straddles me instead.

She bends over to whisper in my ear, "I want to fuck you like this." I feel the long, silky strands of her still-dry hair hit my shoulders, enveloping us like a curtain of privacy. "Can I ride you? Is that okay?"

"The fact you think you have to ask is a problem."

"Do you have a condom? I think we used up the ones in my dresser."

My fingers flex on her hips, annoyed that she'll have to move, even if it's only for a few seconds. "My wallet. In my sweatpants' pocket."

She crawls off and stumbles in the dark until she finally finds it. I hear the foil packet ripping open, then she straddles me again and grips my aching dick with her fingers.

We've been having sex for almost a month now, but I want it every second of the fucking day. However, I don't want to come across as the typical horny male who only wants to get in her pants. Maya means so much more to me than that.

I pull my lip between my teeth when she sinks onto my cock, and it takes an obscene amount of effort not to finish. I think of everything possible to hold back—war, dead puppies, world hunger—but no feeling will ever compare to the grip she has on me. Quite literally.

"You feel *so* good," she whimpers.

My eyes slam shut. "Fuck, don't say shit like that. You're gonna make me come."

"Isn't that the point?" Her hands land on my chest, and when she starts to ride, my fingers dig into her hips. There's no way she's going to keep doing this without me watching, so I lean over to turn on the lamp on her nightstand. Light cascades over her body in a warm golden glow, and I don't know where to look first.

Her tits, which are the perfect size for my hands. Her mouth, which is open in pleasure. The way her nails scrape down my chest while she grinds on my cock in the most delicious way.

"Does this position feel good for you?" I ask.

She nods enthusiastically. "*Yes.*"

But I don't feel right receiving all the pleasure without reciprocating.

My eyes dart to her nightstand. "Is your toy in there?"

She freezes. "What are you talking about?"

"Oh, come on. Don't be shy about it now. The toy you used to make yourself come. You know, the one you intended for me to hear you use? Where is it?"

"You want to use it?"

"On you? Yes. Is that a problem?"

Her cheeks flush. "No, I've just never used it with someone before."

"Then now's the perfect time to start, isn't it?"

After a moment of hesitation, she leans over to grab her vibrator from the drawer, and the sight of the dainty pink toy makes me grin from ear to ear. I know her too well. It's just how I pictured it.

"Switch it to the setting you prefer."

"*Ethan.*"

"What?"

She switches the vibrator on and presses the button once or twice before she passes it over to me. "You're just so fucking hot, it's insane."

I press the toy against her clit, chuckling deeply when her

hips buck in response. "Show me then, baby. Ride my cock while you fuck this toy."

An animalistic sound escapes her and it makes me grow harder. I circle the vibrator around her clit, observing her face to see what she does and doesn't like. Maya is a goddess as she rocks her hips against me, but what does me in is when she trails her hands to my stomach and squeezes. She's full on riding me now, and I'm desperately trying to keep my movements controlled with the vibrator but sweat is breaking out across my forehead from my impending release. The sight of her is too much. Her breasts are bouncing, her face is flushed, and her ass is smacking against my thighs. I'm not—

Maya rips the vibrator from my hands and reaches behind her to—

Oh, fuck.

"Let go," she pleads.

The vibration hits my balls, and I'm a fucking goner.

My eyes roll to the back of my head as I shout to try and compensate for the fact that I'm nothing but smithereens while Maya continues to ride me through all of my muttered cursing. I'm sensitive as hell, but I want her to find release, too, and she does in a matter of seconds.

She cries out my name before collapsing on my chest, and in the blissful aftermath, she rubs circles on my chest and hums happily. "You should take a shower to warm up."

"You should take one with me."

She snorts. "You know we can't do that. There are separate showers for a reason."

"Well, when we're done with school and have a place of our own, we'll save water by showering together. Make up for lost time."

"That sounds like a dream," she mumbles sleepily.

"It's not a dream when it's going to happen."

"You think so?"

"I know so." Then, after a heartbeat, I add, "Don't you?"

While I stare at the ceiling with a ball of anxiety, Maya falls asleep and leaves me waiting for an answer that never comes.

Thirty-two

MAYA

"Oh, hi, Leo! I didn't expect you to pick up Ethan's phone."

I currently have my nose buried in Ethan's sweatshirt. My leg is wrapped around his waist, and his hand is tangled in my hair. However, the second I hear the familiar voice, my eyes shoot open before I attempt to make a hasty exit to the door.

"How could I resist talking to you, Mary? You're always a breath of fresh air." Her soft laugh echoes through the speaker. "Ethan's sleeping, but I didn't want him to miss a call from his beautiful mother. Let me pass him the phone."

My legs are tangled in the sheets now, and Leo doesn't seem to notice my frantic attempt to beeline it out of here. I'm a sitting duck when Leo attempts to nudge Ethan awake because I know my face is visible on the screen, and Mary isn't the type of person to ignore it. I can see the moment realization dawns on her, and the smile that blossoms on her face makes my heart clench.

"Maya, what a surprise!" she exclaims. "I'm sorry. I wouldn't have called if—"

Ethan snatches the phone, jolted awake by the seriousness of the situation. "Mom," he groans. "It's nine in the morning."

She *huffs*. "Well, for some, it's already the middle of their day. I was calling to make plans with you for Christmas break. Can you tell me the exact dates you'll be home?"

Leo, who seems to have returned from a workout, rattles off the dates for her because Ethan is incapable of thinking at this hour. My boyfriend isn't a morning person, but while he's grumpy around everyone else, the circles he makes on my thigh lead me to believe I'm an exception.

"Oh, perfect. Your sister and Cameron are visiting too! Well, Cameron can only stay for a week because of football, but it'll still be nice having them here." A beat, and then, "Should I save an extra seat for your *guest* on Cookie Day?"

Ethan sighs. "Please don't do this."

Mary innocently bats her eyes. "Do what?"

"Make this bigger than it needs to be. I love you, but you have a flair for the dramatic."

"I have no idea what you're talking about. I'm simply asking if you'll be bringing Maya along to frost cookies. That's all."

I slap a hand over my mouth to cover my laugh. I've participated in Cookie Day every year since Maddie and I became best friends, so Mary knows I wouldn't miss it. She's fishing for information about us, and when Ethan glances warily at me, attempting to decipher how I want to approach this situation, I come to his rescue.

"Of course, I'll be there," I tell her. "I'd never miss a Davis tradition."

Her eyes crinkle at the sides with a smile she passed along to her son. Ethan is the spitting image of her with their dirty-blond hair and blue eyes, but it's his heart that I have to thank her for the most. Richard and Mary have raised two incredible children, and I feel extremely fortunate to have found them both.

They've always supported anything their kids have done. Ethan loved playing video games, and Richard and Mary suggested he go to school for animation if that's something he was passionate about, or if he didn't feel the need to go to college, they believed he could be successful as a streamer if he tried hard enough. Expectations were never placed on him like my parents did to me.

"Perfect." Her eyes twinkle with mischief. "Should I seat you next to Maddie or Ethan?"

"*Mom.*"

I let out a giggle at the blush on Ethan's cheeks. It's adorable.

Telling his parents about us should be scary, but Mary and I have always had a good relationship, and I know she'll love whoever Ethan chooses to be his girlfriend. Including me.

I wonder if Ethan realizes how rare it is to have parents like that.

And maybe I'm honest because I know I'll never get this reaction from my parents. Maybe it's because I crave acceptance, even if it's not from my own flesh and blood, but I find myself blurting, "You can sit me next to Ethan. I am his girlfriend, now, after all."

"I knew it!" she squeals. "Oh, honey, I am *so* happy for you two. I want to hear *everything* when you visit. We'll have a girls' day! Nails? Hair? Or maybe you can do it yourself with that talent of yours."

Mary's overwhelming support stirs a rush of emotions inside me, and it's hard for me to figure out which one to focus on first.

I'm relieved she's elated for us, but I didn't expect to feel jealous of Ethan's relationship with his parents. He has their unwavering support about us. Hell, his mom even supports me and my passion for cosmetology.

Why can't my parents treat my passion and the person I choose to be with the same?

With a watery smile, I reply, "I'd love that. Um, I forgot something in my room. I'll be right back."

It's a shitty excuse, but I'm not thinking clearly when I slide off the bed and leave them to finish their conversation. Disappointment that I'll never have that kind of connection with my parents threatens to tear me apart from the inside out, and as soon as the door closes to my room, fat, salty tears stain my cheeks.

I have no right to be jealous when my parents love me unconditionally. They'd put their lives on the line for me, and they've proven it time and time again. I shouldn't wish they were different. I'm a selfish daughter. Selfish, and ungrateful, and—

"Are you okay?" Ethan's eyes flicker over my face, to the tears streaming down it, before he pulls me into his embrace. "Hey, what's going on?"

I didn't even hear him come into the room, but I melt into his arms and sob softly into his sweatshirt. Telling him the real reason I'm crying will only fill his head with doubts. He doesn't know why I ghosted him the first time, but if I tell him my parents disapprove of him, it'll reveal everything I don't want him to know.

He's worked so hard this year to discover who he truly is and is meant to be. Confiding in him and sharing that he's not good enough for my parents will only cause a setback that he doesn't need. All I can hope is that in a few weeks when I go home to visit my parents, they'll let me plead my case and change their minds about him.

And if they don't, *then* I'll tell him their opinion of us, and Ethan and I will figure it out together.

"I just miss my family." The lie feels thick coming off my tongue, but this is in his best interest. "It's been a while since I've seen them."

Ethan rubs my shoulders in soothing, calming strokes. "It's okay, baby. You can FaceTime—" Words stall in his throat when he remembers that I *can't*. My family doesn't have the money to afford iPhones, let alone laptops. They've had the same flip phones for almost ten years now, and I'm lucky if they can afford to put minutes on them. "You're going to see them soon, right?"

I nod and pull away from him to swipe at my cheeks. "Yeah. In a few weeks."

"See? That's not long at all. Then you can share this news with them in person. It'll be even better than telling my mom over the phone."

My body stiffens before I quickly recollect myself. "Right."

"I'd like to come over for dinner sometime. You know, to meet them properly and all. Hell, I can even pitch in for the food. Help your dad grill." My eyes burn with the tears I'm holding back, because damn him. Why does he have to be so perfect?

He thinks he's helping by talking about the future and all of us spending time together, but all it does is put my heart into overdrive. In seconds, my palms are sweating, and the guilt is creeping up my throat, desperate for me to tell him the truth.

But I swallow the feeling and plaster a smile I hope is convincing on my face instead. "I'll ask them," I weakly reply.

And beg them to accept you.

Thirty-three

MAYA

Ethan shows up at my dorm room on Friday at eight in the morning with a bouquet in one hand and a duffel bag in the other. I'm utterly confused, when he says, "Want to go on a trip?"

"A trip?" My heart races at the possibilities. "I would, but I have to work, and—"

"No, you don't. Tabi didn't mind switching shifts with you, so you're working next Friday instead. We'll be back in time for your shift tomorrow night."

"I—" Words die in my throat before reaching my lips. I can count the number of times I've been on a trip on one hand, and after confiding in Ethan about my desire to travel, this gesture feels *intimate*—curated and designed specifically for me.

His lips quirk at the sides, a smug smile at catching me off guard, which is rare. I'm a detective when it comes to surprises. Once, I went through Maddie's closet to find my Christmas present after hearing Ethan mention during dinner that she hides everything in there. He was right. I discovered a beautifully wrapped box with my name on it behind a pile of dresses, and after pleading with Maddie to let me open it, I received the most expensive sweater I've ever owned.

I flick my eyes over his outfit of jeans and a button-down shirt. I'm not used to him wearing anything other than sweatpants or sweatshirts, and even though I'd never change him, he's damn nice on the eyes like this.

A gold watch fastened around his wrist glints in the light from the hallway behind him, and his typically shaggy blond hair is combed back and contained at the nape of his neck.

When a hint of cologne makes my mouth water, I'm positive there isn't a sexier sight than Ethan Davis.

"What should I pack?" I ask. "My hair isn't done, and my makeup—"

"I allotted time for all of this." He strides into the room and sits on my bed. "You have two hours to get all done up."

"But what do I pack? I don't know if I have anything fancy enough based on how you're dressed." I own skirts and crop tops, but I've never had a reason to buy an expensive dress. Although, I wish I had, so this moment wasn't so awkward.

His gaze softens, tugging at my heartstrings. "Don't worry about that. For now, just pack some pajamas."

I arch a brow. "This is an overnight trip?"

I'm entirely feral for him when he nods and leans back on his hands, elongating his body. It's a simple movement, one he doesn't know elicits a reaction from me, but right now, it takes an enormous amount of effort not to straddle him when he looks as delectable as a sweet piece of cake.

I grin from ear to ear before grabbing my toiletry bag. "I think I'll pass on the pajamas," I say. "No use in packing them when I plan on sleeping naked."

~

"Are you ever going to tell me where we're going?" With my feet on the dash, I'm leaning back in the passenger seat while Ethan remains tight-lipped about where he's taking me. We've been driving for almost two hours without a lick of a hint from the signs on the highway.

We stopped at a store before we hit the road, where Ethan bought my favorite road trip snack without having to ask. I didn't pay it much attention the last time we went on a trip with his family to the Grand Canyon when he came into the gas station with me and never left my side. We picked out our snacks together, and then he snatched the Takis from my hands before I could reach the checkout counter. He insisted his mom told him to pay, but the credit card he used had *his* name on it, not Mary's.

My heart threatens to burst when I glance down at the Taki bag in my lap, the same flavor and everything. He's remembered every detail about me, down to my favorite movie and designer brand.

The revelation has those three little words threatening to slip from my tongue until another green sign whizzes past us, drawing me from my stupor. "Sedona?" I ask.

He shakes his head with a smile, reaching over to interlock our fingers. "No. Now, will you stop guessing? You'll see when we get there."

~

"You've got to be *shitting* me! Ethan, tell me you're joking."

I fell asleep at some point, only to awaken in an entirely different universe.

Las Vegas, Nevada, the party capital of the United States, envelops us at every turn. Neon signs and lights are a tease even though the sun is still up, but the city makes up for it with the bustling of people littering the streets. Different vendors are stationed on corners selling a variety of objects, and the buildings are taller than any I've ever seen. I'm craning my neck to try and get a glimpse of the rooftops when I shout, "This is insane! Have you been here before?"

"Uh, no. First time, actually." Something about his tone seems off, and when I rip my gaze from the view to glance at him, I see a version of Ethan I thought had disappeared for good.

He's got a white-knuckled grip on the steering wheel, and his eyes never leave the road in front of him. Cars surround us on every side as we travel down what I'm assuming must be the strip everyone talks about, and although our morning yoga sessions seemed to have helped with his anxiety, he's told me that traveling is a trigger for him.

"Shit. Are you okay?" I feel like an idiot for not remembering his travel anxiety until now. How could I have forgotten? It makes this impromptu trip more meaningful. Bringing me here is taking a lot of courage from him, and I don't take it lightly.

He exhales a shaky breath. "I'm fine. There's just . . . a lot of people here. I'll feel better once we get to our hotel, but we have a stop to make first."

~

I assumed the "stop" would be grabbing food from a grocery store for the night or replenishing the gas we'd burned through to get here. I'm utterly speechless when we walk hand in hand into a little boutique nestled in the heart of the strip. It's girly and pink, with greenery and decor aligning with its aesthetic. The dresses on the racks are so me.

"I don't even want to ask what we're doing here."

"I'm buying you a dress for tonight. Take your pick."

I whip my head to his. "You can't be serious."

"I'm dead serious."

"*Ethan.*" My voice drops into a whisper as the sales associate makes a beeline for us. "With what money? I don't have enough to pay you back for this."

"It's a good thing I'm not asking you to, then, isn't it?"

I *huff* and cross my arms over my chest. The last thing I want is to be a charity case, and while he hasn't given me a reason to feel that way, it's difficult not to when everything, even the purchase of a new dress, is foreign to me. Goodwills were my second home. Everything I own that's in my closet is second hand except for the sweater Maddie got me for Christmas sophomore year. My best friend didn't understand why I cried over it. *It's just a sweater,* she said. But what she didn't realize was that it was the first article of clothing I'd ever owned with the tags still attached.

And now I'm about to add a second piece to my collection.

Ethan, whose hands are still shaking from the anxiety coursing through his veins, squeezes my hand to comfort *me* instead. "I want to do this for you," he whispers. "I set aside the money I got back from taxes the past few years to have moments like these."

I scoff. "To buy dresses for women?"

"No," he replies. "To buy dresses for *you*."

The admission is still hanging in the air between us when the sales associate reaches us and begins rambling about the different sales they're running. My hand is slick as it clutches his, and I'm unable to say anything when he lets go and ushers me ahead of him to walk with the woman to pick out dresses to try on.

"Is there anything specific I should look for?" I call over my shoulder. I'm overwhelmed by the different fabrics and textures flooding the racks. "Length or color requirements?"

The raspy laugh he gives in response makes the hair on the back of my neck stand at full attention. "I've grown quite fond of the color pink when it comes to you, but no, no requirements." His grin grows wider when I feel my cheeks heat beneath his scrutinizing stare.

"Surprise me, Maya."

Thirty-four

ETHAN

I may have splurged on the hotel.

Okay, I *definitely* splurged on the hotel.

The Bellagio is a five-star resort in Vegas, and when we set foot on the marble floors with gold porcelain accents and painted ceilings that could have belonged in the Roman Empire, it wasn't only Maya who felt out of place. This is the nicest place I've ever stayed; we're only here for one night, so I wanted to make it count.

Plus, while I'm unpacking and Maya squeals over the hotel's fuzzy robes, it's 100 percent worth it.

"They're *so* soft!" she coos. I hold back a laugh when she pokes her head out of the bathroom door. "Do hotels always give free samples of shampoo?"

I'm reminded that although this is the most luxurious hotel I've ever been to, it's one of the firsts for her. It's a welcome distraction given I've been on edge since we passed the Arizona state line. Traveling has always been tough, but Vegas? I may be in over my head. Our view of the strip showcases just how busy the nightlife is as we get closer to dinner, and the knot in my stomach continues to grow.

"Ethan?" Maya waves her hand to bring me back to the present.

"What?" I almost forgot she asked me a question. "Oh, sorry. Yeah, there's usually free samples. You can take them home if you want."

She's supposed to be getting ready for dinner since our reservation is in an hour, but I don't even think about reminding her of the time. The worst way to get into trouble with a woman? Rushing them. I've learned from my mother and sister that it's a quick way to get yourself in the doghouse.

"We don't have to go to whatever you're planning," she whispers. "I'm fine ordering room service and staring at this incredible-ass view."

Of course she would be. Maya is always thinking of everyone but herself, and it's one of the main reasons I wanted to bring her here. She deserves a night of luxury. This trip is all about her, and I don't want to make it about myself. It's why I'm pushing through this even though my anxiety urges me to accept her offer and hide away in our room. Just the two of us.

For her, I'm willing to come out of my shell occasionally.

I shake my head. "Nah. I didn't bring you all this way to not follow through with what I have planned."

"Are you sure?"

"Positive. Plus, I'm dying to see whatever dress it is you bought today. You were mighty secretive about it."

"Because I wanted you to get the full picture! I have to touch up my makeup."

I roll my eyes. "You look perfect to me, but if you feel it needs it, then by all means."

"It does." And with an affirmative nod, she shuts the bathroom door and gets to work.

~

"Sorry! I know I took forever, but I wanted to look perfect for . . . well, I wasn't informed what we're doing, but beauty takes time, okay?"

"It's fine. I wasn't—" When I glance up from my phone, every coherent thought leaves my head instantly. My brain cells stop functioning and my world comes to a standstill like someone just hit Pause in the middle of an action scene. "I wasn't—" Nope. Still not functioning.

Maya giggles, biting the inside of her cheek while she gives me a spin to showcase her outfit. It's a tight pink minidress that barely grazes her midthigh. It showcases her legs and silky tan skin, and I'm drooling like a dog at the pink stilettos on her feet, which the saleswoman claimed were the same shade as her dress.

She was right.

Waves of black hair fall like the ocean at midnight down her back, and I'm itching to rake my hands through it, but that isn't even the sexiest part about her tonight. She exudes confidence with every step she takes toward the bed where I'm sitting. I can tell that she *feels* beautiful, and that was the goal. It radiates from the glow of her cheeks to the beam of her smile, and with the city lights reflecting off her face, I've never seen her look more intoxicatingly stunning than now.

I roll my lips together, trying but failing to come up with words. "You look . . ."

"Hot. I know." She grins proudly.

"That's the easiest word to describe you, but it's insufficient. You're so much more than that."

An emotion that I don't recognize flickers in her eyes. "You'd be the first to think so. Men usually wanted me for one thing, so every pickup line consisted of trying to get into my pants. It never went beyond that, which is—oh, fuck. I need to fix my strap."

She glances down at her heel, where the strap has slipped from the buckle. Before she can bend over, I gently grab her foot and place it on my lap. From this angle, I'd have the perfect view up her dress, but I want to savor that sight later. Plus, we're already late for our dinner reservation, and if I catch a glimpse of whatever panties she chose to wear, we'll miss it for sure.

It's an effort not to smile when she sucks in a sharp breath as soon as my hand caresses her ankle. I flit my eyes up to hers, running smoothing strokes along the back of her calf. "You're more than lame, casual terms," I mutter. My eyes never leave hers, thinking if she focuses on me when I say this to her, she'll eventually believe it. "Fierce." I lift her leg to kiss her ankle. "Loyal." Her calf. "Confident." Her knee. "Giving."

"Ethan." Her head falls back when I nip at her inner thigh.

"The sight of you is all consuming, Maya Garcia. Your beauty, inside and out, could rival the heavens." I laugh at the thought. "Honestly, I wouldn't be surprised if you're heaven itself, because every time I'm in your presence, you make me want to fall to my knees and worship."

I nuzzle my nose higher, at the apex of her thigh, before reason washes over me.

I have a mission to accomplish, and we won't have a chance if we're holed up in this room all night. I fully intend to make her my personal religion after the festivities, but until then, she'll have to wait.

When I pull back, leaving her breathless and wanting, she glares at me with an expression that could kill. "What are you doing?"

"We're late for our reservation, and we *really* can't be late for the other thing I have planned." Rising from the bed, I play with the hemline of her dress and place the gentlest of kisses on her lips. "Later. Okay?"

"No," she whines. "You can't suggest *worshipping* me only to leave me hanging. That's just cruel."

"I'll make up for it later. Promise."

I've never known Maya to back down from a fight, so I'm unsurprised when she tugs her phone from the sparkly clutch slung over her shoulder and says, "Two can play this game, Ethan." She taps rapidly on the screen, and then, a few seconds later, my phone pings. "I *was* going to save this for the end of the night, but if I have to be hot and bothered, so do you. Remember when I asked if it would be okay to purchase something extra I thought you'd like at the store today?"

I gulp when I swipe to open the text message, and holy *shit*, I'm a dead man.

Attached is a photo of her in a lacy black lingerie set. Stockings are attached to a garter set securely on her hips, and the bra pushes her breasts together in a way that should *not* be allowed. I'm sure my jaw is on the floor, but then another image comes through of the set from *behind* and—

"It's crotchless?" My mouth suddenly feels like I swallowed sandpaper. Two black straps sit beneath her ass to support it, but aside from that, she's utterly bare. "Do you mean to tell me that if I put my hand beneath your dress right now, there'd be no barriers in my way?"

She gives me a sultry little grin that shoots straight to my cock. I'm raging hard, and I'm seconds away from flipping up her dress until she pats me on the shoulder and strides for the door. "Come on. We've got reservations we can't miss," she says with a breathy laugh. It lets me know that she's fully aware of how sexually frustrated I am and is enjoying every second of this torture.

Payback is a bitch.

Thirty-five

MAYA

"I'm just waiting for you to say it."

Ethan tilts his head to the side. "Say what?"

"That it's my fault we missed our dinner reservations."

Hand in hand, we left the restaurant five minutes ago with rumbling stomachs when the hostess said our table had already been taken. Can't say I'm surprised when Ethan revealed we were an hour late, and now I'm feeling horrible for spending so much time taking pictures in the mirror. In my defense, he didn't say anything, so I had no clue we were on a time crunch.

"It's not your fault. We both contributed to being late."

My lips twitch as I remember him needing an additional ten minutes before we could leave our hotel room due to the raging hard-on he was sporting after seeing my pictures.

"Regardless, we need to figure out something else for dinner. I can google some restaurants nearby." As he slips his phone out of his pocket with his free hand, I brush soothing strokes along the knuckle of the one tangled in mine. His hand has been shaking since we set foot on the busy strip, and every now and then he'll inhale deeply, though I can't understand why.

"How about—" I tug him toward a hot dog stand on the corner, pulling us out of the crowd of people rushing by.

"You can't be serious."

"What? Are you too good for a hot dog?" I tease. "I didn't peg you as the type to be stuck up."

"I'm not, Maya, but it's freezing outside. We didn't bring gloves or hats to keep us warm."

"Then what better way to warm up than a hot dog?" I approach the stand while he mutters under his breath, and after we both have our orders, we find a secluded alley away from the bustle of people. I'd never tell him, but that was my goal all along. I could tell all the excitement was getting overwhelming for him, so this was the closest food option I could find.

"This is so not what I had in mind for tonight," he grumbles.

"What? Eating fantastic food and being in even better company?"

"No," he answers with a mouthful of hot dog. "You deserve better than eating in an alley while you're *shivering*."

I hold up the tinfoil wrapped food. "This is my cure for being cold, remember? And as to eating in an alley, it's definitely a first, but I think I'm rather enjoying myself." I catch him doing the deep inhale again. "What is that?"

"What is what?"

"You keep inhaling like you're not getting enough air."

His forehead scrunches as if he's debating whether or not to tell me, but eventually, he relents and says, "Anxiety is weird. I'll get in these situations with crowds of people and feel like my lungs are constricted. They're not, but my mind tells me they are. So I'll inhale deeply to remind myself I can still take a deep breath." His lips purse. "It sounds ridiculous when I say it out loud. Medication and therapy help, but it's not a cure-all, you know? I'll always battle with it, even if it's only a fraction."

I smile softly. "I don't think you're ridiculous at all. Does it bother you? To inhale?"

"Nah." He shakes his head, contemplating. "It's more of a reassurance than anything."

"Then I'll happily listen to you inhale if it reminds you that you're still breathing."

His stare lingers on mine for what feels like an eternity as we finish our food in companionable silence. The feel of his eyes on me is almost a caress, and his speech at the hotel keeps circulating through my mind on a never-ending loop.

In this alley, I've never been so comfortable, and that's saying something, given there's a dumpster a few feet away from us that smells absolutely foul. The reality of the situation is it doesn't matter where I am with Ethan. It just matters that I'm with *him*.

~

For the main event of our date, I tried to come up with thousands of possibilities about where he could be taking me. No matter how hard I tried, I couldn't understand why he'd want to drive me to Vegas for a day when we'd both never been here before, but as we stand in front of the conference center and my eyes dart to the sign above it, my vision is suddenly blurry from the tears that will no doubt escape.

"*Ethan.*"

"It's a beauty expo," he explains, as if I haven't already pieced that together. "There will be tons of booths with free samples and demos with the latest styling tools and makeup products. It seemed fitting to bring you here with your clientele and portfolio taking off. I figured it'll give you more inspiration."

"*Dios mío.*" I rub a palm over my heart as if that'll calm the pounding beneath.

"I'll say it until I'm blue in the face, Maya, but this is what you were born to do. You know it, I know it, and anyone who's ever met you knows it too. You may not believe in yourself yet, but I do, and until it finally dawns on you, I'll be by your side to remind you." I'm a blubbering mess when he tugs me against his side. "I want you to soak up every minute of this experience and apply it to your future as a *cosmetologist*, because that's what's in store for you."

I swipe at the tears cascading down my cheeks, no doubt ruining the makeup I spent hours on, but Ethan takes over for me and uses his thumb to catch them instead.

This man overcame his fear of traveling to bring me here because he believes in me. He thinks I can do this, and for the life of me, I'm wondering why the hell I let him go to begin with. If my parents can't see he's good for me, then that's their loss.

Ethan Davis is the man I'm spending the rest of my life with.

"I don't know what to say," I whisper through a choked sob. Well, that's not entirely true. Three words are on the tip of my tongue, but I refuse to say them until I come clean to my parents. I can be confident and claim all I want that my parents will have to deal with my decision to be with him, but once I'm in front of them, I have no clue how our conversation will play out. Telling Ethan that I love him will only result in more heartbreak if next weekend, I can't follow through with this newfound courage I imagine I've gained.

"You don't have to say anything at all." He tugs two tickets out of his wallet and passes one to me. "I just want you to enjoy tonight."

I laugh into the night sky. "There's nothing in this entire universe that could ruin my night, Ethan. Although I probably look terrible now. Pretty sure my makeup is ruined."

"Please." He rolls his eyes. "You couldn't look terrible even if you tried. Your setting spray did a damn good job."

I gasp, and at the sound, he tosses his head back and releases a genuine, throaty laugh that leaves me practically giddy. "You're learning!" I squeal.

"Yeah, yeah, yeah." Linking his arm with mine, he leads us to the entrance.

"What else have I taught you?"

When he grins wickedly, I realize I walked directly into that trap. "I'll show you better than I can tell you, but there's time for that later. For now, let's go fuel that passion of yours."

~

The beauty expo reminded me of when I was a little girl and my parents would let me pick out candy at the grocery store. It didn't happen often, but the array of flavors and selections overwhelmed me. I didn't know where to look first, and as Ethan guided me through the different vendors, never complaining when I stopped at each one, I was a little girl picking out candy all over again.

Hair tools, makeup brands, skin products. The list was endless. We got a goody bag for buying tickets, but it nearly doubled in size with all the free samples. It was like freaking Christmas when we finally got back to the hotel room with our arms loaded with bags.

"I can't wait to try these products out on my clients," I gush. "God, tonight has been the absolute best, and it's all because of you." After I put the bags in my suitcase, I twirl around to throw my arms around his neck.

"You're so beautiful," he whispers, drawing me closer. I'm flush against his chest, and my breath quickens when his hands skim the sides of my dress until they reach the hem. "So, have you finally accepted your fate as a cosmetologist, or are you going to deny it for a bit longer?"

"I think tonight has changed my perspective on a lot of things. The whole point of this year was to find ourselves, right?"

He nods as his fingertips rub the backs of my thighs.

"Well, I think by reconnecting with you, you've given me the courage to be true to myself. Finishing cosmetology school was one of the proudest moments of my life, but I thought then that it'd never be my full-time career. I didn't think it would be possible, but you . . ." I blink away tears. "You push me in the best ways, Ethan. You've made me realize that I *can* do this if I want to, and I can't thank you enough."

And next weekend at my parents, I'm not only going to fight for you, but I'm fighting for myself too.

"Well, I'm glad you feel that way because you do the same for me. I've been thinking a lot about myself, too, and I decided to go and change my major on Monday."

My eyes grow wide as saucers. "What? That's *incredible*, Ethan! Are you kidding? I'm so happy for you! It's for sports education, right? Please tell me it is."

"Yeah." A bashful hint to his tone has me melting against

him. "I haven't told the kids or Ronnie yet that I'm accepting the assistant position. Thinking about surprising them with the news next Sunday at the game."

"I'm so proud of you. Seriously. You've worked so hard to figure out who you want to be, and I think coaching is the *perfect* job for you."

We may have been two messes at the start of the semester, but slowly and surely, we've helped each other uncover the layers to see what's underneath. Ethan with his passion for coaching; me with my clients and my love for cosmetology. We've stepped into who we've always wanted to become, and tonight, I realize I don't want to give this up for anything.

Not my clients, and certainly not Ethan.

As if he's thinking the same, he wraps his fingers around the hem of my dress and tugs it over my head. The fabric falls to a heap on the floor, leaving me in nothing but heels and the lingerie I sent him photos of earlier.

My skin heats beneath his gaze. His pupils have darkened into the dangerous stare I've grown to love. One that promises a version of ecstasy that draws a fine line between pain and pleasure. But I trust him enough to know it would never result in pain. No, his torture only coexists with endless orgasms.

"I've been thinking about you in this set all damn night," he mutters more to himself than me. His fingers toy with the bra strap, snapping it into place before he jerks his head to the mattress. "Get on the bed, Maya."

He doesn't have to tell me twice.

I'm lying on my back in a matter of seconds, listening to the sound of a foil packet opening before he crawls on top of me. He pauses when he looks at me again, and the danger that flashed in his eyes a moment ago fades, replaced by an expression far softer.

My hair is fanned out around me on the pillow, and my makeup (despite what he claims) is probably a disaster, but it's impossible to feel anything but beautiful when he's staring at me like that.

He hesitates, but only briefly before he bends down to kiss me.

Previously, our kisses were intended to ravish and fuck each other senseless, but this kiss is different. It's slow. Deliberate. Every move he makes with his tongue against mine is filled with intention.

I used to believe slow kissing would never turn me on, but Ethan Davis has me changing my mind as he presses his lips to the tiny heart tattoo on the inside of my wrist, then to the cross on my forearm before dipping his head down to the belly button piercing I always catch him staring at. He flicks his tongue against the crystal sun charm, and my hips buck at the ceiling before my hands drag through his hair to pull him impossibly closer.

He grabs my leg to hook it around his lower back, grinding his cock against my center, where it's exposed by the lingerie. His motions remain slow and sure, and everywhere his hands touch feels like velvet against my sensitive skin. I can *feel* the emotion between us, and even though we aren't saying it, those three words have made their way into the void. It's hard to deny them when Ethan whispers my name like a sacred prayer.

I whimper at the loss of his lips, but when he reaches between us to sink into me, nothing has ever made me feel more complete. He's kissing my collarbone now as he moves his hips at a slow, sensual pace, and I squirm beneath him from how turned on this new level of intimacy is making me. I've never had sex like this before. Never had a man stare at me like if I'm the last thing he'd ever see in this world, he'd die happy.

"I know." He answers my thoughts, his throat strained from holding back his impending release. "Let go for me, Maya. I've got you."

It's the first of many rounds tonight, I'm sure, so I follow his command and allow him to push me over the edge. He stills seconds later, cursing in the crook of my neck while simultaneously whispering sweet nothings in my ear, and honestly, my life has never felt more complete. I never thought I'd use that word to describe it, but here I am, wishing for nothing else at this moment.

As we're panting down from our high, Ethan rolls onto his back and asks the one thing I wasn't prepared for. "Why did you ghost me all those months ago? And not the fake reason. I mean the *real* one."

Just like that, he took a needle to my balloon of peace, and my post-orgasmic state pops. "You're still thinking about that?"

"Who wouldn't? I mean, I don't want to ruin the mood, but it's a constant fear in the back of my mind that it's going to happen again, and I can't be all in if—" He shakes his head and stares at the ceiling. "I've worked hard to get where I am. That's all. Taking a risk on us is worth it, but I'm afraid of the repercussions if this blows up in my face a second time."

I have no right to be upset that he's curious about it. Anyone would be, and frankly, I'm surprised he lasted this long without demanding an answer. But is it really worth crushing his self-esteem if I'm going to beg my parents to change their mind next weekend? A seven-day stall isn't that long for him to wait for an answer. This way, if my parents react better than I expect them to, I won't have to put a damper on his progress so far.

He may want the truth, but for now, I'm only giving him a fraction of it.

Just a few more days.

I turn on my side to face him in the dark hotel room. The lights from the city cast his cheeks in a moonlit hue. "A part of me was afraid of what I felt for you the first time we had sex," I admit. "It felt too real. Too serious. And I wasn't in the right place mentally to take on a relationship with you or *anyone*."

"But you are now?"

"I mean, I was still scared at first, but then you gave me that styling tool for my birthday, and everything fell into place. You've always been the one, I've just been too afraid to admit it. First, it was because of Maddie, and then it was because of—" I clear my throat when I almost slip up. "There were a lot of reasons to try and avoid my feelings, but you made it impossible for me to run away from them any longer, Ethan, and I'm tired of fighting them. I want you. For the long term."

Does not telling him the complete truth make me an utter ass? Fully. However, it's better this way if I can spare him more heartache.

Besides, I'd never ghost him like I did the last time. I've learned my lesson.

"I'm holding you to that," he says with a sleepy smile. "Thanks for telling me. Feels like a weight has been lifted off my chest now."

And when he comes back from the bathroom to pull me against his chest, when his soft snores fill the silence, only then does the guilt threaten to swallow me whole.

I have to fix this.

Come hell or high water, I'll get my parents approval.

Thirty-six

MAYA

"Are you sure you're ready to do this?" Ethan, who offered to drive me to my parents, slides his eyes to mine as a form of reassurance. I insisted I could take the bus back home, but he refused and wouldn't take no for an answer. And when I panicked and said he couldn't come inside because I was planning on telling them about my decision to pursue cosmetology—I didn't have the heart to tell him about the other reason—he didn't mind one bit. He only wanted to drive me for emotional *support*. He claimed it worked out because he wanted to see his parents anyway, but sitting outside my house now makes everything *real*. "We agreed on me not coming inside, but if you need someone . . ."

"No, it's fine. I've got this." I open the passenger-side door with a deep breath and give him a weak smile. "I'll call to let you know how it goes, okay?"

Something flickers in his blue irises, telling me he's aware something is up, but rather than push me on it, he dips his chin and leans over to squeeze my hand. "Sure."

On my way up the gravel path to my home, I attempt to wipe my hands on the back of my jeans. It's weird. I assumed things would be different when I left for college, but nothing seems to have changed. The flower beds are still flourishing, and the tiny windmill by the rundown porch steps is still spinning.

The only thing that's changed is me.

"*¡Bambina!*" The door flies open, and both of my parents nearly tackle me to the ground. Their scent envelops me and surrounds me with a sense of home I can't get anywhere else. It makes me ashamed that I used to be embarrassed by this tiny trailer when it was filled with so much love. "You got here sooner than you told us yesterday." Even with her thick accent, I can already tell my mom's classes have improved her English drastically. She's annunciating words so much better than she ever had before.

"Yeah, sorry. Change of plans." My heart pounds when my dad glances behind me to where Ethan is still sitting in his car. Realization dawns on him before his eyes narrow into slits.

He points to the car. "*¿Quién es ese?*"

"Papí. English, *por favor*." It seems only my mom has been taking the classes seriously. Don't get me wrong, I love speaking Spanish and would never expect them to forget where they came from, but if I plan on traveling and making my dreams come true, I need to feel confident leaving them alone. I need to know they'll be okay here by themselves.

"Okay. *Who* is *that*? You said you were taking the bus."

"Can we finish this discussion inside, please?" I don't want Ethan to see this fight go down on the front porch, especially when he's unaware that the main subject of the disagreement will be him. I have no clue why he hasn't driven off yet, but his car is still idling outside, and, oddly, it feels nice knowing there's a getaway car in case things don't go the way I plan.

With a *huff*, my dad moves to the side to allow me to pass, but not before casting a lingering glare at the car. As if to ensure he can keep eyes on Ethan the entire time, he only shuts the screen door, and it's an effort not to roll my eyes.

"Is that Maddie's brother?" he asks. "The boy we told you not to see?"

This is the time where I could lie through my teeth and tell them we're just friends, but I don't want to be dishonest anymore about us when Ethan has been nothing but good to me. He doesn't deserve to be my dirty little secret.

I take a seat on the couch, watching them sit in the chairs across from it before I reply, "Yes. We're dating."

My father mutters something beneath his breath—likely a curse word of some sort. "We said no, bambina."

"Yes, but I never got the chance to explain myself then, and I want to now. He's . . ." I shake my head with a smile. "He's perfect for me, and he's going to State. He's majoring in sports education to become a football coach, and if you'd go with me to a game of theirs, you'd see just how passionate and incredible he is with the kids. He treats me right, and isn't that all you've ever wanted for me?"

I've rarely seen my father angry, but it's evident in the redness of his face when he leans forward and says, "No. What we wanted was for you to be taken care of. He parties too much, smokes marijuana, and what about the girls?" He scoffs. "That will not—" He releases an aggravated breath as he struggles to find the words in English. "No. The answer is no."

"Mamí," I plead, tears filling my eyes. "Please. He's important to me, and he's nothing like you guys are painting him to be. If you'll just agree to meet him, I swear you'll change your minds. I *love* him." The admission is surprising to them, but it isn't to me. I've known it for a long time, and it's exhausting to keep holding it inside. For the first time, I'm being truthful with myself, which is why I keep going when I should probably stop. If the dam is already broken, why not ride out the flood? "He's made me realize things about myself, and I—" Fuck, here goes nothing. "I'm meant to be a cosmetologist, and if I'm going to get a degree in business, I want to use it to pursue that. It's all I've ever wanted to do, and he believes in me, you know? I can do this if you guys give me the chance to prove—"

My rambling stops when I notice my parents' gazes bouncing from my mouth to my eyes. They're having trouble keeping up, so I snap my mouth shut and wait for them to process it.

Papí is the first one to speak. "You want to struggle like us?" He waves a hand around the living room. "Is this what you want?"

"Ricardo." Mamí tuts and cuts a glare in his direction.

"No. I'm not going to stand by and watch her throw her life away!" Tears track down my father's face when he stands and begins to pace. "We worked too hard for this. We came here so you could be *happy*, and—"

"Do I look happy to you right now?" It's been fixed in my head since I was a little girl to never cross my parents, but this is important to me, and if I don't stand up for myself now, I never will again. It's now or never. "Working in finance isn't going to make me happy. Will it give me a paycheck? Sure. But it's not what I want for myself. It's what *you* want."

Papí looks as if he'll keel over at any given second from the tone of my voice, and Mamí has a sheen coating her eyes as she watches our argument unravel.

"*Increíble.*" He laughs like he can't quite believe this is happening before he forgoes English altogether and switches to his native tongue. I hold my chin high while he lists every possible reason Ethan isn't good enough for me. He harps about coaching not being enough to support a family. Then he's shouting as he insists Ethan's personality hasn't changed despite never getting to know him, and he tells me it's impossible to have a future with him if both of our careers are *unrealistic.*

My father, who always supported my dreams as a little girl, is shooting them down one by one. But I should have known they were just that when I was younger. *Dreams.* He used to listen to me as a child gush over different nail polishes and even partook in some makeovers, probably thinking it was a phase. It never occurred to me then that he disapproved of it. He never thought I'd be able to make it on my own if I wanted to pursue it for a living.

But the one man who does is—

The sound of a floorboard creaking has all three of us whipping our heads to the screen door, and the sight of Ethan on the porch makes my world come to a halt.

Papí moves to tell him off, but my mother grips him by the shirt and whispers something in his ear that sounds an awful lot like a threat, just as Ethan throws his hands up placatingly.

"You forgot your bag," he explains, setting it gently on the porch. His eyes seem adamant about not meeting mine. "Then I heard shouting and wanted to see if everything was okay, but I, uh, got my answer."

How much of that did he overhear?

"Ethan—" My voice breaks when he shakes his head.

"I'll talk to you later, okay?"

And then I watch him walk away from me and down the gravel path to his car. His shoulders are slumped and his body is rigid, and seeing him so devastated has a newfound rage surging through my veins.

"Is this what you wanted?" I whisper through my tears. "Ethan *is* a good man, Papí, whether you choose to see it or not, and I'm not going to sit here and listen to you degrade him and attempt to prove to me he isn't. I've spent my entire life trying to please you both, but I want something for myself for once. *He* is what makes me happy. *Cosmetology* is what makes me happy. The only missing thing is your approval, but I refuse to continue killing myself fighting for it if it means hurting myself and the person I want to be with."

I am stepping toward the door when my father clears his throat. "Bambina." A warning. Plea. I can't decipher the agony behind the word, but there's no time for that when the man I love is walking away from me.

"We can talk about this," Mamí says. I'm convinced she's the only one with a rational mindset. "Just sit back down and—"

But I'm already closing the screen door behind me.

Thirty-seven

ETHAN

"Ethan!" My name is a desperate plea on her lips, but I can't focus on her with the ringing in my ears. My head is pounding, and my heart feels flayed open at her betrayal. "Ethan, *please*."

A strangled sob escapes her throat when we reach my car, and because I still can't stop myself, the sound of her crying makes me glance over my shoulder to check on her. She *lied*. We had multiple conversations when she could have mentioned her parents loathed us being together. It would have explained everything, and I wouldn't have walked around with all these insecurities over what the hell I did that caused her to ghost me when the answer was so obvious.

I'm pissed I didn't figure it out sooner.

"Listen—" she starts, but I cut her off before she can finish.

"Nothing you can say right now would make any of this okay, Maya." I inhale deeply, trying to rein in my emotions. She's the only person on the planet who can make me lose control so quickly. "When did you plan on telling me that your parents despised me? When I came over for the *cookout* you said you'd ask them about?"

She flinches at my words, and dammit, I shouldn't be this weak. I shouldn't want to console her. I *should* be trying to piece myself together since my sense of self just fucking shattered all over her porch steps.

Every bit of work I did to fix myself, every therapy session, every pill, and every stupid yoga lesson she put me through was all for nothing. I was an idiot to believe I'd healed my self-esteem. My confidence, which I thought she was helping me rebuild brick by brick, was a mirage. She might as well have used twigs that could snap under the weight of a feather because that single rant from her father was the only match needed to send my soul and me up in flames.

She grasps the sleeve of my sweatshirt, whirling me to face her. "I wanted to tell you, but you've been working so hard to find yourself this year. I didn't—"

"And how did that work?" I fling my arms up in frustration. "You think hearing your dad say all of that stuff about me was easy? Do you think hearing I'm a lowlife who smokes weed all day didn't wreck me regardless? If I had known, I could have better prepared myself for this. I wouldn't have walked into something that caught me completely off guard. You should have told me the truth the second they disapproved."

Maya's brows are scrunched together, but for the life of me, I can't figure out why.

"How did you. . . . How did you understand what he was saying?" she asks.

Well, shit. I'm already gutted and bleeding out before her eyes, so I might as well get everything off my chest since I'm already perpetually embarrassed.

"Why do you think I chose to learn Spanish in high school?" I ask. "And why do you think I continued it in community college? Why do you think I've been having weekly language sessions with Ronnie, since he's fluent?"

"Ethan."

"I always knew your parents were more comfortable with Spanish. I know how important they are to you, and if I had any chance in hell at winning you, I knew I'd need to fit in with your family too." I laugh at the sky, at what a fucking joke this has become. "I've been pining for you for *years*, Maya, waiting for the opportunity to have a chance, and it just sucks that it has to end this way when I'm—" I snap my mouth shut to prevent myself from saying something I shouldn't, but what do I have to lose at this point? I've already lost my sanity. Might as well lose my pride too. "When I'm in love with you," I finish, with a shaky exhale.

Tears stream down her face, dripping from her chin and onto her T-shirt. It's an effort not to reach for her. Takes every ounce of willpower not to kiss those tears away, but at some point, I need to prioritize myself and my feelings. I've bent over backward trying to make this work for us, and has she stuck up for me at all to them? I have no clue. Does she feel the same? Is she also concerned that all I'll ever be is a coach who can't support a family?

My mental health is already tanking, so I bite those questions back rather than ask them out loud. After all, I can already piece the puzzle together about how this will end. Her parents mean everything to her. I wouldn't expect her to choose me over them, nor would I ask her to. This is just one of those situations that really fucking sucks, and no matter how much I want to change it, I can't.

Her father is still glaring at me from behind the screen door, so it's not like I can fight for her parents to change their minds when I wouldn't be surprised if he's got a shotgun lying around inside the house. There's not an ounce of me that feels like fighting for something when judging by the darkness in her brown eyes, it seems like I've already lost.

She sobs harder, practically gasping for air. "I don't deserve you, Ethan. I never have. I should have told you the truth from the beginning, before we started things up again, but I didn't want to ruin all the effort you've put into your future. I knew if I told you what my parents thought, it would destroy all your hard work. And I thought once they got to know you, the *real* you . . ."

I *huff* out a defeated laugh, sliding my eyes to the screen door where her parents haven't moved an inch. "It's a little too late for that, Maya."

"Things don't have to end," she begs. "We can work this out. Please."

"I'm not in the right headspace to decide something like that, and neither are you. The truth of the matter is that you hid this from me, and until you figure out what it is you *truly* want and can start being honest with yourself, I can't keep putting my heart on the line when it keeps getting destroyed."

She shakes her head furiously, clutching my sweatshirt with a force I'm afraid will rip it, and dammit, I'm not strong enough to hold back my tears. One slips onto my cheek when she whispers, "I do know what I want, and it's *you*. Please don't go. I'm sorry. I'm *so* sorry."

The sobs rocking her body pull the rope in me that seems to be tethered to her. I have no idea where we go from here, but watching her cry is physically painful for me. "Maya." I pull her into my chest, cursing under my breath when she flings her arms around me as if it's the last hug we'll ever share. Maybe it is. Maybe she knows something I don't. "I can't stay and hash this out now. I need some space to think things through, and I can't do that when your dad looks ready to murder me."

She pulls away to swipe at her face. "Promise me you'll give me the chance to explain myself. Don't disappear on me."

My eyebrows shoot to my hairline. "You're seriously making me promise that when you've done the exact same thing to me?" Raking a hand through my hair, I take another wide step back from her and add, "That isn't fair of you, Maya. Not when you've hurt me twice now. I've done nothing but bust my ass for us, and to have this relationship thrown back in my face hurts more than you realize. You knew before we started again that things could never work if your parents didn't approve. That's why you ghosted me the first time, right? The *real* reason? So why put me through the heartbreak again? Did you even consider my feelings?"

"Of course, I considered your feelings, Ethan! The reason I didn't tell you was to *protect* your feelings, but I—"

"*Maya!*" her father shouts. "*Entras. Ahora.*"

I don't need the years of Spanish under my belt to understand he's telling her to come inside. This conversation is over for now, and although it's frustrating, we need space. Nothing will be solved while our emotions are running high and her parents are breathing down our necks.

I wouldn't blame her if she sided with her parents. I'd understand.

At the end of the day, I'll be what her father described me as.

Just a coach.

And that'll never be enough for them.

Thirty-eight

ETHAN

"All right, I gave you seven days, man, but now it's getting pathetic." Leo rips the covers from my head, ruining the perfect nest I'd made for myself. "Jesus, you reek. When's the last time you showered?"

"Go away." I groan, but with no covers left, I'm forced to stare up at Leo towering over me with a pinched expression. "I'm perfectly fine here."

"Do your professors feel the same?"

"I emailed them," I angrily retort. "So again, leave me alone."

"Can't do that," Leo replies. "Someone's here to see you."

My head snaps at the prospect of *her* showing up unannounced, but Mark's bulky figure steps into my vision instead. I should have known it wouldn't be her. Why would it be when I said I needed space? She's respecting my wishes, so why am I disappointed?

Mark is shoulder to shoulder with Leo now, and when he crosses his arms over his chest, it's a lot more intimidating than when Leo with his slender frame does it. It's like comparing a rhino to a field mouse.

Mark's voice leaves no room for bullshit when he says, "Get up."

My body stiffens, but I make no effort to move. Truthfully, I've succumbed to the depression that overtook me on that gravel pathway of Maya's house. That whole situation was a bone-chilling reminder that I wouldn't amount to anything. I'm a nobody and still undecided about what I want to do with my future. The minute I thought I did know, Maya's father threw it back in my face like a joke. As if it wasn't a career to be proud of.

And I shouldn't care what Maya or her parents think, but I do. I care what *everyone* thinks about me. It's what drove me to have anxiety attacks when I was playing football. It's why I felt overwhelmed by the pressure to amount to something great, like those around me. Cameron, the star football player. Maddie studying to become a freaking *doctor*. I'll never measure up to half their success, and after hearing Maya's father say it out loud, I've accepted it. I've *become* it.

Mark scoffs. "If you think I won't drag your ass out of this bed and throw you in the shower myself, you're sorely mistaken. Now get the hell up. Leo's been coddling you for the past week, so now I'm here for the tough love."

"Hey, I didn't coddle him," Leo retorts. "He did that by wrapping himself up in that fucking comforter like he was preparing for metamorphosis."

I roll my eyes. "I didn't ask for help or for you guys to get me out of bed. I want to be left *alone*."

"Well, that's not going to happen." Mark puts his hands around my ankles and arches a brow. "What'll it be, Davis? Are you going to hold on to a fraction of your manhood, or am I going to carry you to the showers like a child?"

"Has anyone ever told you both that you're goddamn insufferable?" The thought of Mark carrying me is ridiculous, so I sit up, wincing at the soreness of my muscles. It's ironic since I haven't done shit after leaving Maya's house. I was supposed to change my major on Monday. I was supposed to attend a game for the boys this past Sunday. Neither of those things happened.

"It's normal to lick your wounds for a day or two after a breakup," Mark explains.

"We didn't break up. We . . ." Well, did we? I asked for space and haven't contacted her in seven days. Maybe she considers it a breakup, but regardless, we have to speak at some point to get everything out in the open and officially declare it.

"Took space," Mark finishes for me. "Leo filled me in. How much *space* are you planning to take? Girls don't wait around forever."

"Maybe I don't want her to." My fears slip out like word vomit. "Who am I kidding? I was living in a fantasy world, thinking we could actually be together. I was waiting for the shoe to drop, knowing it was too good to be true, and learning her parents disapproved of me made everything make a whole lot of sense. She's better off without me, or maybe I'm better off without her. I don't know. She kept this from me, knowing that once I found out, I'd be heartbroken again. That's not easy to forgive."

"Didn't say it had to be easy to forgive, but at some point, you've gotta pick yourself back up." Mark's hand lands on my shoulder. "Any girl who doesn't want you is missing out, Ethan. *She* was lucky to have *you*."

"Ditto." Leo hums in agreement.

"Please. Have you seen her? She's way out of my league."

Mark shakes his head. "Looks aren't everything, dude."

"That's rich coming from the guy with two different hair gels," I drawl.

Leo cuts Mark with a glare. "You use two different hair gels?"

"They're used to create different textures," Marks says, in an attempt to defend himself.

"Do you mean curly or straight? Or, like, hairstyles?"

"Different—" Mark sighs deeply. "We're getting off topic. The *point* I'm trying to make is you've got a heart of gold, Ethan. It's why we're your friends. It's why the kids love you." The scowl he makes next makes the pit in my stomach grow larger. "It's why they were so disappointed you didn't make it to their game, and it's why I'm here to get you out of whatever funk you've found yourself in."

"They wouldn't have wanted me at their game," I mutter. "They've idolized me and turned me into someone I'm not. Those kids have their whole future ahead of them, and the last thing they need is a failure who's barely keeping his head above water telling them what to do with it."

"You're wrong." Mark clears his throat, forcing me to meet his stare. "Is that why Jake made his first sack last game? Are you going to look me in my eye and tell me you had no part in that after staying after practice repeatedly with him to help with his form?"

My heart races, and then a surge of regret washes through me that I *missed* it. It's something he worked so hard to do, and it probably devastated him that I wasn't there to witness it.

But it's hard to shake the self-loathing when I heard a grown man ranting about how horrible I am. It would make anyone feel insecure, at least a little bit. Especially when that man helped create the woman I'm head over heels for. He has a shit ton of influence with her. Both of her parents do, so this silence between us speaks volumes. I don't want to knock on her door only for her to tell me she's siding with them, and I don't want to make up only for her to go back on her word and change her mind. She may think she doesn't need her parents, but she does. They're everything to her. I refuse to be the reason a rift forms between them.

If I'm being honest with myself, I don't know what the fuck I'm doing when it comes to her. To *us*. Which is probably why I haven't moved from this bed. I know that, regardless of what her response is, our happily ever after will more than likely come to an end.

"Look." Mark pins me with an expression that makes me swallow thickly. "Continue to sulk if you want, but your actions affect more than just you. I know you were reluctant about being a coach to these kids, but it's already happened, and their last game before winter break is this weekend. It'd be a shame for you to give up on them now."

I open my mouth, but he holds a hand up to stop me.

"The way I see it? You're left with two options. You can be the guy Maya's father is claiming you are, or you can continue to create a new image of yourself that you're proud of. The choice is yours."

With that, he turns to the door, but not before glancing over his shoulder to say, "Make sure he gets in the damn shower, Leo."

I roll my eyes when Leo sends him a salute. "Aye, aye, Captain." The door shuts, leaving us alone, and just when I'm expecting Leo to provide me with the humor deflection I'm seeking, he comes out of left field and does something even more annoying.

He's *mature*.

"I know you probably want to return to sulking in that little pity cocoon of yours, but we're just looking out for you, man. It's tough seeing you like this. Even Cameron texted to ask—"

"*Cameron?*" How the fuck—oh, right. I forgot the gossip train runs between him *and* Maddie now that they're together. Maya must have confided in Maddie, who in turn relayed it to Cameron. I didn't know whether or not Maya wanted them to know, so I kept my mouth shut and hid away in my room rather than talk to the one person who has the ability to get me out of this downward spiral I've found myself in. But talking to Cameron would pull out all the insecurities I've tried to hide for so long, and opening up that can of worms doesn't sound inviting.

There's enough on my plate at the moment.

"Tell him I'm fine," I grumble.

"Really? Because you still smell like a piece of fish that's been basking in the garbage all day. Could have fooled me."

"For fuck's sake." Rising from the bed, I snatch my toiletry bag off the hook next to the closet. "I'm going to shower. *There*. Happy?"

He snaps a photo with a wide grin. "Ecstatic, actually. The group chat will be *thrilled* you're coming out of hibernation."

"*Group chat?* Since when do we have a group chat?"

When a notification *ping*s on my phone, he throws his head back and laughs. "Since now. Enjoy your shower."

Thirty-nine

MAYA

With a thundering heart and trembling hands, I knock softly on Ethan's door.

It took a lot of hyping myself up to do this, but I've given him more than enough space. Eight days felt like an eternity when I was so used to being with him. Morning yoga. Late-night study sessions. Watching *The Bachelor* with the girls because, despite what he claimed, he was *very* invested in it.

My chest clenches at the memories when he opens the door and stills on the other side. His hair is mussed and sticking up at the ends, and judging by the bags beneath his eyes, I'd guess he's had trouble sleeping like me. I've never been the type to hole up in my room all day, but this fight between us has revealed a different side of me. I couldn't gather the energy to put makeup on or do my hair when there were more important things at stake, like the future of my relationship with the one guy who has ever mattered to me.

"Hi." It comes out as a choked whisper, but I lack the

confidence to be my bubbly self. I've messed up twice now with Ethan, so I have no idea how this conversation will go. What I do know? I can't take another second without hearing his thoughts. "Can I come inside?"

I hold my breath while he considers, finally nodding and stepping to the side for me to pass. My shoulder brushes his chest, and his body freezes for a heartbeat before he clears his throat and steps away from me.

Not a good sign.

Silence follows me as I take a seat on his bed. I twist my hands in my lap as I try to figure out where to start, but he beats me to it.

"You had every opportunity to tell me that night at the hotel, Maya. I asked you why you ghosted me, and you lied to my face. Whether it was to protect my feelings or not doesn't matter. I deserved to know the truth. I deserved better than that."

I nod, internally cursing when my vision blurs.

"That being said, I can sympathize with how hard it must be for you. It fucking sucks, to put it plainly, and I never—" He swipes his hands over his face. "Fuck. I never knew the truth behind the saying 'If you love something, let it go' until now, but I can't be the reason for a rift between you and your parents. They mean everything to you, Maya. Everything you've done, everything *you* have sacrificed has been to make them proud, and I won't allow you to live in constant guilt by choosing us. And selfishly, I won't allow *myself* to be put in the middle of something you're not sure about. I keep getting my heart wrecked by you, and I'm not saying I don't partly understand your reasoning, but at some point, I have to value myself too."

If you love something let it go?

No. No, this is all wrong.

I was supposed to come in here and we would apologize to each other and kiss and make up. That's how every romance movie works. It's how every rom-com I've ever watched ends, and I refuse to accept that this is over between us. Really, truly over. My expectations aren't unrealistic. He told me as much, so dammit, he needs to live up to this one too. My happily ever after is with *him* and no one else.

"I am sure," I whisper. "You're the *only* thing I've ever been sure about, Ethan."

He smiles, but it's not a genuine one. It's a smile filled with pity. "I meant what I said outside of your parents' house. I'm in love with you, Maya, but I've learned to love myself, too, this year. Truthfully? I'm tired of wearing masks in front of people, and if we were to stay together, I'd have to pretend to be someone I'm not to prove to your parents that I'm worthy of you when the truth is I'm worthy of you now. Just as I am. And trust me, it's a shitty realization because you are—" His voice catches. "You're everything to me. Always have been. But I can't stay in a situation where I'll never feel like I'm enough. I hope you understand that."

I laugh at the ceiling in frustration, desperately trying to hold my tears back. "You're more than enough, Ethan. You're the man of my dreams." *And I'm in love with you too.*

The sentence feels meaningless when he doesn't intend to stay with me, but I can't find it in me to be angry with him when I understand. He's worked so hard to get to where he's at in life, and my parents' opinions threaten to tear his progress to the ground. Even if I was to disregard what they think and run off with him, it would always be in the back of his mind.

"I was unworthy of *you*," I whisper. "You've always thought it was the other way around, but I envy the woman you choose to end up with because she's going to be *really* lucky." My chin wobbles but I push through it. "And I'm proud of you for finally realizing your worth and figuring out your passion this year. No matter what my dad says, being a coach is *nothing* to be ashamed of. You're impacting kids' lives, and that's one of the hardest jobs there is. I just . . . I wish things were different, and I wish my parents would change their minds, but—"

The mattress dips beside me, and he doesn't think twice before tugging me into his chest. Sobs rack my body as he squeezes me tightly and buries his head in my shoulder. I want to scream at the unfairness of all of this. I want to tell him to run away with me and never look back, but that would only make things more complicated. He's right. My parents do mean the world to me, and although I'd be happy with him, it'd kill me to drive a wedge between us.

"That means a lot to me, Maya, and maybe your parents will change their minds one day, but that day isn't today or probably anytime soon. And you *are* worthy of me, don't think for a second that you aren't. I can't imagine ever ending up with someone else because in every dream of mine, it's always been you, but I love you too much to rip you away from your family."

I fall apart in his arms, hating that this is the last time I'll ever hold him. I don't want to let go, and it seems he doesn't want to, either, because we stay locked in an embrace far longer than we should. Seconds pass, and then minutes before finally, he pulls away and wipes his eyes with the sleeve of his sweatshirt. They're red and puffy, likely a reflection of mine, and no matter how hard I try, I can't make sense of this situation.

We both love each other. We both want to end up together. And yet we can't make this work. Outside factors are forcing us apart, and I can't do anything to stop it. It's exhausting trying to fight the inevitable.

Right person, wrong time has never rung more true.

"I hope you get everything you've ever wanted out of life." His words are like a kiss to my fractured heart. "I hope you recognize how talented you are, and I hope that if your parents can't accept us, they will accept *you*. Your aspirations, passions, and everything that makes you so unique. You're one of a kind. Never forget that."

I'm a blubbering mess when he presses his lips to the crown of my head and rises to his feet. There's so much I want to say, but I can't bring myself to speak when it won't make a difference. Everything we've built over the past three months is crumbling to the ground. It's fading into a barren wasteland filled with the possibilities of what could have been, and all I want is for my feelings to vanish with it.

I'm self-aware enough to realize that's a lie, though. I don't want to forget a single minute with Ethan Davis. From sharing the last bite of ice cream to playing chicken with his sister in the pool. Our first kiss in his parents' car. Our first night together in the hot tub. All those moments led to me becoming the person I am today, and this year, not only did he discover himself, but he helped me discover *myself* too.

My only regret is not being truthful with him from the very beginning. I thought it was in his best interest, but it only turned around to bite me in the ass.

The truth is, I deserve all the repercussions.

Including losing him.

"I'm so sorry for everything, Ethan. For not being truthful with you, and for everything that went down at my parents. You didn't deserve it. Any of it. But I also need you to know that I don't choose them over you. I made my decision a while ago, and if you asked me to today, I'd run away with you without any hesitation to start a life together. I'd pick you over them."

His gaze softens, and his fists are clenched at his sides, like he's physically incapable of keeping his distance from me. "I know," he whispers through tears of his own. "But I can't allow you to make that decision. I *won't.*"

When I reach his door, I turn to get my last fill of him. Blue, glassy irises, full lips, and messy hair I love to run my fingers through. He's my favorite person. He's *my* person, and although my parents don't approve of him now, maybe they will in time, and if that ever happens . . .

There's not a single person on this earth who could keep me away from him.

~

Two hours later, I'm back beneath the safety of my comforter with my laptop playing a Hallmark holiday movie that Maddie swore would make me feel better. I know I look like hell because she *hates* these types of films, and yet she practically begged me to stay on a video chat so we could hit play at the same time and watch it together.

My eyes are swollen and red after confiding in Maddie about the breakup with Ethan. I had to come clean sooner rather than later before word got back to her about the *real* reason we had to end things. The secret I kept not only from Ethan, but from her too.

"Oh, look! Daniel is driving through the storm to get her back." Maddie sighs like she's genuinely into this movie, which couldn't be further from the truth.

"Can you stop trying to make me feel better? You're itching to turn this off. Tell the truth."

Maddie's a terrible liar, so in seconds, she gives in and *huffs*. "Okay, you're right. This is awful. How is risking his life romantic? He couldn't wait until the morning to apologize to her? You know, when there isn't a blizzard outside?"

My best friend's critiques of the movies I enjoy normally irritate me, but I find comfort in them this time. I've never missed her more than I do right now. I'd give anything to have a sleepover in person, where I'd paint her nails or braid her hair while we talked about everything new in our lives or the latest gossip in town. It's not the same without her here.

"You're right," I admit as Daniel swerves to avoid a patch of black ice. "He's an idiot."

Maddie pushes a stray blond curl behind her ear, and I can't glance away fast enough to avoid catching what I'm assuming is an expression of pity. Her ice-blue eyes are identical to Ethan's, but that's what I get for dating my best friend's brother. I'll be reminded of him every time I look at her. "I hate seeing you like this," she whispers. "You've never been this down about a guy before."

"Because I haven't. Ethan was different. In so many ways." My vision blurs with tears threatening to spill. "I'm in love with him, Maddie, but there's nothing I can do to fix it. My life isn't going to play out like Daniel's and Theresa's." I fling a hand at the laptop in annoyance. "I'm not going to get a happily ever after because it doesn't happen in the real world."

"Don't you dare." Maddie narrows her eyes into slits. "I hate these movies, but I watch them for you because you always claimed it would be a dream for your love story to play out this way. And it *will*, whether it's with my brother or not." A pause, and then, "I don't know why you didn't tell me about your parents. I could have been there for you."

"Because I didn't want you to think badly of them. My parents are kind people, and they've always wanted the best for me, like any parent would. It's just, sometimes I think they replace my dreams with theirs. They want me to have what they never did, but what if that isn't what I want? If I'm being honest, I'd take the struggle they went through if it meant I could go through it with Ethan."

"Fuck." Maddie grabs a tissue from her nightstand and blots her cheeks. "You know I'm a crier. I can't help it. Have you told your parents that?"

"Well, I tried to, but it resulted in that huge fight. After Ethan left, I wasn't in the right headspace to talk to my parents, and I didn't feel like staying. I took the first bus back here and haven't spoken to them since. Their phones aren't in service."

"Maybe you should talk to them again now that everything has cooled down."

I bite nervously on my lip. "I'll have to at some point. I can't stay angry with them forever."

"Exactly. I've never seen two people made for each other like you and Ethan. Yeah, he's my brother, and you were nervous about telling me at first, but I wasn't shocked because it just made sense. I think it always has."

I sniffle and wipe away more tears with the sleeve of my shirt. "Really?"

"Totally. I suspected he had a thing for you growing up. I mean, who pays for someone to go to Disneyland if they're just friends?"

My entire body stills.

I'm certain I'm not breathing.

There's no *way* I heard her correctly.

"What did you just say?"

Maddie gets flustered, her cheeks reddening by the second. "Wait, didn't you know? Cameron told me a while ago that it was never a scholarship. Ethan gave the money to their coach since he was a chaperone on the trip. I assumed he told you."

No, he hadn't, but I should have known it was him when that random scholarship popped up a week after I vented to him about it in his kitchen. It's not like this is a revelation or anything about how much he cares for me, because he's shown it every time he's with me. This is just another item added to the never-ending list of how perfect he is for me.

He may not be interested in a career that'll rake in six figures a year, but the more time I spend around Ethan, the more I realize that wealth comes in different forms than money. I wouldn't mind living in a small house with a tiny picket fence if it meant sharing all my days with him, because he brings everything important to the table. Love, stability, patience, compassion. I could go on for hours.

When a knock sounds at my door, I tell Maddie to hold on and check to see who it is. No one is out in the hallway when I open it, but when I glance down, a smile forms on my lips for the first time today.

It's a pint of cookies and cream ice cream with a plastic-wrapped spoon on top.

And when I bend down to pick it up, I see a yellow sticky note on the front with handwriting I'd recognize anywhere.

Since I can't wipe away your tears (thin walls), I figured this would be the next best thing that could.

God, why is he so *flawless*? The man couldn't have one thing wrong with him if he tried. We're both hurting from this breakup, yet he still took the time to grab something to make me feel better. He's the kind of man who would do anything for me. He'd share his coat so I could stay dry. He'd spend his summer savings so I could go on a trip I've always wanted. He'd learn a second language to fit in with my family. He'd share the last bite of cookies and cream ice cream because it's my favorite flavor. He'd—

"Are you laughing?" Maddie's voice seeps from my phone into the room. "What happened? Who was it?"

I pick my phone up and shake my head in disbelief. "I'm just now realizing that Ethan is Daniel."

"What?"

"From the movie," I say. "The guy who's an idiot driving in a blizzard to get to the girl because he can't wait until morning? It's Ethan. He'd be the type of man to do the same for me." He's everything I've ever wanted. Everything I've been searching for. He's met all my high standards and then surpassed them, and it's time someone does the same for him. "But he doesn't need to drive in the blizzard. For once, I'm turning the rom-com stereotype on its head. The guy doesn't always have to chase the girl, Maddie. Sometimes, the girl needs to risk her life in a blizzard for the guy, you know?"

"I'm not following." Maddie seems concerned. "Are you okay? What's going on?"

A flood of determination enters my system, and rather than

wait for it to pass, I'm going to grab the bull by the horns and try this rodeo again.

Ethan deserves it after all he's done for me.

"I'm buying a bus ticket tonight back to Wickenburg to fight for what's mine."

Forty

ETHAN

Leo [Attaches photo of a pissed off Ethan with his toiletry bag in hand]

Leo Here's our sunshine boy in all his glory

Mark Sweet. You actually got him to shower. I'm impressed

Cameron He wasn't showering?? Is it THAT bad?

Leo Yup. Smells like ass in our room

Mark He'll feel better afterward and return to normal in a few days

Leo What is "normal" to you guys? Because the version I live with is a sarcastic ass ninety percent of the time. Not that I'm complaining, though. I live to get under his skin. It's what makes our friendship so special

Mark Sarcastic ass is accurate, but we love him

Cameron Basically, yeah

Ethan You all realize that I'm INCLUDED in this group chat, right?

[Silence]

~

I've never felt such agony.

Depressed? I've felt that before. Anxious? Practically my entire life. But letting Maya go was single-handedly the hardest thing I've ever done, and it's taken every fiber of my being to pick myself back up instead of giving in to the temptation to hole up in this room forever.

Life keeps going regardless of what's happening to my heart, and where I didn't have a clue how I wanted my life to unfold when I got here, I do now. Kids are depending on me this weekend, at their last game before winter break. I have a major to change because, despite Maya's father's opinion, coaching is what I've fallen in love with, and after spending a week and a half stewing in my anger, I refuse to let one person change the course of my life.

I've worked hard to get to this place. I have friends who want me to succeed, and for the first time, I want the same for myself because I can envision an end goal. I can vividly picture what I want to accomplish, so although this breakup threatens to tear me apart from the inside out, I have to keep going.

One step at a time.

But at ten o'clock on Thursday night, I open the door to one of only two people I'll allow myself to fall apart in front of.

Cameron is on the other side with his hands shoved in the pockets of his sweatpants, and judging by the way he sweeps his eyes over my face, he's debating whether or not to crack a joke. He must notice the exhaustion lining my features, or maybe he can tell how emotionally taxing it's been for me to pretend that I'm okay when, in reality, it's difficult to get out of bed each morning.

Whatever the reason, he pulls me in for a hug, and it's everything I need and more.

I have no clue how he got here, or how long he's staying, but him showing up for me means more than he'll ever know. Cameron is my brother, through and through. If anyone can help me sort through the shattered pieces of my heart, it's him.

My best friend pulls away to study me and frowns at whatever he sees. "Fuck, man. You look worse than I thought."

"Yeah." I clear my throat and swipe at my face, cursing the tears that slipped out. "What the hell are you doing here? It's the middle of the season."

"Do I need a reason to visit you?" He sticks a thumb over his shoulder and adds, "I ran into Leo downstairs, and he gave me this." Pulling a blunt out of his sweatshirt pocket, he shakes the plastic bag in front of me and wiggles his brows. "Shall we light her up?"

"You can't smoke with football."

"No, but you can."

It doesn't take much for me to give in. In fact, nothing sounds more enjoyable than escaping from my thoughts for a bit, so I follow him outside to my car. Rather than climb inside, we opt to sit on the hood, since Cameron doesn't want to risk getting a contact high. The memory of Maya giggling in my passenger seat sends a stabbing pain to my chest that nearly brings me to my knees, but I push the thought away and spark up the blunt, inhaling deeply before blowing a ring of smoke into the crispy air.

After a minute or so, he asks, "Do you want to talk about it?" Darkness envelops us, a single streetlamp providing enough of a golden glow to make out our expressions.

"There's not much to say." I shrug. "I can't change anything about the situation. Letting her go was in the best interest of both of us, you know? But it doesn't mean it doesn't hurt like hell." Cameron leans back to rest his elbows on the hood of my car, nodding as if deep in thought. "It wasn't going to work out anyway. Well, I keep trying to convince myself of that, at least. We want different things out of life. She wants to travel, whereas I prefer to stay in Arizona for the rest of my life. She's outgoing, and I'm shy. Hell, I couldn't even play college ball because performing in front of large crowds had me going into a full-blown anxiety attack."

Cameron tilts his head to the side. "Do you wish you could have played in college? I mean, now that you've gotten the medication to keep your anxiety under control, do you regret it? Not playing?"

I've thought about this question a lot. When I told my parents I wouldn't accept my full ride to State, it kept me up at night wondering if I'd made the right decision by giving it all up. My parents were nothing but supportive, but I could tell they were concerned, too, even though they'll never admit it.

"I did at first, but when I started volunteering in the youth program, it made me realize there was a different side to football, one where I didn't have to be in the limelight as much but could still enjoy the sport. It still makes me feel like I'm letting people down or like coaching is some downgrade, but traveling around the world with the media breathing down my neck if I ever made it professionally sounds like a nightmare. I'm not—" Fuck. I didn't expect to have this conversation tonight, but I'll blame it on the weed loosening things up. "I've come to terms with the fact that I'll never be you."

While the admission hangs between us, I feel Cameron's body tense beside me. "What are you talking about?"

"Oh, come on. Don't act like you didn't know I strived to be you growing up. You've got it all, Cameron. Always have."

He snorts. "You, out of anyone, should know looks can be deceiving, Ethan."

"I understand that *now*, but when we first got into high school? You towered over the rest of the guys in our grade. You had the game to pick up any girl in school. People flocked to you everywhere we went because of your confidence, and you played football so *effortlessly*. The pressure didn't matter, and it irked me that I couldn't be the same way. Even now, you're about to graduate college and enter the draft while I'm a year behind, probably even further behind now that I'm changing my major."

"But that's okay," he replies. "There isn't a rule book to life, man. Sure, I went to college straight after high school, but that's not everyone's destiny. Our accomplishments come at different times, and whether it's one month or five years from now, all that matters is that they *happen*, right?"

I take another long pull from the blunt, rendered speechless.

"And being anxious about traveling and wanting to stay in Arizona doesn't mean there's anything wrong with you. It's simply your preference. Being a homebody is normal. Wanting to play video games rather than go out and party isn't a bad thing. All of these things that you've tried to change about yourself? I promise you'll enjoy life ten times more if you accept the things that make you who you are rather than run yourself into the ground trying to fight them." He bumps his shoulder reassuringly into mine. "The truth is no one wants to change you. You're enough, and I'll bet anything you're enough for *her* too. Fear of traveling and all."

Allowing his words to sink in, I laugh softly to myself. Leave it to Cameron to give me life-altering advice. "It's more complicated than that. I may be enough for her, but I'll never be enough for her parents, and I won't get in the way of their relationship when they mean so much to her."

"That's fair." He sighs and slings an arm over my shoulder. "Well, I hope they change their minds, but if they don't, you've got a pretty kick-ass group of friends who'll help you through it."

"You mean, when they aren't calling me a sarcastic ass?" I can't help but smile at the sound of his laugh. It makes me want to call my sister and thank her for making him happy enough to bring it back after so many years of him silencing it.

"Are you going to deny it?"

I roll my eyes, and a comfortable silence falls between us while I finish the last of the blunt before sliding off the hood to stamp it out with my shoe. "Not that I'm complaining or trying to sound ungrateful, but you realize you could have said all this over a video call, right? How long are you here for, anyway?"

He checks the time on his phone. "I have to be back at the airport in three hours for a red eye."

"*What?* Why the hell would you fly out for only a few hours?"

"Because." He holds my stare, the cocky, arrogant jokester nowhere to be found. "You've been there for me at my absolute lowest, Ethan, even when I didn't deserve it. It doesn't matter how many miles apart we are—if you need me, I'll be here. You don't have to go through this heartbreak alone, and you won't so long as you have me by your side. *Brothers*, remember?"

Through the liquid sheen coating my eyes, I pull him in for another hug and clap him on the back. The bond between us is unbreakable. "Brothers," I affirm. "For life."

Although it's torture living next door to the girl of my dreams while simultaneously not being able to do a damn thing about it, having the support of my friends makes it tolerable. Cameron's right. I don't have to go through this alone. I've avoided leaning on others in the past, opting to wear a mask to become the version of me I thought they wanted. But tonight, I'm back to being fully myself with Cameron, just like we used to be as kids, and it's a reminder that I've come so far from where I started.

There's still a gaping hole in my chest where Maya should be, but I can't allow myself to be consumed by that feeling and retreat back into the version of myself at the beginning of the semester when I used to *dream* of having my life figured out. Now I'm here, enjoying college for once, and I've discovered a career that'll be fulfilling for me.

I can't give that up.

All I can do is continue to take steps toward the future I want, and pray to whoever the hell I need to that one day Maya can be part of it too.

Forty-one

MAYA

My entire life, I've tried to please everyone around me. My parents, my friends, romantic interests. Any room I entered, I'd imagine how to make others smile, and I didn't even realize that by doing this, I was hurting myself in the process. But my eyes have been opened after losing Ethan, and now I find it laughable that I ever thought I was selfish. Yes, I respect and appreciate everything my parents have sacrificed, but I'm also worthy of everything America has to offer, and that includes my career and the person I want to be with.

Which is why I knock on the door of my childhood home at midnight with more force than I intended. After a minute or so, a golden shimmer of light flickers inside, and then I see my mom peek out the blinds of the living room to check who it is. I hear a tiny gasp, and then she's throwing the door open and hugging me so hard that she knocks the air from my lungs.

"Oh, bambina." A strangled sob works its way up her throat, and although crying is what I want to do, too, I refuse to let my tears fall. I need to be strong. I've turned this over and over in my head on the way here, and I won't leave this house until they agree to my terms and conditions.

But still I take a brief moment to nuzzle my head into my mother's fluffy robe before I pull away. I've never fought with my parents, and leaving them with no way to contact me wasn't the wisest decision on my part. "Is Papí here?"

"Yes, but . . ." She rolls her lips together. "Let's sit for a minute."

"I don't want to sit, Mamí. This is important."

She nods. "I understand, but it won't take long. I have something to share with you."

Despite the adrenaline coursing through my veins, I sit beside her on the couch, unable to help the nervous jitters as I bounce my leg. She places her hand on my knee and squeezes gently before sending me a teary smile. "When your father and I were younger, we came from different backgrounds. My parents owned a successful farm in our village, and his—" She shakes her head. "He didn't have the greatest influences around him. Born into a family of criminals who created a bad name for themselves around town."

"Why didn't I know this?" I've heard plenty of stories from their younger days, but I was never told about my father's childhood.

"He didn't want you to, but I think you need to hear this because . . ." She sighs. "Your father and I fell in love quickly. I caught him trying to steal an apple from our stand in the farmer's market in town, and after finding out he was just hungry, I gave him a bag of fruit for free and continued to do so for the next few months until he finally offered to take me on a date." She smiles at the memory, and it's so bright that it lights up her entire face. "The more I got to know him, the more I discovered how charming he was, and it didn't take long until we made things official."

My heart clenches as tears spring to my mother's eyes. I can't help but wrap an arm around her shoulder and hold her close, giving her the reassurance to finish.

"I got pregnant with you shortly after, and when I told my parents"—she frowns, a crease appearing between her brows—"they kicked me out."

"*Abuela* and *Abuelo* kicked you out?" I can't hide the shock in my voice.

She smiles grimly. "We had no money or future in Mexico, so your father convinced me to come to America, and it was many, many years before I spoke to them again. Your father thought we could have a better life here, one free of judgment and away from his family, which was no good with him." It's *for* him, but I don't correct her. "Papí promised we wouldn't struggle here. He always dreamed of having a big house. One that had one of those pretty . . ." She searches for the word. "Porches?"

I nod, swiping a few stray tears.

"It was harder than we thought, but what Papí didn't realize until you left a few nights ago was that I didn't need a big house or a pretty porch. We created a *family*. It wasn't easy, but we had a roof over our heads and food on the table. Most importantly? I had *him*." She searches my eyes, regret shining in them. "Your Papí thought I was unhappy with our life, so he was scared for a boy to do the same to you."

"It's true." My father's deep voice rumbles, surprising us both. He joins us on the couch before kissing my mother on her cheek. "I couldn't forgive myself for taking Mamí away from a family with money only to throw her into a life of hard work."

She nudges his shoulder. "And I'll tell you again, I'd choose to do it all over if it meant being with you."

I'm caught up in their pure adoration for one another, almost forgetting why I came here in the first place. Their love is one I've already found with someone else, and if my mother is saying they had a long conversation after I left, I can only pray that it means they changed their minds.

But first, my conditions.

Sitting straighter on the couch, I roll my shoulders back and say, "Ethan is the man I want to be with. He's the man I'm *going* to be with. You've raised me to be a strong woman who only deserves the best, and he's exceeded all my standards. I love you both more than life itself, and the last thing I want is my relationship to come between us."

Mamí frowns. "We don't want that either, bambina."

My brows lift, and I'm desperate to ask what they mean, but I have to get all of this out while I'm on a roll. "And I have no problem graduating from business school. I understand education is important to you, and it is to me too. *However*, I'll use my business degree to open my own salon. It may not rake in six figures a year, nor will Ethan's coaching job, but we will be *happy*. And just like you and Papí, any struggles we might face down the road will be worth it to me because I'll have him by my side. I love him, and if you give him a chance, I know you will too."

With it all out in the open, I hold my breath and wait for the backlash that never comes. Instead, my father nods thoughtfully and says, "I was harsh, and I owe him an apology."

"You do," I agree.

"And I'm sorry if I made you feel you couldn't chase your *pasión*. I'm still nervous, but we came here to give you a chance, and we'll support you."

Mierda. My heart is racing.

This is everything I've wanted to come out of this conversation and more. I bite my lip to keep from smiling because as much as I want to celebrate, I need this last piece of my life to click into place.

"And Ethan?" I prod.

Papí leans back on the couch with his arms folded across his chest. "I'll need to meet him," he says, "but the last thing we want is to treat you the way Mamí's parents did to us. We'll give him a chance. *Pero—*" He holds a finger up. "If he so much as looks at you wrong . . ."

I don't bother to hear the rest of what they're saying. I tackle them both on the couch and hug them close, happy tears tracking down my face. "Thank you, thank you, thank you!" I squeal. "Te amo."

Papí kisses the crown of my head. "Te amo, princesa. Now, I have to get to bed. I have to be at work at four. Will you be here tomorrow?"

My first instinct is to rush back to campus and tackle Ethan with kisses, but honestly? I didn't get to spend any time with my parents on my last visit, and now that things have been patched up between us, I want to bask in the comfort of home, even if it's only for a few days. I've grown homesick being away from here for so long.

I'm confident a little more time apart won't change the connection Ethan and I share.

"Yeah, I'll stay for a few days and head back this weekend."

His smile grows wider just as Mamí stands and walks to the kitchen. "I don't have to work until tomorrow night, so why don't I make us some hot chocolate? You can tell me more about Ethan."

"Only if you tell me more about you and Papí. It's so romantic."

Papí laughs from the bedroom. "I was a thief who didn't deserve her time of day. I *still* don't."

"*¡Silencio!*" Mamí scolds him with a laugh.

I sit at the tiny kitchen table, allowing the warmth from the stove to feed the mushy sensation flooding my chest. I expected coming here tonight to result in another screaming match, but when Mamí passes me a steaming mug of hot chocolate and we stay up late telling each other how we both fell in love, I'm eternally grateful it didn't.

I fought for what I wanted, and it paid off. Now, nothing stands in the way of Ethan and me being together. If he'll still have me, that is. The world's worst blizzard could hit the town of Wickenburg this weekend, and without having to think twice, I'd be the idiot driving through it to get to him.

Because sometimes the girl has to chase the guy, and I'm totally all right with that.

Forty-two

ETHAN

"Looks like it's about to pour any minute." Mark squints at the ominous sky overlooking the field. Thick, dark clouds swirl above us and cast the bleachers in shadow. "I hope the game finishes before." He holds a clipboard to his chest as the ref whistles a time-out.

It's the fourth quarter, another close game. With only forty-five seconds left on the clock, we're up by a single touchdown; so as long as the Stingrays don't get close enough for a field goal, we'll win. But the ball is in their possession and it's third down, so it's on the defense to make this final stop.

Jake looks as white as a ghost.

Mark rambles on about the play he suggests we run, but my gaze is fixed on Jake. He's rubbing his palm against his heaving chest, squeezing his eyes shut tight. The kid is about to have an anxiety attack on the field. Not that I can blame him. The pressure is a lot, especially since we'll advance to sectionals if we win this game.

"Jake. Come over here." I jerk my chin away from the rest of the team, watching as he runs over on shaky limbs. Mark nods in understanding after he takes one look at the poor kid's face, then returns to the remainder of the kids to coach them through the play. "What's going on, man? Talk to me."

"I can't do it," he says breathily. "What if I can't stop him? I haven't been able to nail the play once."

I arch a brow. "That's not what I was told. I heard you got your first sack last game."

"Yeah, but it was a lucky play. I haven't been able to do it since." His eyes dart to the field, a new shade of pale washing over him. "I'm sorry," he stutters. "This is stupid. I shouldn't be so nervous about this."

My chest squeezes when I put a hand on his shoulder. "You have no reason to be sorry. You're anxious about performing your best, and that's understandable. It would be weird if you *weren't* worried. It means you care."

"I just don't want to let anyone down."

"Let anyone down? Let me tell you, kid, at some point in your football career, it's bound to happen. You won't always be the best player on the field, but that's what being part of a *team* is for. I believe you can do this, and Mark and Ronnie do too. But win *or* lose, we'll have your back. There's no need to feel pressure, all right? My only expectation is that you go out there and try your best because you love the game. You shouldn't be playing for any other reason."

The ref blows the whistle, signaling the end of the time-out, and with bated breath, I wait to see what Jake will decide to do. Thunder rumbles in the distance, and the football moms on the sidelines are already packing up their gear, ready to make a run for it if it starts raining.

"All right," he says with a decisive nod. He bounces from toe to toe, and I smack his helmet and signal for him to get on the field, pride surging through every chamber of my heart. "Thanks, Coach."

Before I can correct him, he jogs toward his teammates, while the new title reverberates deep in my chest like a seed waiting to blossom. A whistle falls around my neck, and it isn't until now that I realize Ronnie was behind us and overheard our entire conversation. "I know I said I'd wait for you to accept the position, but tough shit. Welcome to the team."

I clench the whistle tightly, unable to come up with a rebuttal when it feels so right. *Assistant Coach*. God, the smile on my face is cheesy as hell.

"Thanks, Ronnie," I say when Mark approaches my side. My friend punches me on the shoulder, and although it's meant to be joking, it causes me to wince. "Jesus," I hiss, rubbing the sore spot. "I don't think you understand how freakishly strong you are."

He tips his head back and laughs. "Or you're just weak."

Our laughter fades when the play starts. The opposing team hikes the ball, and their quarterback looks around for someone to throw it to. The tight end, wide receivers, running back. . . . Our team is doing a damn good job at blocking, but my eyes remain glued on Jake, who drops his shoulder low and shoves the offensive lineman with enough brute force to send him flying backward.

Mark throws the clipboard in disbelief and I take off running along the sidelines to watch it play out. "Yes, yes, *yes*! Sack him, Jake!"

Adrenaline rushes through my bloodstream as I watch Jake take the quarterback to the ground.

The crowd on the bleachers and sidelines goes wild. The

ref signals the end of the game, declaring us the winners, and I run onto the field to tackle my little superstars. We're a mess of a huddle when the sky opens up and rain streams down to coat their sweaty, sticky skin, but the thing they don't tell you about coaching? You feel so much pride and love for one group of kids that it fills all the empty spaces inside you until they're numb. I haven't felt this good in weeks.

"Do we get pizza tonight?" Devonte shouts.

"Oh, most definitely. Pizza is on me tonight, guys. You made me proud."

Mark races over with a few umbrellas, Leo sidling up beside him with his own. I'm happy he came out to the game to show his support, but I roll my eyes the second he opens his mouth.

"Congrats on the win!" he shouts over the downpour. "Bummer about the rain, though. I was going to try and score one of the football moms." He scans the almost deserted bleachers, spotting Tabi on the sideline with her dad and Annie before he gets that mischievous grin. "Well, *actually* ..."

"*No.*"

A single word from Mark makes Leo's spine straighten. Mark's tone leaves no room for debate. Leo flicks his eyes from Tabi to Mark before realization dawns on him. "Oh, I get it. Off-limits, huh? I'll respect that."

Mark doesn't reply; he only clenches his jaw before fixing his attention on the kids celebrating in the rain. Even with the umbrella, water pelts my skin like an ice-cold shower, and in seconds I'm shivering and craving the warmth of my car.

"I'll meet you guys for pizza?" I shout over the storm.

They nod in unison, opting to celebrate with the team for a few more minutes.

I'm walking off the field when a flash of neon orange catches my attention in the stands.

I squint through the rain at the person sitting on the bleachers in the middle of a fucking downpour with no umbrella, only to still at the sight of eyes I'd remember anywhere. Eyes that I've tried to forget with no luck. Eyes that appear in my dreams each night like a hauntingly beautiful fairy tale.

Why is she here?

Fuck, that's not important.

She's *here*.

Without wasting another second, I jog over to the bleachers and dart up the risers to reach her at the top. She's drenched, droplets of water trailing down her face and dripping onto the gaudy jersey below. Mascara stains her cheeks from the rain, or maybe she's been crying. I honestly can't tell. Whatever the case, she's the prettiest fucking girl alive, and perhaps the craziest.

"Are you insane?" I shout. "It's freezing out here!"

She shakes her head when I offer her the umbrella. "Take it," I insist.

"I don't want it, Ethan. This isn't a blizzard, but it might as well be."

What the hell is she talking about?

Christ, she's probably already sick from the weather.

I grab her wrist to pull her closer, sheltering us from the rain under the tiny umbrella. She trembles beside me, shivering from head to toe. "What the hell are you doing here?" I ask. "You're going to catch pneumonia. You *hate* the rain. And didn't you say you'd never wear orange because it isn't your color?" I'm rambling, but truthfully, it's only to distract myself from my nerves regarding the real reason she decided to watch the game.

"I'm here for you."

Her words knock me off kilter.

"Maya." Damn my sky-rocketing pulse. This can't mean what I think it means. I refuse to get my hopes up only to have them shot down again. "I meant what I said. I would never ask you to choose—"

"I came here to ask if you're free for a cookout next weekend." A tiny grin tugging at her lips gives her excitement away, and my mouth dries out in seconds. My heart pounds as hard as a drum in my chest, and I'm unsure if she means what I'm assuming is a formal invitation from her parents to give me a shot.

"I'm here to fight for you," she continues. "Because you deserve someone who gives you the same effort you put into them. You taught me to believe in myself, which is why I'm going to finish this business degree to open up my own salon after I graduate. Because not only did I fight for us, but I fought for myself, and I couldn't have gained the courage to do that without you by my side every step of the way. I'd do *anything* for you, Ethan, including taking a bus back home in the wee hours of the morning to change my parents' minds. I'll sit in the rain for you even though I despise it. I'll wear orange because it's your team's color. I'll—" She laughs when I wrap an arm around her waist. "You've done whatever you can to surpass my high standards, but it's time I do the same for you."

"*Maya.*"

"I don't deserve another chance, not by any means, but I promise if you agree to try this one last time, I'll never lie to you again. You can trust me."

"Maya."

"Because I'm in love with you, Ethan Davis," she reveals, with a shaky exhale. Rain batters the bleachers around us, drowning out all the other voices but hers. In this moment, the universe includes no one but us. "This isn't the traditional rom-com ending I always imagined I'd have, but it's *mine*, and I'm righting my wrongs and coming clean right here, right now, because if I can't have you, I don't want anyone."

The words I've craved to hear spill from her lips for years leave my mind reeling. I've been in love with this girl for as long as I can remember, convinced it was an unrealistic dream to think of her as a possibility for my future. But now she's here, right in front of me, professing her love in the middle of a rainstorm like one of the cheesy movies she loves so much. She's *wooing* me as she thinks she needs to, when that's simply not the case.

I'd choose her in any lifetime, alternate universe, or different dimension. There's never been a choice when it comes to her, and there never will be.

I glance around us with a smile, attempting to hide the fluttering in my stomach. "I mean, the weather tracks. I guess all that's missing is a happy ending, huh?"

Her eyes dart to my lips before scanning my face. "Well, the ball's in your court, s—"

Maya doesn't see it coming when I press my lips to hers with a blistering, passionate heat carried from the very depths of my soul. She should know better than to ask questions she already knows the answers to, and if she got her parents' approval, there's nothing standing in our way. This woman is my soulmate. My best friend. She's the only thing that's been missing in my life, and now that I have her again? I'm never letting her slip from my grasp.

"Wanting you has never been a question," I pant against her lips. "Now kiss me like you mean it."

I don't have to ask her twice. She plucks the umbrella from

my hand and jumps into my arms instead, and, with rain pouring from above, I push my fingers into her hair and devour her blindly, unable to see because of the water in my eyes. My hands travel down her back, feeling the jersey plastered to her skin, and it's a damn shame we're in the middle of a public field, because if we were anywhere remotely private, weather be damned, I'd take her right there.

Maya smiles against my mouth before she pulls away and whispers, "*Now* it's a traditional rom-com ending. Congrats on the win, *Coach*." Her fingers are wrapped around the whistle, and she gives it a little tug to place another kiss on my lips. "That has a nice ring to it."

"It's *boyfriend* to you." Placing her back on her feet, I notice she's still shivering, so I lean over to grab the umbrella again and force her to take it. "I'm not letting you get sick on my watch. Come on, let's head to the car."

"Maybe I took the wooing a little too far." She huddles into my side when we step off the bleachers, but we quickly run into Mark and Tabi having a heated debate with her father. Or is it *their* father? I don't know. The situation is fucking weird, and honestly? Maya and I have a lot to catch up on. It's only been a week since we last spoke, yet it feels like a lifetime.

"I am *not* bringing him with me!" Tabi shrieks. "Dad, this was supposed to be a trip for me to have to myself. It's for me to grow my blog and build my portfolio. Not bring *him* along for the ride. Why are you even insisting he goes? What is *so* important that he has to tag along with me to the East Coast?"

Mark tilts his head to the side under his umbrella, a tiny Annie latched onto his legs. "Oh, come on, Tabi cat. It won't be that bad."

She whips her head to his. "You planned this, didn't you?"

"I wish I had, since it's getting such a reaction out of you, but no. This was all Ronnie's doing."

Ronnie sighs aggressively. "I don't have time for this right now. We're meeting the kids for pizza, and the last thing I need is for two grown adults to rip each other's throats out. You each have a reason to travel to the East Coast, and since *I'm* the one funding both trips, it's saving me money to have you travel together. Mark said he'd drive his Mustang."

Tabi gasps. "Please tell me you're joking. No way in *hell* am I riding in that death trap. I refuse."

Mark barks out a laugh. "Sheila's been nothing but good to me. Be nice. I saved up for three years to buy her."

Tabi sends pleading eyes to her father. "He *named* his car, Dad. He's insane."

Ronnie shrugs and pulls his keys from his pocket. "If you choose not to go, that's on you, and you'll miss your trip. Just know you won't have a free babysitter next time. I'm using this paid vacation over break to take full advantage of my grandfatherly duties." He smiles warmly at Annie. "Besides, I think it'll be good for you to be stuck in a car for two weeks together. Gives you time to bond."

"Over my dead body," Tabi sneers.

"Uh, hey, don't mean to interrupt, but I'm taking Maya back to the dorm to change. We got a little . . ." I trail off, unsure of how to describe what the hell just happened in the stands.

"Wet?" Mark supplies with a grin. "That's what tends to happen when you make out in a monsoon." He wiggles his brows. "Glad to see you're back together. Leo's gonna have a field day when he finds out."

I roll my eyes. "We'll meet you at the pizza place. Just give us a half hour to change."

"And by that, you mean an hour," Mark calls as we walk away. "Seriously, Christmas is right around the corner! Just buy the man some headphones!"

"Shut it." I can't see it, but a loud *thwack* echoes behind me, which I'm assuming is Ronnie hitting Mark with a clipboard.

Not even my friends and their asshole comments can get me down when I'm feeling on top of the world today. Rather than send him a snarky rebuttal, I toss a grin over my shoulder and say, "Hey, Tabi? When he stops to fill up the tank, put diesel in it!"

She explodes into hysterical laughter and says, "Noted!" just as Mark shouts, "Fucker!"

Hand in hand, Maya and I walk to my car, then turn the heat on full blast as soon as we get inside. Even with makeup running down her face and water clinging to her skin, she's so fucking beautiful, and I'll spend the rest of my life cherishing and worshiping everything about her.

With flushed cheeks and a broad smile, she clasps her shivering hand in my free one as I drive back to the dorm.

We started this semester unsure of ourselves and scared to take a chance on what we were born to do, and on the silent ride back, I can feel us basking in the warmth of each other and what our new future holds.

I spent so many years worrying about finding something I'm passionate about. I worried about not keeping up with others I graduated with, fearing that I was straying from the trail everyone else was walking when the truth is? Multiple trails can wind up at the same destination, and I've learned that it's okay to take the scenic route on this journey called life.

Because holding Maya's hand while we discuss what I should bring to the cookout with her parents doesn't have me worrying about how we got here.

It just makes me grateful we did.

Acknowledgments

I can't believe we're already celebrating another book! I loved each and every minute writing Maya and Ethan's love story, and I hope the characters resonated with you as much as they did with me. Different works take me on different journeys, and this one provided me with an unexpected healing process that I didn't realize I needed.

That being said, there are so many wonderful people who helped me create this book to thank.

To Tyquane—you are the best husband I could ever ask for. The belief you have always had in my writing career doesn't go unnoticed, and I love you more than you'll ever know.

To Rebecca—I wouldn't be where I am today without your constant support as not only my writing partner, but one of my ultimate best friends. Thank you (and Jamie) for always offering advice when I need it and for seeing me through my mental breakdowns and writer's block. It's an absolute honor to have you by my side.

To Ashley—thank you for creating the coolest merchandise *ever* to send out to influencers and for flying across the country for my signings. I love you more than words can describe! I'm so lucky to have you as my best friend.

To Fiona—your insights and critique are such a talent you bring to the world. Where would I be if I hadn't been awakened to my overuse of italics? In all seriousness, I couldn't have chosen anyone better as my editor. It's truly been a privilege to work with you.

To my readers—I am so grateful for everyone who has picked up a copy or has read my stories on Wattpad. Because of you I'm able to do what I love, and I'll never take that for granted. I'd be nothing without you guys.

To Sanah—I'm still in disbelief my books are in the UK, and I'm so grateful for you and the team for always keeping me in the loop and answering all of my incessant questions!

If you enjoyed *Game Changer*, please consider rating it on Goodreads and Amazon. It helps me immensely as an author. Also, I love seeing social media posts! Color stacks, flat lay collages, etc. I'm primarily on Instagram, so please tag me so I can share the beautiful photos you take! @deannafaisonbooks.

I hope to continue creating smutty little stories for you all.

Perhaps an enemies to lovers next?

Until next time,
Deanna <3

About the Author

Deanna Faison is a romance author residing in Clayton, North Carolina, where she writes from home full time. If she's not hunched over her laptop creating bad-boy heartthrobs and independent female leads, she's likely chasing her Marvel-obsessed four-year-old around the house or cheering on the Baltimore Ravens with her husband. One day she hopes to travel around the world so she can meet the readers who have made her success possible.